*His kiss was hungry,
his caresses urgent.*

"You make me feel so good," Mitch said. It was the closest he could come to expressing whatever it was he felt for Jamie Withers.

There was more he could have told her, so much more, had he been the kind of man who was able to share such things. He couldn't believe how utterly beautiful she was to him. He felt soothed by her touch, even as he was inflamed by it. She gave so much, awakening feelings in him he hadn't even known existed: the desire to possess, to cherish.

He wanted to give back some small part of everything she had given him, of everything she was giving him now.

But he was fighting a losing battle. The way he wanted to love Jamie just wasn't possible....

Dear Reader,

Welcome to Silhouette **Special Edition** ... welcome to romance. Each month, Silhouette **Special Edition** publishes six novels with you in mind—stories of love and life, tales that you can identify with— romance with that little "something special" added in.

June has some wonderful stories in bloom for you. Don't miss *Silent Sam's Salvation*—the continuation of Myrna Temte's exciting *Cowboy Country* series. Sam Dawson might not possess the gift of gab, but Dani Smith quickly discovers that still waters run deep—and that she wants to dive right in! Don't miss this tender tale.

Rounding out this month are more stories by some of your favorite authors: Tracy Sinclair, Christine Flynn, Trisha Alexander (with her second book for Silhouette **Special Edition**—remember *Cinderella Girl,* SE #640?), Lucy Gordon and Emilie Richards.

In each Silhouette **Special Edition** novel, we're dedicated to bringing you the romances that you dream about—stories that will delight as well as bring a tear to the eye. And that's what Silhouette **Special Edition** is all about—special books by special authors for special readers!

I hope you enjoy this book and all of the stories to come!

Sincerely,

Tara Gavin
Senior Editor
Silhouette Books

CHRISTINE FLYNN
Beyond the Night

Silhouette Special Edition

Published by Silhouette Books New York

America's Publisher of Contemporary Romance

For Dawn, my daughter and my friend

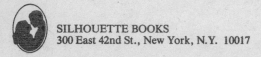

SILHOUETTE BOOKS
300 East 42nd St., New York, N.Y. 10017

BEYOND THE NIGHT

Copyright © 1992 by Christine Flynn

ISBN: 0-373-09747-6

First Silhouette Books printing June 1992

All the characters in this book have no existence outside the imagination of the author and have no relation whatsoever to anyone bearing the same name or names. They are not even distantly inspired by any individual known or unknown to the author, and all incidents are pure invention.

Printed in the U.S.A.

Books by Christine Flynn

Silhouette Special Edition

Remember the Dreams #254
Silence the Shadows #465
Renegade #566
Walk upon the Wind #612
Out of the Mist #657
The Healing Touch #693
Beyond the Night #747

Silhouette Desire

When Snow Meets Fire #254
The Myth and the Magic #296
A Place To Belong #352
Meet Me at Midnight #377

Silhouette Romance

Stolen Promise #435
Courtney's Conspiracy #623

CHRISTINE FLYNN

is formerly from Oregon and currently resides in the
Southwest with her husband, teenage daughter and
two very spoiled dogs.

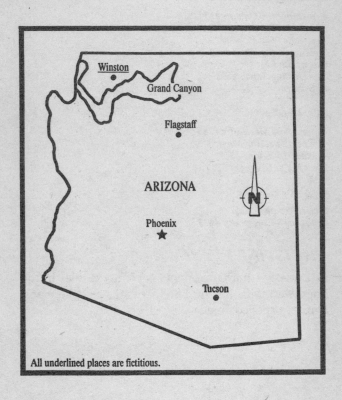

All underlined places are fictitious.

Part One

Chapter One

Thursday, 3:00 p.m.

Jamie knew there was a problem the instant she answered her telephone. Stan Hubbard, the local sheriff, was calling from the emergency room and he wasn't wasting time with preliminaries.

"We've got a bad one," he began, his faint drawl lacking its customary laziness. "I picked up a guy out on the highway about half an hour ago. Seems he and a buddy were hiking up around Thunderhead Cliffs yesterday and his friend took a header. The guy's been there since last night and the fellow I've got here says he wasn't moving much when he left to get help. Sounds like he needs medical attention as soon as we can get it to him."

Jamie understood the problem. Unlike more populated areas in Arizona, remote Winston didn't have a sophisticated emergency-rescue system. What it did have was an arrangement with the community hospital, where Jamie worked, to provide medical personnel when the need arose.

With the flu making the rounds, personnel was at a premium.

Today was Jamie's first day off in nearly two weeks. Taking a deep breath, she glanced toward the oven. It seemed little Tammy Robinson's birthday cake would have to wait a while longer. "Do you want me to drive out with you?"

Stan hesitated. "Not quite. It seems this fella's in a ravine and it's going to take some climbing to get to him. That's why I'm calling you. You've climbed out there before."

"I've *hiked* out there," she corrected, suddenly uneasy. Hiking and climbing were two different skills. Stan knew that. "Just how far down is he?"

"Not all that far. Not according to his friend, anyway. It's getting to him that's the problem. You can't drive anything in there close enough to do any good. I talked to Red about using one of his helicopters and he's calling in a pilot. Can you fly out with it?"

Stan wouldn't ask her to do anything he didn't think she could handle. He also wouldn't ask her for help without a real need. That need cut off any further hesitation. Doing what she could for others was second nature to Jamie. Saying no was next to impossible.

Some lessons, it seemed, were never learned.

"I'm on my way," she told him, and turned off the oven, leaving her half-baked cake.

Ten minutes later, dressed in jeans, a heavy black sweatshirt and hiking boots, and with her golden brown hair swinging in its customary single braid against her back, Jamie pushed through the emergency doors of Winston Community Hospital.

Even as the automatic doors closed with a quiet hiss behind her she could see the sheriff on the telephone at the nurses' station. His tan uniform with its sharp creases pressed into the shirt and his wide black belt with its row of bullets leading around to his gun and holster gave him a definite look of authority. His bald head and slightly crooked nose gave one the impression of a bully. But as he glanced up from the map he'd spread on the elbow-high counter, his smile for Jamie was kind.

He raised his hand in greeting as she passed. Jamie smiled in return, her footsteps never faltering as she skirted the counter and headed into the area divided into curtained-off examining rooms.

At the sound of her approach, Martha, a gruff-looking, gray-haired R.N. with a heart of pure platinum, turned from a supply cabinet. The older woman had a no-nonsense way about her that Jamie respected, as well as a remarkable talent for being right.

From the gleam in Martha's bespectacled eyes, it appeared that she'd again called the outcome correctly.

"I told Stan you'd do it," she said, taking in Jamie's attire with a self-satisfied nod. She turned back to take two elastic bandages from the shelf. "Knowing that, I went ahead and checked out the med-evac pack for you. There's heat packs in there along with cold ones. As cold as it was last night, you'll be dealing with hypothermia as well as whatever else he did to himself."

"Is it anyone from around here?"

"They're both from Utah. The boy I'm working on is Jim Kilpatrick. Can't recall offhand what he told the sheriff the other boy's name was. But they're both nineteen."

The cabinet door clicked shut as she lifted her chin toward a cubicle behind her. "The one in there sprained both wrists and is likely to lose a couple of fingertips from frostbite. Aside from being worried about his buddy, all he's concerned about is whether he'll be able to climb again. Says he needs his fingertips to get good holds on the rocks."

Shaking her head, she turned away, the soles of her white oxfords squeaking on the beige linoleum floor. "I never will understand the mentality inclined to such things. The human body suffers enough without such deliberate abuse. If God had meant for people to climb around on rocks, He'd have given them feet like mountain goats."

Martha also felt that if God had meant people to fly He'd have given them wings. Had they been meant to cavort like fish in water, He'd have given them fins. A person's feet should remain planted firmly on good old terra firma. All manner of difficulties could be prevented if people would heed that simple admonition.

Reminding herself that Martha's philosophy about keeping one's feet on the ground could also be applied in less literal ways, Jamie concentrated on checking through the bright orange pack on the counter. It wasn't that she didn't trust Martha's judgment about supplies. She just needed to know what she had to work with as well as making sure that what she might need was there. Heaven only knew in what condition she would find her patient.

She had just repacked a bag of saline when Terese Hadley, their incredibly efficient admitting clerk, hurried past with a quick, "Hi, Jamie," on her way to answer a ringing telephone. Stan was still on the nearest one, so the petite brunette grabbed the phone farther down the beige Formica counter, signaling Jamie as she did. Answering the call, she quickly scratched out a note on a memo pad and handed it to her. Four hastily scrawled words were written on the pink paper.

"Mitch is the pilot."

Jamie knew how to remain calm in a crisis. Many times a patient's life literally depended on her ability to remain detached, to focus on what had to be done immediately and not be overwhelmed by the scope of the problem. She tried to apply the same principle now.

It didn't work quite as well on a personal level.

Outwardly, not a single muscle moved in her face. Inwardly, she felt as if the air had just been sucked from her lungs. She raised her glance from the note to Terese's sympathetic expression.

"Emergency," Terese said into the receiver, even as her eyes said, "I'm sorry."

Jamie forced herself to take a deep breath. It was startling, and enormously disappointing, to find the wounds still so raw. Mitch Kincaid had walked out of her life nearly four months ago. Four months of chastising herself for getting involved with someone who'd warned her from the beginning that he wouldn't stay, and four months of promising herself she'd get over him. Just this week, she'd begun to think she was getting it all back together. The four words staring back at her from the paper in her hand had just shown her how little progress she'd actually made.

Handing the pad back to Terese, she avoided the younger woman's knowing eyes and zipped up the pack. Jamie had learned long ago that there was little about life that could be considered fair. She'd seen good people suffer enormously and real flakes get off scot-free. But she couldn't begin to imagine what she'd done to deserve this particular twist of fate. In all of Mojave County, she would think that there *had* to be someone other than Mitch Kincaid who could fly a helicopter. But even as she prayed for a reprieve, she knew there wouldn't be one. Arizona's Kanab plateau was as vast as it was remote and choices in Winston, the only town for hundreds of miles with a population of any consequence, were limited. On this particular winter afternoon, she seemed to be the only qualified medical support available and, apparently, Mitch was the only pilot the owner of the air service could send.

Jamie hadn't even known he was back.

. The quality of her apprehension changed as the sheriff hung up the telephone and clipped his pen into the pocket of his tan shirt.

"Red said a chopper's warming up. Should be here in about three minutes." He looked at his watch, then to the large clock on the wall above Jamie's head. Time was critical. But Stan knew he didn't need to tell her that.

"I really appreciate you doing this, Jamie. I'd go myself, but there's only room for two in the chopper and with the guy needing medical attention, it's better you than me. It'd be over three hours before we could get help in from anywhere else and that's more than the daylight we've got left."

People in Winston were accustomed to handling their own problems. They did the best they could with what they had available. The best they could do today was put a nurse who liked to hike around in the rocks together with a helicopter from a nearly defunct airline specializing in air tours of the Arizona Strip and the Grand Canyon. It was incidental that the chopper came with Mitch for a pilot.

Jamie didn't think to question the need for her presence. It was Mitch's she wanted to avoid. "Red couldn't fly it himself?"

Being a friend, Stan knew why she wanted to know. Being a gentleman, he avoided mentioning it directly. "Red's back is out again. But he said that if anyone can handle this, Kincaid can. He's qualified, Jamie. And he's available."

"I never meant to imply he wasn't qualified."

He looked from her. "I know."

"I just didn't know he was back."

"I didn't either. But you can handle this. Right?"

Jamie hoisted the strap of the med-evac pack over her shoulder. The strap caught the end of her braid and, wincing, she tugged it out to swing back between her shoulder blades. Stan didn't even notice that she hadn't answered him. He was too busy sucking in his stomach when Terese walked by for him to pay any attention to much else. It had been obvious to everyone but the lovely young widow that he had a thing for her. Now, from the suddenly self-conscious way Terese lowered her eyes, it appeared she had finally noticed.

When Terese got busy with Martha, Stan realized he had little excuse to hang around much longer and joined Jamie by the doors. She stood just inside, her expression carefully blank as she peered out toward the cloudless horizon. The land around Winston was mostly gently rolling rangeland and on a clear day, it seemed a person could see forever. Especially to the south where, twenty miles away, the Grand Canyon split the northwestern corner of Arizona in a ragged gash. The earth there fell away in a chasm so wide, astronauts had actually seen it from outer space. She remembered standing at the edge of that chasm, looking three thousand feet straight down and feeling the sudden necessity to back up before some inexplicable force pulled her over. She felt the same sensation now—the urgent need to turn and run.

"He'd better hurry up," said Stan, settling his Mountie-style hat over his sparse fringe of blond hair. "It's almost three-thirty. Sun sets about five-thirty or so."

Jamie touched the glass, feeling the chill against her fingers. "Do you know how cold it is?"

"Last I heard it was thirty-seven degrees. That was about two o'clock."

From what she understood, the young man they were to rescue—Tim Webster, she'd finally been told—had been injured about twenty-three hours ago. The temperature last night had reached thirty degrees. Tonight, the weather forecast had called for a low of twenty-five. The mercury would drop like a rock once the sun set.

The weather was just another problem to add to her growing sense of trepidation. She tried to think of others that might present themselves, of conditions and contingencies that might affect the rescue. But a person couldn't be prepared for everything, and all she could think about at the moment was that she was about to face the man who'd turned her neatly ordered life upside down, then walked away without so much as a backward glance.

A knot the size of a small fist formed in her stomach when she heard the drone of a helicopter. Within seconds the sound was directly overhead. Not giving herself time to consider the irony in what she was doing, she hurried out the double doors. The distinctive whap-whap of rotor blades drowned out the soft thud of her hiking boots on the pavement and Stan's shouted, "Be careful!" before the doors closed.

Nearly every decision Jamie had ever made in her life had been shaded by two inherent tendencies: to avoid confrontation and to help where she was able. Those needs were never so at odds as she ran toward what would be anything but a pleasant encounter.

The rotor wash flattened the scrub grass and sent a cloud of dust billowing upward as the helicopter eased down like a giant yellow-and-white insect on the vacant land next to the parking lot. Ducking her head, Jamie darted through the churning air. She wouldn't think about the knot in the pit of her stomach. She'd consider only what she had to do to get her victim to safety and, somehow, get through the next couple of hours without falling apart. She rarely drank, but she was contemplating getting royally stewed when this was over. The bottle of apricot brandy her former college roommate had sent her for Christmas six years ago should be nice and smooth by now.

The helicopter door swung open. With an efficiency of movement common to those intimately familiar with the difference seconds can make, she tossed her backpack behind the seat and climbed in. An instant later, she was handed a headset.

She'd have been all right if she hadn't looked at him.

The face she'd spent countless nights trying to forget was suddenly very real. And though she'd tried, she found she'd forgotten very little, after all. She'd remembered the weathered lines bracketing his mouth and how they deepened when he smiled. She'd remembered, too, the scar in the slash of his left eyebrow, the imperfection making his rugged features even more compelling. There was a hardness about him, an edge that, in some elemental way, prevented a person from thinking him handsome. Yet that same edge made it impossible to think him otherwise.

No expression marred the rugged angles of his features and his eyes, the deep blue of midnight, betrayed nothing. Mitch had always masked his emotions well. It would seem he hadn't changed on that score.

The thought both hurt and compelled. She'd have given her left lung to never see him again.

He lifted the headset for her to take and indicated a switch on the microphone arm attached to the one he was wearing. The headsets were a means of cutting the deafening noise of the rotors as well as a means of communication between pilot and ground and pilot and passenger. Settling the two cup-like pieces over her ears, she pushed the switch as he'd indicated.

Through the headset she heard him say, "Buckle up," as he turned his attention to the controls. He didn't spare her so much as another glance, but she'd no sooner snapped her shoulder harness into place than the craft pitched forward and up.

Jamie had the vague sensation of having left her stomach behind when she heard his voice again. The words came quieter this time, yet their impact equaled hitting a brick wall.

"I've missed you, Jamie."

Except for his first brief glance, he still hadn't looked at her. For that, Jamie was infinitely grateful. He'd always known what to say to get to her, though he probably had never even realized the kind of power he'd had. Yet, despite the hurt she'd suffered from him, she didn't believe he'd hurt her on purpose. It would have been easier for her to hate him if she could believe that. But he wasn't that kind of man. Some people simply built their emotional barriers so well that they could never break free of them. Mitch seemed to live in that kind of prison; the kind where no one could get in and he couldn't get out. As hard as it was to love a man like that, she couldn't help but feel it had to be harder still for him.

She looked away, off to her right, so he couldn't see the uncertainty in her expression. "Why did you come back?"

Several seconds ticked by before she felt him look at her. Another long moment passed before his voice extinguished her faint flicker of hope. "Red needed some help."

She should have known he hadn't come back because of her.

"Look, Jamie," she heard him say when she failed to comment. "Red's business is in trouble and he thinks I can help him build it back up. Is there anything wrong with that?"

Even through the filtering static of the headset she didn't miss the defense in his tone. But she wasn't going to fight with him. He was so much better at it than she. "I'm sure he's glad you're back. He's missed you."

So had a lot of other people, but she wasn't going to tell Mitch that. The idea of him being around again filled her with an aching emptiness. There had been a time when they could have been friends. They *had* been friends. Once. Before they'd become lovers. But it was too late for friendship now and she hoped with all her heart that he wouldn't insult what they had shared by suggesting it.

It was a little late to start protecting herself from him, but she had to start sometime. As Martha would say, there was no time like the present.

Below them, the grade school and the park across from her own little house disappeared. They flew over the tract houses that bordered a wash, then past the trailer park marking the outskirts of town. Ahead stretched the flat floor of the high desert, ringed in the distance by the high mesas and plateaus that gave an eerie, other-planet effect to the endless reaches of the land.

She'd left the communication channel open. "How long will it take us to get there?"

Mitch's hesitation could have meant he was concentrating on his flying. She supposed, too, that he might be considering her abrupt and obvious change of subject. She never had understood what his silences meant.

When she finally heard his response through the headphones, his tone was cool. He told her that it shouldn't take more than twenty minutes to reach the area they needed to search, then added that her guess was as good as his as to how long it would take to find the man once they got there.

The guy the sheriff had picked up on the highway had said they were hiking near an area known as The Pinnacles. Mitch told her that he planned to take a swing below the ridge line leading up to the spires before the sun sank much farther and put the valley floor in shadows. The area was a morass of crevices and ledges, and once the sun dropped below the horizon it would be even harder to spot their victim.

They had roughly an hour and a half of daylight left. It took the twenty minutes Mitch had estimated—most of which passed in excruciating silence—to reach the area where they began their search. As much as she hated the thought of a person being injured or in pain, Jamie was relieved to have something to concentrate on other than the tension snaking between her and the stone-jawed man in the left seat.

Ten more minutes passed in a painstaking sweep of the ridge. Below them, slipping beneath the elongated shadow of the helicopter, slab rocks and boulders, winter-killed vegetation and gray-green Joshua covered mile after mile. In startling contrast, less than fifteen miles away rose Mount Trumbull with its stands of ponderosa pine forests and quaking aspen.

Jamie kept her eyes on the terrain. Mitch did too, at the same time handling the helicopter with a kind of skill Jamie couldn't help but admire. She'd never flown with him before, but she knew he loved to fly. He lived for it, actually. Even now, as his subtle shifts of the collective pitch stick caused the craft to dart forward and back, to hover, then to inch along the craggy slopes before speeding up to double back, he was more relaxed than he would have been sitting in an easy chair.

Jamie couldn't have relaxed had her life depended on it.

"Hey!" Mitch leaned toward her, then banked left. Jamie grabbed the sides of her seat. "Did you see that?"

She hadn't seen anything other than endless stretches of pink and salmon, and sand-colored rock. The striations were incredible and had it not been for their search she'd have been left a little breathless by the sheer stark beauty of the place. "I didn't see anything." Her eyes narrowed as she craned her head. "What did you...? Wait! That flash? Is that what you mean?"

Something far below them glinted in the sun, flashing gold against the deep umber ground. Mitch brought them as low as he dared, but the walls of the little canyon were too narrow to risk flying between them and though they couldn't get close enough to do them any good, they were able to see what had caught their attention. A backpack was caught on a rock near the base of a shallow ravine, its frame catching the beam of the searchlight Mitch had turned on to sweep the shadows. About twenty feet below the pack, a man lay on his back, motionless. It seemed they had found their hiker.

All they had to do now was get to him.

As Mitch eased the helicopter upward, Jamie watched Tim's ominously still form shrink with the distance. "What are you doing?"

"We'll have to set down up here," came Mitch's reply as he rose to hover over the tabletop mesa above the narrow canyon. "There's more of a slope on the other side of this. It'll be easier to get him if we hike down that way, then follow the ridges to the bottom of the ravine. I'll try to rig pulleys to bring him up some of the steeper faces. It'll be easier than both of us trying to carry him out the long way."

Skeptical, not wanting to be, Jamie gave an agreeing nod. The back side of the mesa did have an incline rather than sheering straight down as it did from where the hiker had apparently fallen. If they cut across at an angle, maybe following the boulder-strewn wash, the trek down wouldn't be so bad.

That reassurance was tested when she glanced over at Mitch's brooding expression. She was sure he'd have preferred to rappel straight down the face, taking the same route as the hiker. Mitch thrived on that sort of thing. But in no way was Jamie interested in dangling over the side of a cliff like bait on the end of a fishing line. She liked climbing around in the rocks but only so long as one foot could always touch the ground.

It was entirely possible, of course, that Mitch wasn't even thinking of that. Maybe his expression looked so dark simply because he was no happier being forced into their present situation than she was.

Despite the fact that the surface hardly looked large enough to play marbles on, Mitch set the helicopter down and cut the power. For a fraction of a second he thought of forcing himself to do what he'd avoided from the moment he'd seen Jamie run out the hospital doors—to look into her eyes and see if she hated him as much as he feared she might. He'd never known her to be as distant as she'd been the past twenty minutes.

Without further thought, he climbed out of the cockpit. The breath he'd just drawn had brought her scent with it; some subtle combination of soap and baby powder and something that reminded him vaguely of wildflowers. With a swiftness he'd always found disconcerting, that scent elicited a surge of memories that had his body tightening and his gut feeling as if he'd just been rammed by a linebacker. All too easily he could recall the sweet taste of her skin, the feel of it beneath his hands and how just looking at her could make him hard.

The cockpit door slid shut behind him. There would be enough time later to confirm what he suspected—that coming back hadn't been such a hot idea after all.

"Open that door over there. We're going to have to take the stretcher out on your side."

He hadn't meant to sound curt, but he didn't waste time apologizing for his less-than-pleasant tone. They had a job to do, and he knew Jamie was just as anxious as he to get it over with. Fortunately, she simply did as he'd asked, sliding back the door to expose a scoop stretcher lying where the two back seats had been removed.

It only took minutes for Mitch to secure a rope and pulley to the struts of the helicopter and pitch the end of the rope over the edge to a narrow ledge some twenty feet below.

Once that was done, he put his own pack with another coil of rope and some crampons into the stretcher with Jamic's pack, checked the pistol he always carried climbing in the wild and, each taking an end, they started their descent.

Mitch knew from personal experience that Jamie was in excellent physical condition. She was five feet seven inches of lithe, athletic grace—something he couldn't ignore watching her sweet backside precede him—but hauling a man up a mountain in a stretcher was not an easy task.

"I'll rig up another pulley when we get to where the first rope is," he told her. "It'll be easier if we can bring him up by carrying him over the more horizontal surfaces and pulling him up on the vertical ones."

Lack of time dictated speed. The terrain demanded caution.

As Jamie's boots loosened bits of vermilion shale to skitter down the incline, she couldn't help but think that falling was a distinct possibility. She was accustomed to hiking with the weight of a backpack. Hanging on to a six-foot-long mesh-and-aluminum stretcher while remaining upright on a slant was something new.

"How do you want to work the pulleys?"

"I'll use the rope to climb up. Once I'm up, you secure it to the stretcher and I'll raise it."

"Then I go around the back way and meet you on the next ledge to do it again?"

"Unless you want me to send the rope back down to you."

"We'll see." She had a while before she had to make that decision. Right now, it was one thing at a time.

Mitch was behind her, letting her choose the way she wanted to take. He moved with the ease of a panther: surefooted, silent. Since he had scaled the likes of Mount McKinley and K2, this particular switchback route probably looked like a stroll in the park. Label an activity dangerous and he'd no doubt try it. Heli-skiing, parachuting, scuba diving. The steeper, deeper, higher or faster something was, the more it appealed to him. She'd never figure out how he'd managed to survive to the ripe old age of thirty-four.

Ten months ago, he almost hadn't survived. She didn't want to think about that now.

Instead, as they made their way along the precipitous route, cautious of the loose rock and the scorpions and snakes making their home among them, she focused on the man they'd come to help. She couldn't see him yet, but she was sure he wasn't conscious. He'd been ominously still when they'd spotted him. Not even the noise of the helicopter had made him move. With the walls of the canyon concentrating the sound, there was no way a conscious person couldn't have heard them.

She mentioned that to Mitch. Conversation, minimal as it had been, had been limited to the task at hand. She intended to keep it that way.

"The noise would have been enough to wake the dead," she said, then wished she hadn't put it in quite those terms.

"I hadn't wanted to mention that he might not be alive. But it sure looks like a possibility." A rock loosened by his boot clattered past her. "I'm sorry it had to be this way, Jamie."

The breeze, cooler now than it had been even minutes ago, carried his words to her. The strange calm in them bothered her, but she couldn't look up from her footing to see what might be in his expression. "What do you mean?"

"That circumstances aren't better. I knew we'd run into each other, but I hadn't thought it would be like this." She thought she heard Mitch sigh. The faint sound could also have been the wind. "I didn't know whether my coming back would matter to you or not."

"What you do is your own business." She hoped she sounded open-minded, mature; the way they did on the glitzy nighttime soaps her next-door neighbor always watched. "Not every relationship works."

He had the decency not to push for more. But even as she wondered what he wanted from her, she knew she wasn't being fair. Though they had parted on less than amicable terms, they had been important to each other. Mitch had become important to a lot of people. In some ways, his leaving had been a betrayal to them all.

She had the feeling Mitch realized that. But what he didn't understand was that of all those people, only she had understood that it had been impossible for him to stay.

Chapter Two

It took the better part of an hour for them to reach the bottom of the wash leading into the ravine. By then Mitch's silence seemed defensive, and Jamie was so edgy that she dropped her end of the stretcher with a gasp when a lizard darted over a rock in front of her. She normally didn't startle so easily, and when Mitch realized what had caused her to jump she saw his initial disapproval give way to curiosity.

Without a word she picked up her end again, silently daring him to comment. He knew that crawly things didn't usually bother her. Two ornery brothers had cured her fear of bugs and such long before she'd moved to the desert— and the desert was full of insects, snakes and scaly critters the likes of which her city-dwelling family had never seen. Most people eventually grew accustomed to sharing space with the natural inhabitants of the area and, like Jamie, developed a healthy respect for the poisonous varieties. Even the small gray lizard now blinking back at her from the shelter of a nearby rock seemed puzzled by her behavior.

"We don't have much farther to go."

Grateful for the assurance, Jamie sighed and picked her way over the jagged boulders centuries of rain had washed into the ravine.

Those boulders were the last obstacles between them and their victim. As soon as that barrier was cleared, Jamie could see the inert form of Tim Webster lying less than twenty feet away. He lay with his arms flung out and his right leg tucked awkwardly beneath him, the position exactly the same as it had been when they'd seen him from the air. Only from here she could see that his clothing—blue sweatshirt, jeans and boots—wasn't as insulating as she'd hoped. The freezing cold last night could easily have taken its toll.

Swallowing her trepidation, she grasped the professionalism that made her separate emotion from knowledge and focused her thoughts solely on her patient. Without waiting for Mitch, she lowered her end of the stretcher and grabbed the bright orange med-evac pack. Pebbles and sharp shards of rock crunched beneath her boots as she hurried to the man's side. Landing on that unforgiving bed would have been like landing on concrete. She tried not to shudder as she glanced up at the ridge rising so far above them. His friend said he'd fallen from nearly halfway up, easily a couple hundred feet.

Watching her, Mitch approached more slowly. He felt certain that Jamie knew that the guy they were going to so much trouble for was already dead. It wasn't always the fall that killed a climber. It was the delay in getting help. Shock, internal bleeding, heatstroke in hot weather, hypothermia in cold. Any one of those could compound what may have begun as a relatively manageable problem. Having suffered a couple of those delays himself, he was intimately familiar with their effect on the human body.

"Tim?" he heard her ask. "Can you hear me?"

The young man didn't move, but the sound of Jamie's voice drew Mitch. It had a seductive quality to it, a soft huskiness that soothed and aroused at the same time. He liked those contrasts. Always had. What he didn't like was the track his thoughts were taking. Thinking about her in terms of arousal or seduction wasn't at all appropriate at the moment. But it sure beat thinking about the poor kid sprawled on the rocks.

Leaving the stretcher by one of the huge clay-colored boulders a few feet away, he hunkered down opposite Jamie. Her fingers were pressed to the side of the hiker's neck; her eyebrows were knitted in concentration. With her free hand, she fumbled with the zipper on her pack.

Without thinking, Mitch reached over to unzip it for her. The moment their hands collided, she drew back.

"Sorry," she said, as if apologizing for having given something away by her reaction.

He pulled back, unable to describe how it felt to have her shrink from his touch. With a quiet "It's okay," he let her open the bag herself and made himself concentrate on the form between them. He wondered if there would be a response to her ministrations. There didn't seem to be any life left in the lean, young body.

He's just a boy, Mitch thought, seeing the baby-fine stubble of hair on the unnaturally pale cheeks and chin. The young man's lips were a dull gray blue around the edges, and when Jamie asked if he could hear her, they remained as still as the encroaching twilight.

Mitch thought that the kid was gone.

Jamie obviously knew otherwise. Her left hand dived back into the pack; her right rested reassuringly on Tim's chest.

"Is he alive?"

"Barely," she said, her tone hushed. Then, hanging a stethoscope around her neck, she spoke again to Tim.

"We're going to take care of you. Just relax," she said, which Mitch thought an odd thing to say to someone already as limp as leftover pasta. "We're going to get some fluids into you and get you warm. Can you hear me, Tim?"

She kept up the quiet banter as Mitch, not knowing what else to do, watched. He had no right to feel proud of her. He had no rights at all where she was concerned. But he felt the pride, anyway. She sounded so calm, so sure, and her movements as she cut through the arm of the blue sweatshirt with scissors she'd taken from the pack were quick and decisive. She seemed relieved to find long underwear under the shirt and cut through the sleeve of that, too. Within seconds she had an IV going and was injecting something from another syringe into it. Then she was leaning back over him, listening to his chest with the stethoscope and laying her hand over his abdomen to test its rigidity.

It was impossible for Mitch to tell anything from her expression as her small, slender hands worked over the length of her patient's body. Only her voice carried any emotion—and there only assurance—and it unnerved him to know that he couldn't read her as easily as he once had. He hadn't been with her for two hours, yet he sensed a defensiveness, a kind of self-protectiveness he'd seen her hide behind with others, but never with him. He hadn't wanted her to change. He'd liked her just as she'd been.

Maybe, he thought, he should have let her know that it was his fault things hadn't worked out between them.

Grim self-deprecation voided the value in his conclusion. She'd no doubt already figured that out. It had been he who hadn't seen it at the time. He hadn't seen a lot of things. Just like now. He would have given this young man up for dead. Yet Jamie had found the life still struggling in him and was doing everything in her power to make the boy hold on.

She'd once done the same for Mitch. She'd seen a spark of something worth saving buried deeply inside his battered soul, but he'd already given up on it.

"We haven't got much longer." He glanced up the rock walls of the canyon above the ravine to the deepening blue of the sky. "If we don't hurry, the sun's going to set before we can get him out of here. I have no desire to get stuck halfway up there in the dark."

She raised her head, not looking particularly appreciative of his reminder. "I am hurrying. But we can't move him yet. Here." She pulled a long plastic bag from the pack. "Help me get him into these."

Mitch frowned at the object she unrolled. "Put him *in* there?"

The thing grew longer as she spread it out. "They're mast trousers," she explained. "He's bleeding internally and his right leg is broken. When these are on and inflated, they'll immobilize the lower part of his body and equalize the flow of blood. Easy, now."

Jamie didn't bother with further explanations. The young man in her care was in the advanced stages of shock and he needed far more help than she could give him. She secured his broken leg and inflated the plastic trousers, then hurriedly tucked small heat packs under the green wool blankets they put around him after lifting him onto the stretcher. She could only hope she'd done enough. It was incredible that he'd hung on for so long. But then, she didn't count out miracles when it came to human life. Some people were born fighters.

Mitch had been like that.

With a curse for her persistent memory, thinking a touch of amnesia might be nice, she secured the safety straps over Tim's legs and waist. Mitch had already fastened the one over their patient's chest and she was aware of his quiet scrutiny as he waited for her to finish. She hated it when he watched her that way, as if her every thought were exposed to his inspection. It didn't help to know that he *had* known her better than anyone ever had; touched her on the most intimate of levels and plowed past barriers she hadn't even known she'd erected.

Glancing away, she wished with all her heart that she could forget—and knew without a doubt that she'd never be able to.

The medical pack was behind her. Reaching around, she dragged it from the foot-wide flat rock where it rested, tipping the rock sideways in the process and leaving a trail in powdery pink dirt. She'd heard the clatter when the rock fell but paid no attention to it as she stuffed the stethoscope and a pressure cuff back into the bag and began to zip it up.

"Jamie?"

Mitch's tone was strangely quiet, the question in it decidedly cautious. Thinking some change in Tim must have prompted his odd tone, her attention immediately focused on her patient. Tim still looked the same. The medical term for his appearance was *cyanotic*. The layman's term was *lousy*.

She glanced up, puzzled. But Mitch wasn't looking at her, so he didn't see her confusion. His focus was riveted to her left.

"Stand up as slowly as you can." A calculated calm hushed his voice. "Whatever you do, don't make any sudden moves."

She didn't have to ask what the problem was. Without having to see it, she suddenly knew. The ominous rattle started with an almost syncopated rhythm. The only sound in the deep ravine. It grew louder, faster, and as she breathed a whispered, "Oh my God," her muscles tensed to spring.

"Move!" she heard Mitch shout.

She jerked back, adrenaline pumping furiously. Less than three seconds had passed since Mitch's warning. The snake had only allowed her two.

The coiled rattler struck just as her knees left the ground. Horror met disbelief. For a fraction of an instant, time stopped in a surreal freeze-frame. Almost at once, Jamie saw the deep indentations below the black eyes on the viper's triangular head and the scales on its beautifully patterned skin. Then she felt the sting of its needle-like fangs punch through the denim of her jeans and sink into the flesh of her calf above the top of her leather boot.

Pain, white hot and staggering, radiated through her leg. Scarcely halfway up, she grabbed her knee, drawing her leg up as she fell. Rocks poked at her back, sharp edges jabbing the length of her spine. She didn't notice. Little registered beyond the intense, searing sensation in her leg. It felt as if lightning were being shot through it, every bolt burning hotter than the last.

Through a haze of pain she heard the crack of a pistol, the sound reverberating against the canyon walls. She heard another shot, its echo meeting the first, and rolled to her side as if to defend herself from it. A moment later, Mitch crouched over her and she felt his hand at the back of her neck.

He rolled her toward him.

This couldn't be happening. They were supposed to be leaving now, climbing out with Tim. "Oh, God, Mitch. It hurts."

"Easy." His large hand cupped the back of her head, cushioning it. "You've got to stay still."

"We've got to get Tim out of here."

"Are you crazy? We've got to get *you* out of here."

She'd argue Mitch's conclusion later. Now she commanded herself to think, even as she wondered if she really felt a faint tingling in her fingers and feet, or if she only imagined the sensations because she knew what symptoms to anticipate. Weakness, numbness. The feeling of suffocation. Sometimes knowing what to expect wasn't all it was cracked up to be. Maybe she was only hyperventilating. She was entitled to that, wasn't she? But she didn't have time for it. Calm. She had to stay calm.

Mitch snagged the orange pack. "Do you have any antivenin in here?"

She should have thought of that herself. Would have, once she'd become more accustomed to the fog of pain. The antidote for snake bites was always carried in this wilderness.

Sucking air through her teeth, she nodded and reached for the pack.

Mitch pushed her hand away. Taking her by the shoulders, he eased her into a sitting position, then drew her to him so she could lean against his solid chest. Jamie fit there like a child. And like a child, she wanted very badly to turn into him so he could make the pain and the hurt go away.

With one arm around her, he dug through the contents of the pack. "Tell me what I'm looking for."

In a way, she was grateful for the concentration it required to describe the package and then for the effort it took to get her jacket off and her sweater sleeve pushed up. But having made it that far, she encountered another problem. She was shaking so badly that Mitch had to break open the packaging for her. Then he had to help her get the serum into the syringe.

He sat beside her holding the alcohol wipe he'd just used on her inner arm. "Can you do this?"

She heard the worry in his voice, felt it in the tension in his body.

"Can you?"

"You know me and needles. But if you need me to, I will."

She appreciated the effort. He hated needles; used to go pale at the sight of one. Martha's never-ending litany of truisms flashed through the fear and the pain. *The bigger they come the harder they fall.*

"It's okay." She wanted to smile. The effort was beyond her. "All we need right now is for *you* to pass out. Just steady my hand. Okay?"

It took her two tries to get the vein, but somehow she managed to inject herself. Somehow, too, they managed to get her leg splinted to immobilize it and a cold pack in place to slow the circulation and ease the pain.

She had no choice but to let Mitch take over. Actually, no one *let* Mitch do anything. He was too much his own man to allow anyone the control that would require such permission. But he did what needed to be done, asking what to do only when he couldn't figure it out for himself. She'd seen this no-nonsense side of him before; his ability to concentrate so absolutely. At first she'd been impressed by it. At the moment she was thankful for it. But she'd forgotten that his determination could be rather aggravating, too.

"I don't suppose there's any chance that you can walk on that."

Walking was a bad idea for a number of sound medical reasons, but just the thought doubled the pain. "Afraid not."

"Then I'm taking you out first."

As calmly as she could, she refuted his decision. "He has to get to the hospital." She nodded toward the hiker lying so still in the stretcher. "He's barely hanging on now."

"I'm not leaving you here."

"He needs blood, Mitch. They can't do anything more for me at the hospital than we've already done. The antivenin will either work or it won't," she added, and she couldn't believe how scared she suddenly was. The tingling was *real.*

believe how scared she suddenly was. The tingling was *real.*
And the weakness was already pulling the strength from her
limbs.

Don't panic, she warned herself, praying Mitch wouldn't
argue with her. The antivenin would work. It had to.

Mitch didn't argue. Turning, he bent over the stretcher.

"Mitch. Don't!"

He ignored her. The metal buckles of the safety straps
clunked dully against rock as he flipped the straps back.
Removing a blanket and two of the four small heat pack-
ets, he set them aside. But instead of taking Tim out of
the stretcher as she'd feared he would, Mitch resecured the
straps and put the two remaining heat packs back under
the young man. His expression a study in stone, he took the
blanket over to a smooth curve in the side of an enormous
boulder and kicked away the scattering of rocks and debris
at its base. When that was done, he came back and picked
her up.

"I don't want to do this," he told her, acutely aware of
the trembling of her slender body. He'd carry her out of here
if he could, but that was impossible, and he couldn't be responsible for Tim Webster's death by taking the decision
from Jamie's hands. He had to trust her with this. "But I
don't see that I have a choice. Have you got something for
pain in that bag of yours?"

She nodded, wishing she could sink into his solid strength.
The pain wouldn't be so bad if she could just concentrate on
something else. But the old catch-22 was in full operation.
The intensity of the pain made that concentration nearly
impossible.

"What?" he wanted to know.

"Morphine. But I don't want to use it. I wouldn't be able
to think."

She could barely do that now.

He didn't question her decision. It only mattered that he was at least leaving her with some means of alleviating what had to be sheer agony.

Lowering her to the blanket, he took off his jacket. He stuffed her right arm into it, then her left, and refused to consider throwing her over his shoulder and hauling her out that way. If he'd thought for a moment that the idea would work, he'd have done it. But it wouldn't. And the guy on the ground behind him was dying. "I'm leaving my pistol with you. As much as you're shaking, I doubt you could hit anything with it. But the noise might scare off a prowling coyote." He pulled the pistol from the back waistband of his jeans and laid it on the ground beside her. He also placed her pack within easy reach.

"How are you going to get him out?"

From the frown darkening Mitch's features, it seemed he'd been wondering that himself. A little awkwardly, since he wasn't in the habit of dressing other people, he buttoned her into his jacket as he tested his plan aloud.

"He doesn't seem to weigh much over a hundred and forty or fifty pounds. I think I can drag him up past where his backpack's hanging up there, then leave him while I climb up to where we dropped the last rope. I should be able to manage from there like we talked about. I'll either have to tie the stretcher to the rope then climb around the long way and pull him up, or climb up the rope after I've secured the stretcher to it." With his jacket buttoned over hers, he tucked the blanket around her legs. "Probably better that the guy's unconscious. Since he's already taken a header over that cliff, I doubt he'd be too crazy about the idea of dangling over the edge of it."

"Be careful."

"Don't worry, I won't drop him."

"I meant you."

A rebellious flicker of hope, undaunted by her acceptance of its futility, punched through the urgency of the moment. He cared. She knew from the bleakness in his expression as he touched her cheek with his knuckles.

"You, too." He drew his touch along her jaw, looking for the words he knew she needed to hear, something to leave her with that might ease her fear. And his own. He thrived on fear. Was, he supposed, addicted to it. But not this kind. Not the kind where he feared for someone else.

He searched for the words, but couldn't find them. He never had been able to.

"I'll be back" was all he said before turning away.

She watched him go, power and purpose concentrated into his every movement as he lifted the head of the stretcher and started up the incline.

"I'll be back," he'd said, and she knew he would. She could trust him with her life. She just couldn't trust him with her heart.

Gripping her arms around herself in a futile attempt to stop the shaking, Jamie closed her eyes and rolled to her side. It had taken every ounce of strength she possessed to keep him from seeing how badly she was trembling. He had to take the injured hiker out first, but if Mitch had thought she was getting worse, she doubted he would have listened to her. No one knew better than she how infinitely stubborn he could be. And as weak as she was getting, she knew she couldn't have argued with him. She'd made him think she was stronger than she was. But there was nothing particularly unusual about that. She'd pretended to be strong all of her life.

What she'd never told Mitch was that her entire life was an act. She was nothing at all like the calm, composed, rational person she wanted the world to see. All that was only a defense. Against herself, possibly. Against others, certainly. She could be brave for others. Being brave for herself was impossible. She knew herself too well. And right now she was so frightened she could scarcely breathe.

The fear increased. One of the sensations of the body's breakdown was a feeling of suffocation. The venom could cause respiratory paralysis and circulatory collapse. Already, an intense itching had begun and her calf had swollen to the point where the leg of her jeans was skintight. How long did it take for the antivenin to have some effect? Seconds? Minutes? With the foreign elements fighting each other in her body, she couldn't remember.

She rolled to her other side, agitated, restless, trembling. She couldn't remember ever being so cold. But her leg was hot. The notion was silly, she thought as her head began to ache, but if she could somehow wrap herself around her leg she might be able to warm up.

She opened her eyes, then shut them again, preferring self-induced darkness to the blackness encroaching upon the ravine. In the distance she heard the yip of a coyote, and closer, the skitter of pebbles dislodged by some nocturnal inhabitant of the shadows. The sounds registered, but she was beyond fearing them. She thought only of the dark and sought its oblivion. That is what Mitch had told her he'd found there. "It was like floating in nothing. Just empty blackness. That's all I remember."

When had he told her that? When she'd first met him? No. Later. Much later.

The oblivion finally came, easing the fear and taking her back. Back to when she'd first laid eyes on the man whose voice she could almost hear in the surreal state that claimed her....

Part Two

Chapter Three

Ten Months Earlier

Jamie's first thought when she saw the gurney roll past the nurse's station was that the man on it should have been in a body bag. He was covered with blood, his body limp and broken; and when Stan told her that the guy had run his motorcycle into Graffiti Rock, a huge boulder on the outskirts of town, "Going a good sixty miles an hour when he took the curve," she feared that Dr. Moody's presence would be necessary only to pronounce the date and time of demise.

Moving alongside the gurney, she directed the driver of the town's only ambulance to push it into the largest of the four emergency units. The code room contained specialized lifesaving equipment, as sophisticated as the county budget could afford. It wasn't quite the Star-Wars array owned by the urban E.R. in Los Angeles where she'd honed her battle skills, but the basics were all at hand. From the looks of it, this guy was going to need everything they had.

The soles of Martha's shoes squeaked on the checkerboard tiles, announcing her arrival even before her ample frame appeared on the other side of the gurney. "The doctor's on his way." She glanced down then, her terse "Oh, boy" indicating that she'd just taken a good look at their newest patient. "Have you got a pulse?"

Jamie's fingers were on his neck, her eyes moving over his blood-streaked face as she quickly assessed the color and feel of his skin. "Yeah. I do," she said, and the action began in earnest.

Jamie and Martha moved with the tense efficiency of people trained to one single purpose. Monitors were attached and an IV started even as clothing was cut away. Temporary compresses were applied to the deep gashes on his forehead, jaw, shoulder and legs to staunch the life-draining flow of blood. Torn and bloodied jeans, shirt and leather jacket were dumped unceremoniously into a white plastic bag along with harness-style brown boots. The bag was tossed into the basket under the gurney just as the curtain whipped back.

Balding, bespectacled and ever-rumpled, Dr. Theodore Moody snapped on rubber gloves as he hustled in, issuing instructions and asking questions already anticipated by the nurses.

"What have we got?" he wanted to know, and sighed when he looked at the man filling the table.

Within minutes, surgery was notified that the tonsillectomy Dr. Moody had scheduled would have to wait and Dr. Thompson, the town's orthopedic man, was called in from the golf course to assist. Dr. Thompson would handle the compound fractures of the left leg—the most obvious injuries at the moment, though X rays could easily reveal more—and Dr. Moody would do the interior work: what he suspected to be a ruptured spleen at the very least. Blood was sent to the lab to be typed and cross-matched, and the patient's vital signs were constantly checked. Considering the extent of his injuries, everyone thought it incredible that he was breathing on his own.

As Jamie worked to secure pressure bandages, she heard Martha return with the chart Terese had prepared. Dr. Moody had already departed to scrub.

The silver cover on the chart caught the bright overhead light as Martha opened it. "The sheriff took a wallet off the patient at the site," she said. "According to a Texas driver's license in it, he's thirty-four years old, six feet and one inch tall, weighs one hundred ninety-five pounds, has black hair, blue eyes and was born on November 17. His name is Mitchell Alexander Kincaid III, and he has an address in Houston. But," she stressed, closing the cover, "when Terese called to get a telephone number, there was no listing."

Jamie checked the flow on the IV. "Unlisted?"

"No, I mean there was no Mitchell Alexander Kincaid. Not a first, second or third."

"I hope she finds a number for him soon."

"Me, too," Martha agreed and Jamie set the matter of contacting this stranger's family aside.

A cuff had been attached to his arm, monitoring his blood pressure and showing it on a digital display. A pulse oximeter on his index finger indicated his pulse. Needing to unhook him from the equipment to get him to surgery, she'd started to take the lead from his finger when she noticed the sudden increase in his pulse rate. His fingers twitched. Then, incredibly, they closed around hers.

She hadn't realized he'd regained consciousness.

She squeezed that large, very masculine hand, understanding the contact he was seeking. "We're taking care of you," she told him. "Take it easy. Okay?"

His lips moved, but she couldn't hear him. So she leaned closer, still holding his hand. "Say it again," she urged, hating the effort it would cost him.

"Please." His fingers tightened. "Don't let go."

The words were barely audible, but the plea struck her as if he'd screamed it.

Her glance darted to his face. For the first time she truly looked at him, seeing past the abrasions and the gauze and the pallor distinguishing the patient from the man. He hadn't moved except for that one small effort to clutch her hand and his eyes remained closed, his features still.

Those features were strong and even. His jaw was chiseled, with a hint of determination about it that she truly hoped he possessed. Incongruously, she remembered Martha saying that his eyes were blue, and Jamie found herself thinking they might be very nice eyes, banked as they were by lashes most women would envy. Those lashes were as thick and dark as his over-long hair that, even now, made him look rather rebellious.

He was an attractive man. Disturbingly so. And it was easy enough to see that, until a short while ago, he'd been a healthy, vital one. His body was strong and beautifully muscled, even as battered and broken as it was now. He had that raw masculinity some women found appealing, most found dangerous, and Jamie had never, in twenty-nine years, come even close to encountering on a personal level. The few men in her life had been quite tame. But then, so was she, so it was pointless to feel any sense of regret, much less the odd sense of loss that came with the thought of how someone so strong should be so vulnerable.

She squeezed his hand again, but there was no response this time. Mercifully, he'd slipped back under, his body's response to unbearable pain. "You hang in there," she told him, even though he probably didn't hear.

Terese came up behind her. "Surgery's ready for him."

Letting his fingers slip from hers, Jamie finished removing the cuff while Martha covered him with a white blanket for the trip down the hall. A few moments later he was no longer in her care. Martha and an orderly rushed him out and Jamie was left to inventory the supplies they'd used, replace them and make sure everything was ready for the next time someone drove into a rock, suffered a heart attack, or whatever else nature and human error could come up with.

"I've got a call in to the Houston police." Terese swept the curtain fully open and started peeling little white stickers from Jamie's blue surgical scrubs, the uniform in emergency. The stickers were bar-code labels removed from supplies they'd used and would be run through a scanner in accounting. The nurses always stuck the stickers on themselves so they wouldn't lose them in the sometimes frantic action. "They're sending someone out to that address on his license to tell them what's happened and have them call here." Her dark curls bounced a little as she slowly shook her head. "Lord, but I feel for the person who answers that door."

Jamie added two more stickers to Terese's clipboard. It had been a while since she'd seen that lost look shadow their clerk's pretty features. "I'm sure you do, Terese. Hopefully, they won't be alone."

"I mean, it's been over a year, but I can still remember Sheriff Hubbard standing there with his hat in his hand saying how sorry he was. It's not something I'd wish on anyone." She glanced down at the clipboard, her brilliant fuchsia lips parting with a deep breath.

"Anyway," she went on, seeming to send the memories of the day she'd lost her husband back to their private place, "I hope we hear from someone soon. You know how nervous Hazel gets when we admit someone without knowing his financial condition or without getting permission for surgery."

Hazel was the hospital administrator, a formidable matron who thrived on the kind of paperwork and red tape that tended to make Jamie's eyes glaze over. It had been Hazel's idea to put computer stickers on everything.

Jamie pulled a sticker from the bottom of her white, soft-soled shoe and handed it to Terese. "Sometimes we just don't have a choice."

"No," the young woman agreed, looking at the empty spot where Mr. Kincaid's gurney had stood. "Sometimes we don't."

Jamie saw the shadows return. He'd affected Terese, too, Jamie realized, then tucked the thought away as the two women headed toward their separate tasks. Terese answered a ringing phone. Jamie went to see what she could do for a young couple who'd just come up to the admitting window, looking nervous and distinctly expectant.

Since the woman said her contractions were still five minutes apart, Jamie directed them to delivery with a smile and a "Good luck," and glanced at her watch.

She couldn't help but wonder how the man with the blue eyes was doing. They probably hadn't even started surgery, she thought, and stuffed her hands in her pockets.

In a way, it bothered her that he was so much on her mind. She had held countless hands in her seven years as a nurse. Yet, with this stranger, she'd felt her cloak of professionalism slip. It wasn't that she didn't usually feel for her patients. An instructor had once remarked that her compassion was her best asset—and her biggest problem. It had taken her a long time to learn how to detach a part of herself so emotion wouldn't cloud professional judgment and, selfishly perhaps, to protect herself from the hurts and inevitable losses. Usually, now, only the children really got to her.

But, somehow, Mitchell Alexander Kincaid III had gotten to her, too. Something about him and his plea had touched her. For an instant she'd glimpsed his fear and, by that, he'd unwittingly brought a fear of her own to the surface. He might be dying. Yet as she'd stood there looking at his beautiful, battered face, something about him made her wonder if *she* would ever live.

She thought it very sad that he might not even make it.

Chapter Four

"Oh, Jamie. I really wish you wouldn't do this." Doris Becker, one of the nurses from the medical floor, leaned over the break-room table, eyeing a pan of fresh cinnamon rolls. "My waistline can't afford your baking." She leaned closer and took an appreciative sniff. "And you used nutmeg, too."

"She always does." Martha shrugged out of her ancient pink mohair sweater as she walked in. "That's what makes them better than anyone else's. Lord, girl, you must've been up at the crack of dawn doing this. Couldn't you sleep?"

Martha was right on target, but Jamie's only response was a smile as she dug under the sink for coffee filters. Night shift had been too busy to make a fresh pot and she desperately needed a cup. Her own coffeemaker, a relic from her college days, had finally given up the ghost.

Doris lost the battle with her willpower. Cutting two of the fragrant rolls from the pan, she put them on a paper towel, told Jamie she'd probably hate her in the morning for this and with a wink departed for her floor.

Seeing what Doris had done, Martha headed for the pan. "I'd better set one of these aside for Terese. At the rate they're disappearing, she's not likely to get one. She's out there on the phone with the sheriff," she added, picking up the knife. "He's still trying to get some information on that fellow we had in here late yesterday. The motorcycle accident. Remember?"

Slowly Jamie turned from the coffeemaker and pushed her hands into the pockets of her blue scrubs. Remember? she thought. She couldn't have forgotten had she tried.

Please. Don't let go.

The words had haunted her all night.

"Has the sheriff got anything?"

"Not from what I overheard. Sounds like the address on his driver's license wasn't any good. They're just trying to figure out where to pick up another lead." She plopped a roll onto a paper plate. "There," she pronounced before licking icing from her finger, "that ought to help put some meat on her bones. That child is entirely too thin."

Jamie didn't think there was a thing wrong with Terese's shapely little figure. Personally, she wouldn't have minded a few curves like that herself, especially since Jamie considered her own basic shape to bear a strong resemblance to an ironing board. But Martha equated happiness with food, and if a person didn't look as if she enjoyed eating—and didn't carry around the padding to prove it—then they must not be happy.

That Terese had a right to be less than thrilled with her life for the past year didn't daunt Martha in the least. The older woman had taken her on as a project and she seemed to feel personally responsible for the girl's care and feeding. She'd done the same with Jamie when Jamie, not knowing a soul in town, had first come to Winston. Martha was a good person, but she had no family of her own and she had a way of insinuating herself, wanted or unwanted, into other people's lives. Jamie had never begrudged the friendship and Terese responded well to the grandmotherly concern, but there were those on the staff who only felt sorry for Martha and others who considered her interest as meddling. Her whole life was the hospital and what went on in it. She had nothing else. Except for her cats.

Jamie never meddled and, unlike Martha, she steered clear of handing out advice—especially since she hadn't done such a hot job of running her own life. But there were times when she greatly feared she would wind up like Martha. It was that fear of not really mattering to anyone, of going through life without having experienced it, that Mitchell Alexander Kincaid III had reminded her of yesterday.

Oddly, she hadn't thought she was missing all that much until then.

Two minutes later, coffee cup in hand, Jamie leaned against the white wall behind Terese, blatantly eavesdropping on the young woman's conversation. Since Terese wasn't saying much more than an occasional "Right" or "Sure," there wasn't much to hear. The squiggles she made on her notepad weren't too enlightening, either.

The receiver was barely back on the cradle when Jamie lowered her cup. "What did Stan say? Have they found a relative for him yet?"

The clerk found nothing odd in Jamie's interest—or in the fact that Jamie knew who she'd been speaking with. Martha's presence at Jamie's elbow explained it all.

"Not yet. When the Houston police called me back yesterday, they said that the address on Mr. Kincaid's license is an apartment house. According to its manager, Mr. Kincaid hasn't lived there for over a year."

"What about a forwarding address?"

"He didn't leave one. None of the other tenants knew anything about him, either. Apparently, he kept to himself when he was there. Which wasn't often, from what the manager told the police. He paid his rent on time and left as quietly as he came. He'd been there for about three months."

Martha, who fancied herself something of a sleuth since she never missed *Murder, She Wrote* and had read every one of Agatha Christie's novels twice, clearly enjoyed the little mystery. "What about references? Didn't the manager check him out before he rented to him? I had a rental once and I always checked out their references. You never know who you're going to get, you know." She turned to Jamie. "You did the same when you rented your spare room to that student teacher last fall, remember? Of course, you had to be especially careful there because she was living right in your home. But you certainly checked her references before you gave her a key, didn't you?"

Actually, Jamie had offered to rent her spare room for the term after a five minute conversation in the supermarket with the grade school principal. Jamie knew the principal, and the principal knew the woman she was entrusting to teach the children, so that was enough for her. The young woman had gone back home at Christmas break.

Jamie answered the question with a nod, then smiled at her coworker. "You're digressing, Martha."

Terese stuck her pen behind her ear. "All I can tell you is what the police told me. They have no information on him. He doesn't seem to have any friends, relatives or traffic tickets, and Stan said without something more current to go on, that's about the best they can do. Unless someone calls in looking for him, of course," she added. "He's bound to be missed by someone and when they call to report him missing, they'll be told he's here. The lieutenant I spoke with said he'd notify missing persons."

Terese was right, of course. Sooner or later someone was bound to miss him. Jamie reminded herself of that several times throughout the course of the day, mostly, she assured herself, because things were pretty quiet and there wasn't much else to do. Working the emergency unit was a catch-22 of sorts. It was good to be busy, but being busy meant someone's well-being was in jeopardy, and she hardly wanted someone to be hurt or ill so she didn't have to be bored.

Today, though, having time on her hands wasn't good, either. When things were quiet, the nurses tended to read or do needlework. But she'd been in a fog this morning and she'd forgotten the crib quilt she was making for her new niece. The book she did have lay unread on the counter in front of her. She couldn't seem to concentrate on it. Her thoughts kept drifting to the man she'd heard had been admitted to 16A.

She was still thinking about him when Dr. Moody came in to stitch up a carpenter's finger—the sole emergency of the afternoon.

Winston Community Hospital was small enough that news about anything or anyone unusual traveled just short of the speed of light. Usually the grapevine stuck with gossip about staff. But occasionally a particularly interesting, difficult or unique patient found his or her way into the circuit. Though Winston got a lot of tourists during the season, and on occasion one would be admitted for an illness or injury, it wasn't often that a stranger traveling alone arrived in Kincaid's condition. Word had long ago filtered back to emergency that the motorcycle accident admitted yesterday was in critical condition and, like everyone else, Jamie knew from Terese that still no contact had been made with his family.

As the carpenter left with his finger sporting Martha's neat bandage, Jamie followed the rumpled-looking physician to the sink.

"Do you have a minute, Doctor?"

At Jamie's quiet inquiry, Theodore Moody tipped his balding head back to peer through his bifocals. "I've actually got two. What do you want with them?"

"I'd like to know how Mitchell Kincaid is doing."

"Kincaid," he muttered, lathering his hands. "Not good. He's not responding to any stimuli. His blood pressure is too low. I could name a half-dozen other problems, but the bottom line is that we've done all we can. A lot will depend on him now." He rinsed off the suds, gave his hands a shake and took the paper towel Jamie offered him. "Between you and me," he added, since she'd worked on the patient and he respected her professional concern, "I'll be surprised if he makes it."

Though Dr. Moody tended to look as if he lacked the presence of mind to remove his clothes before going to bed, thus accounting for the permanent creases in his permanent press, he was a competent physician. He was also not particularly prone to pessimism. If he felt Mitchell Kincaid's chances were slim, they undoubtedly were.

After tossing the towel into the trash, the doctor squinted through his bifocals again. "Was that all you needed?"

"That was all," she told him and watched his pant cuffs drag on the floor as he shuffled away.

Her conversation with the doctor was still on Jamie's mind when her shift ended. Standing at the nurses' station, she was drumming her fingers on the counter, looking alternately resigned and uncertain, when Martha wandered by. Terese had already gone home and the second-shift clerk was in the break room putting on fresh coffee. Clearly, Martha wondered what Jamie was still doing there.

Martha's eyes narrowed behind her glasses. She'd changed into her street clothes, a flower-print housedress that had gone out of style twenty years ago. Jamie still wore her blue scrubs. "Aren't you going home?"

"I think I'll hang around for a while."

"Going to check on the motorcycle accident?"

Inevitably, the staff referred to patients by disease or injury. The labeling was an occupational tendency that served a practical purpose. Perhaps, subconsciously, it helped the people who worked every day with pain and its attendant suffering to maintain a protective emotional distance from their patients. Most of the time, though, that emotional distance wasn't so great as they'd have liked to believe.

A self-deprecating smile touched Jamie's mouth. "Yes," she admitted, feeling as transparent as cellophane. "I can't stand the idea of him being all alone." Unconscious or otherwise, she couldn't let him linger all by himself. No one deserved to do that. "I'm just going to sit with him for a while."

The older woman said nothing. She patted the back of Jamie's hand as if she'd known all along what Jamie would do and turned her perpetually stern look to the mustached janitor running a damp mop over the floor of the waiting room. "He needs to shave," she muttered, and headed out the door.

Jamie turned in the other direction. She didn't question her actions. She simply did what she felt was necessary as she moved through the shining corridors of the compact, single-story hospital. In the back of her mind she could still hear the desperation in the man's plea when he'd reached for her hand. It echoed in her mind even as she slipped past the double doors that led to maternity and pediatrics and headed down the wide green hall of the medical floor. Since the hospital didn't have a separate intensive care unit, critical patients were kept in the rooms most accessible from the U-shaped nurses' station.

Jamie motioned to the nursing assistant pulling charts at the station, indicating that she was going into 16A. Receiving an acknowledging nod, she pushed her hands into the pockets of her scrubs and stopped in the doorway. Inside it was dim, the space bathed in the sort of perpetual twilight peculiar to a windowless hospital room. The glowing, oscillating monitors above and beside the bed indicated that the man in it was, for now, holding his own.

She stepped past the threshold, not even conscious of how quietly she moved, and stopped at the foot of the bed. His left leg was braced and suspended; an array of tubes provided medications and nourishment. The sheet and blanket covering him were drawn smooth to his right shoulder, leaving his left exposed. Where the neck of his hospital gown had been tucked aside, she could see the electrodes attached to his chest above his bandaged ribs. His jaw was swollen, as was his left eye, and the bandage covering the stitches on his forehead was stark white against his tanned skin. There was a definite pallor beneath that tan, and an incredibly nasty bruise darkened his left shoulder.

She moved closer. A layman walking into this room might find the array of tubes and machinery alarming. For most, this was an alien environment and, while not hostile, certainly intimidating. Jamie barely noted the medical apparatus. Like the antiseptic smells, it was all too familiar to give her pause. She saw past it, seeing only the man lying so terribly still.

"Hi," she said, just in case he could hear her. How frightening it would be to have strangers moving about and not know why they were there. "I just thought I'd see how you were doing."

And to see, too, she added to herself, what it was about you that has made me think of you so much.

"We met yesterday," she went on, wondering if explaining it to him might help her figure it out herself. "When they first brought you in."

She looked to where his left hand rested on the sheet. Moving alongside the bed, she reached over the raised rail and touched it lightly with her own. "You took my hand," she said, her tone hushed. "And asked me not to let go. I didn't. Not until I had to." With the tip of her finger, she smoothed the fine hairs above his knuckles, careful not to touch where the skin was scraped raw. "I guess I just wanted you to know that I was here for you. I'm pulling for you, Mitchell."

She didn't know if that was what he called himself or not. With a name like Mitchell Alexander Kincaid III, he had several options. Mitch. Alex. Even "Mac," she supposed, if he used his initials. Not knowing, having no way to know, she preferred Mitchell. It sounded strong. Maybe even a little noble. And that appealed to the romantic in her. Most people didn't even know that side of her existed. They saw her as practical and matter-of-fact, satisfied with the little roles she played in the community and not demanding or wanting too much for herself. No one seemed to consider that she might yearn for what other women took for granted.

What did they know, anyway?

"So, Mitchell," she repeated, thinking the formality particularly suited because of the Roman numeral tacked on to his surname. "You hang in there. Okay?"

She fell silent then and, after a while, not knowing what else to say, she pulled the room's only chair over to the bed.

Because it was what he'd asked of her before, she slipped her fingers between his, gave a gentle squeeze and sat by his side for the rest of the evening. He'd asked her not to let go. So, for now, she wouldn't.

* * *

For the next two days Mitchell's condition remained stable. No better, no worse. Still, there had been no word about his family—or who Mitchell Alexander Kincaid III was.

The second day she sat with him after her shift, Jamie brought a newspaper and read him the headline articles, concentrating on the sports page and basketball scores, just in case he was a sports fan. Then she read him the financial page, since Raye Anne, one of the nursing assistants, figured being a "Kincaid-The-Third" might mean he was "rich or something." It didn't seem likely that a man who carried no credit cards and had only six dollars in his wallet was heir to a fortune, but everyone was entitled to his or her own speculation. Or suspicion.

As sheriff, Stan possessed a naturally suspicious mind, and he ran through criminal records and various Wanted lists. All, so far, had come up zero.

Martha, a mystery buff, figured he was a government operative.

Doris, the day-shift charge nurse, thought he might belong to a motorcycle gang, since he had long hair and had been riding a motorcycle. Given his physical size, maybe he was even the gang's leader.

Jamie didn't know what to make of him. She knew only that she felt a very real need to do what he had asked of her. So when she wasn't reading to him in her spare time, she sat beside his bed working on her new niece's brightly colored quilt and telling him about where he was and what was being done for him. And when she started getting tired, she just sat with her hand over his to let him know—if he was capable of knowing—that someone was there.

She did the same the third night.

On the fourth, she was working evening shift herself because one of the E.R. nurses was ill. She'd come by to tell him as much, feeling badly that, other than regular checks by the staff, he'd be alone all evening. "I'll check on you later," she promised him, and touched his shoulder before slipping out as quietly as she'd come in.

I'll check . . . later.

The words registered, yet their meaning was unclear. They seemed to echo softly among the other faint and unfamiliar sounds.

Mitch fought to surface. He wanted to reach the voice. But it had seemed too far off. He strained toward it, struggling through the dense, terrifying fog. But he couldn't hear it anymore. Only the other sounds remained—mere echoes in that same insurmountable distance. A faint blipping. The gentle whoosh of air. A soft click. Something squeaking. Like tennis shoes on a shiny floor. Then the calm came again and the sounds faded.

Until he awoke again.

He knew he wasn't really awake. If he had been, he'd have been able to move, to see, to respond. All he could do was absorb. It was as if he were caught in a time warp. Suspended. Lost. Floating. Things seemed to happen around him, rather than to him. Disjointed, irrational things. Thought wasn't organized or sensible. Consciousness was merely an impression. Full thought took too much energy, so he went with the perceptions.

At times he tasted citrus. Lemon, maybe. The taste of it registered faintly. Smells taunted, too. Antiseptic smells. Alcohol. Disinfectant. And sometimes, the scent of jasmine. Exotic. Warm. Sensual.

Hours passed. Minutes. Seconds. He felt himself come out of that void, but sometimes there would be nothing there. Only the rhythmic blip and the antiseptic smells. Sometimes when he'd smell the jasmine, he'd hear the voice. Different from the others. Soft, melodious, gentle. It asked him to hold on, but he didn't know what he was supposed to hold on *to* because there was nothing but emptiness all around him. So he hung on to the sound of that voice, wanting to respond but not knowing how. Just the effort it took for the impressions to register seemed to exhaust him. But he clung to the sounds of that voice. Whenever he heard it, he could smell the jasmine and when he smelled that soft scent the anxiety eased.

He smelled the jasmine now.

Jamie touched his hand as she stood by his bed. It had been one of those days where everything had happened at once and she hadn't had a chance to see him at all until her shift was over. She didn't know if she was only hoping, or if he really did look a little better than he had last night.

Jamie quietly studied his face. The swelling above his left eye was going down, but the bruising had fully surfaced.

"I can't stay very long." She noticed that the heavy shadow of his beard had been shaved sometime today. He had a very nice jawline, firm and angular. "I've got to go to a meeting tonight," she explained, because she wanted him to know why she wouldn't be here. "We have a big celebration here in July and I'm working on it, so I have to be there. I just didn't want you to think I'd forgotten you."

Footsteps shuffled behind her. Glancing around, she saw Dr. Moody stop at the foot of the bed. He had Mitchell's chart open and his head tipped down to look through the top of his glasses at his patient. "How's he doing? Any changes in the last two hours?"

Since Jamie wasn't his nurse, she told the doctor that she'd just come by on her own and offered to get the floor nurse for an update. With a wave of his hand, Dr. Moody muttered, "No need," and lowered the side rail.

The wrinkles in his forehead matched those in his lab coat as he leaned over to check his patient's pupils. "I hear you've been spending time with him."

"Some. I've been reading the paper to him, talking to him."

"Did you notice any changes while you were doing that?"

"No," she admitted, though she had carefully watched the monitors for any fluctuation in blood pressure or heart rate that might indicate Mitchell was aware of her presence. She didn't realize how disappointed she'd been by that lack of change until she said the words aloud. "I haven't seen any at all."

"Well, keep it up if you can. The stimulation might reach him on some level. We never know in this type of coma. His last EEG showed good brain-wave activity, so it could be that his body has just shut down everything it doesn't need to give him time to start healing. Or," he said, since there were so many mysteries medicine had yet to answer, "maybe not."

He snapped the file shut and removed his glasses. Pushing them into his pocket, he gave his head a tight little shake. "Too bad we can't locate his family."

Dr. Moody left, and though Jamie had intended to leave, too, she found herself staying a while longer. Committee meetings never started on time, anyway.

Since she planned to leave by one of the back exits rather than through emergency as she usually did, she had her bright pink canvas tote with her. Reminding herself, when she saw her week-old grocery list, that she really did need to stop at the grocery store one of these days, she pulled out the gardening magazine that had come in her mail yesterday. She'd read it aloud to him, she thought, since it was all she had with her. But when she sat down beside his bed, she left the magazine closed in her lap and leaned forward.

With her elbows on her knees, she rested her chin on her fists. "Who are you, Mitchell? Who's waiting for you to call? Wake up so you can tell me."

He remained as he was. Motionless. Silent.

She slipped one hand through the railings and touched her fingers to his. He had such strong, capable hands. Broad and blunt-fingered. A working man's hands, judging from their calluses.

Who had held that hand? she wondered. Whose face had he touched? The face of a child? A son, or daughter? Was there a woman somewhere, at this very minute anxiously waiting to hear from him? A wife? A girlfriend? He wore no ring and as tan as his skin was, she could see no evidence of a telltale paler band of skin to indicate recent removal. But the lack of a ring didn't mean anything.

That no one seemed to be looking for him was odd, though. Terese's daily checks with missing persons had revealed no inquiries about him at all. The sheriff's investigations hadn't netted anything, either.

Jamie hated that he didn't seem to have anyone who mattered to him here for him. All he had was her. A stranger in a strange place.

"It's kind of windy outside today," she told him, watching the dark hairs on the back of his hand spring back as she ran her finger from his knuckles to his wrist. "I saw some children flying kites in the field across the street a while ago. There was a bright pink one with purple triangles all over it and a yellow one shaped like a banana."

Maybe she could make him visualize the colors. See the shapes. "The sky is the prettiest blue. Kind of soft, like a robin's egg. We don't have robins here," she said. The information was unimportant but it was something to talk about. "We had them where I grew up in Los Angeles, though. When I was a little girl, they would build their nests in the eaves over my bedroom window. If I stood on the sill and held on to the shutter, I could lean out far enough to see the eggs sometimes."

A soft smile touched her mouth as she remembered. The smile entered her voice. "I wouldn't tell anyone they were

there. It was my secret. My sisters never paid any attention
to them. Linda always had her head in a book and Catherine was only interested in her mirror. But if my brothers had
found them, they'd have pulled down the nest to show their
friends, and broken the eggs to see what was inside.''

As she spoke, she continued to stroke the back of his
hand. She meant the contact to reassure him and she hoped
that, somehow, it did. Oddly, she found the motion quite
soothing for herself. ''I never even told my mother about
them. If she'd known I was hanging out a second-story
window, she'd probably have grounded me for the rest of
my life.''

The truth was, she'd tried to tell her mother, wanting to
share the excitement of that first discovery. But Constance
Withers had been too busy telling a neighbor about yet another award one of Jamie's brothers had won to be bothered with her middle daughter's silliness. There wasn't much
Jamie had been interested in or cared about that her mother
hadn't treated as a waste of time.

Jamie didn't want to think about her mother. Or any of
her family. So she changed the subject, surprised that she'd
even allowed it to come up, and found herself frowning at
Mitch because, in a way, it was his fault she'd thought about
the robin's eggs in the first place.

But the frown faded quickly and in the same quiet con-
versational tone she mentioned that she'd never told anyone else this story because it was every bit as dumb as it
sounded and wouldn't have mattered to him had he been
conscious. Then she asked him to forgive her for boring
him. All she wanted was to reach into the world where he
was lost and help him fight his way back. She even told him
she wished she could do that, because she felt he was a
fighter.

She knew without a doubt that he didn't want to give up,
so she wouldn't, either. No one had ever asked for her help

as he had. She'd just have to ignore how much more disheartened she became every minute he failed to respond.

"I wish I knew if you could hear me." She studied the strong, clean lines of his profile, wondering if her words were reaching him. Research had shown that some coma patients—those who recovered to tell about it—were at times aware of their surroundings and of what was being said. A few even remembered entire conversations. But most, according to the studies, remembered very few specifics—only that they heard voices.

That was enough for Jamie. If he could hear her voice, even if what she said didn't compute, then he might know he wasn't alone.

With a sigh she looked at the digital readout that indicated his pulse rate. There had been no change in all the time she'd been talking to him. She frowned, needing to try one more time. "Can you move your hand for me? Even a little? Try. Please?"

If she could have willed him to move, the intensity of her concentration now would have done it. She watched his hand for the slightest movement, but it remained perfectly, absolutely still.

She knew her disappointment was in her voice. "I'm really sorry, Mitchell. But I've got to go now," she told him, having completely abandoned the idea of reading to him. It felt better when she just talked to him. "You hang in there." She squeezed his hand, then let it slip from hers. "I'll see you tomorrow."

Quietly, she moved from the room. It was nearly ten o'clock.

She'd missed her meeting.

He tried. She wanted him to move his hand. And he tried. But it felt detached from his body. Just as his mind felt detached from the rest of himself. Focus, he thought. Concentrate. But concentrating was so hard when his thoughts kept drifting off.

He fought the encroaching fog, anyway, refusing to give in to the nothingness. Somewhere inside him he knew he could succeed. He had always been able to focus his thoughts so acutely that he could block out all but the challenge. That ability was the one thing he always counted on. It had saved him before. He sensed that in the very essence of his being. It had to save him now.

He willed himself to do what the voice had asked, to make his hand do as his mind bid.

He waited for the voice. He'd smelled the jasmine and for a while he'd felt connected. He knew when it was her now and he'd tried desperately to reach out. Other people came and went from his room and sometimes he was aware of being alone. But she was the only one he seemed to wait for. She was his line with whatever lay beyond this void he was trapped in. Now there was only the void. The link was no longer there, and again he was alone. Of all else, being alone terrified him the most.

His arm rested at his side. He tried to focus. To draw the energy. And he did. The movement was negligible, but his index finger edged toward his thumb.

It was all the effort he could manage, but he knew he'd done it. He'd done as the voice had asked.

But the voice was gone.

Chapter Five

"Hey, Jamie!" The sharp report of a car door slamming sailed across the parking lot. "Pretty morning. Isn't it?" Stan's west-Texas drawl carried on the fresh morning breeze.

"Sure is," she called back, shoving closed the door of her own battered blue convertible. She loved mornings such as this—the sky a clear, brilliant blue and the sweet scent of spring heavy in the balmy air. If she hadn't had to work, it would have been a perfect morning to hike up the ridge and spend a few hours with her sketch pad.

Trading thoughts of what could be for what was, she watched Stan lean his lanky form against the fender of his white police car. He'd followed her into the hospital parking lot, pulling up to the curb by emergency while she'd gone on to the employees' section beyond a low wall of red-blossomed oleander shrubs. Now he waited for her, grinning, as she hoisted her pink tote to her shoulder and headed toward him.

"I missed you at the meeting last night. I'd thought I'd take you out for coffee afterward," he said when she was close enough for him to see the smile in her eyes.

"That can only mean that you wanted something. What is it this time?"

If Stan's face hadn't been all but hidden by the shadow of his Mountie-style brown hat and reflective sunglasses, Jamie could have seen the smile behind his crestfallen expression. She didn't doubt it was there, anyway.

"Aw, Jamie. All I wanted was the pleasure of your company."

"And?"

He hesitated. "And to see if you'd do the safety program at the elementary school with me again this year. All those little kids make me nervous."

She didn't doubt he made some of those same kids a little nervous himself. The man was the size of a small mountain and when he wasn't smiling he reminded Jamie of a bulldog. Fortunately, he smiled often.

Jamie and the sheriff had an easy relationship, one her next-door neighbor, Barb Robinson, thought Jamie should try to push past the "just friends" stage. But Stan reminded Jamie too much of her oldest brother to incite anything but platonic feelings, and Stan had never made any overtures toward her in that direction. Long ago she had accepted that she wasn't the kind of woman men made passes at. She was what her outspoken friend Barb called "wholesome," which Jamie knew was just a kind euphemism for "plain." Her own mother had even confirmed that to her when—trying to help during a puberty-induced crisis—she'd said that not everyone could look like Catherine, Jamie's drop-dead beautiful sister, and she should be grateful that she had such a nice personality.

By twenty-nine, Jamie had finally learned what eventually happens to plain women with nice personalities. They become everybody's kid sister. A buddy. The type of woman men turned to to discuss their girlfriends. Someone to depend on for advice, or to ask out for coffee when a favor was needed. Someone who was known to be reliable, generous and available. All nice qualities, she supposed, but hardly the stuff of men's romantic fantasies.

She certainly wasn't Stan's idea of what appealed on that level. His preference ran to the dark-haired, petite variety. Specifically, Terese. But Terese was still mourning her husband, and Stan seemed to sense that it was too soon for him to make a move.

As they headed into the building, she wondered if he was anticipating seeing Terese even now. He seemed a little preoccupied with his muttered "Great" when she said she'd be glad to do the program. She asked him about what she'd missed at the meeting to plan this year's Fourth of July celebration.

"You really didn't miss much," he said over the hiss of the automatic doors. "Just the usual preliminary stuff about who's heading up what committee and such. What kept you last night, anyway?"

"I was sitting with the man you brought in a few days ago. The motorcycle accident," she clarified.

It was on the tip of her tongue to ask if he'd learned anything else when Stan made the question unnecessary.

"Kincaid?" Now that he didn't need them, he pulled off his sunglasses. "The one who ran into Graffiti Rock?"

She nodded, wondering at the seriousness in his craggy features.

"Have you been able to talk with him?" he wanted to know.

"Not yet. He was still unconscious when I left him last night."

"How is he now?"

She looked at him with indulgence. "I just got here, Stanley."

They had entered the unit by a side door and now stood at the nurses' station. From off to the right, she could hear Terese talking with someone in the break room, saying that Joshua, her five-year-old, had just lost his first tooth.

Setting her tote on the elbow-high counter, Jamie reached over it to the desk and picked up a telephone. Punching three numbers, she waited for the medical floor to answer, glad for the excuse to see how Mitchell was this morning. She hadn't wanted to admit how much she'd worried about him, but now that she was here she could give herself that permission.

Actually, she'd almost called from home, then changed her mind. It was one thing for her to sit with him. The other nurses had accepted that with little question because she didn't have a family and they figured she had nothing else to do. But calling would have been too revealing, both to the nurse taking the call and to Jamie herself. Jamie needed very much to keep Mitchell in the little mental box labeled Patient. That was exactly where he belonged. He was a patient with a past she knew nothing about and a future that could end at any moment. Many people like that had passed through her life—especially during the year she'd spent working emergency at L.A. General.

She refused to consider that the more time she spent at this patient's side, the more of an emotional investment she might be making in his recovery.

"Critical but stable," was the report from the medical floor.

As Jamie passed that on to Stan, he pulled a piece of paper from his shirt pocket.

"Tell that nurse I've got some more information on him. I'll get it down to her."

smoked salmon

A Gift from . . .

HEGG & HEGG

801 MARINE DRIVE   PORT ANGELES, WA. 98362

4150D

Relaying the message, her own inward curiosity evident to no one, she noticed Stan looking toward the break room. She was sure he was looking for Terese, officially because she was the person to whom he first needed to give his information, but more likely because he just wanted to see her. Sure enough, when the diminutive young woman appeared in the doorway and gave him the faintest of smiles, the tips of his ears turned pink.

The phone rang, as it did dozens of times a day. Terese snatched it up, totally oblivious to the disappointment in Stan's expression and his annoyance when the mobile-unit phone attached to his belt went off a second later.

Both calls dealt with the same matter. Within moments, the casual atmosphere was charged with urgency. There had been an accident at the quarry fifteen miles west of town. Three men were on their way to emergency and should be arriving any minute. Workers were still trying to free two more from under a collapsed crane.

The sheriff headed one way and Jamie the other; he out the door to his car to race off with the siren blaring, and Jamie into the locker room to change from her street clothes to her scrubs. In the ensuing chaos, she forgot how anxious she'd been to hear what Stan had learned.

Much later that afternoon—after the first three quarrymen had been released, the last two admitted and an unrelated case tended to—Jamie was able to piece her sporadic conversations with Terese together to learn what the sheriff had discovered.

According to Terese, the owner of the Hi Desert Motel out on the highway had called the sheriff's office this morning. One of his guests had checked in five days ago, then disappeared. The maid said the room hadn't been disturbed at all and the guest's leather duffel bag and shaving kit were never moved from the bed. When Stan had gone over to check on the matter, he'd found that the mysterious guest had registered as M. A. Kincaid and used a Houston P.O. box for an address. A quick look in the duffel bag revealed enough evidence to convince Stan that M. A. Kincaid was the same Mitchell Kincaid who'd nearly been DOA at the community hospital.

In his duffel had been a leather folder containing a pilot's certificate, a pilot's logbook and a passport. Mitchell had logged an incredible amount of flying hours in a number of truly out-of-the-way places. His passport was positively ragged from wear. The last entry was to Saudi Arabia six months ago. Stan also mentioned having seen stamps from several European and Scandinavian countries, Australia, and even Pakistan.

The information everyone wanted, however, wasn't there. The page of his passport for whom to notify in case of death or accident hadn't been filled in.

Before Stan left the hospital that morning, he'd put in a call to the Airman's Certification branch of the FAA in Oklahoma City, hoping to get some information. But by the time Jamie got off duty late that afternoon, she hadn't heard that he'd learned anything.

At least she knew something concrete about Mitchell now. He liked planes and motorcycles; the latter, she decided, since that was what he'd been riding when he ran off the road. Taking the conclusion a step further, she thought it logical that he'd been drawn to power and speed. Maybe, she thought, letting her imagination go, he even enjoyed the freedom some found in flying or racing along an open highway. She didn't think that so unlikely to believe about him and rather liked the images those thoughts evoked. Images that had an eerily realistic quality about them when she remembered the leather jacket and harness boots he'd been wearing when he'd been brought in.

Why she remembered what he'd been wearing could only be explained as being one of those odd details stored away in the frenetic activity of an emergency case. She added those details to more explicable observations. The injuries he'd sustained hadn't diminished the raw masculinity in his powerful physique, and his over-long hair gave him a roguish quality she found alarmingly appealing. She could easily see him astride a great black beast of a motorcycle, his brooding features masked by the black-visored helmet he'd worn, and his broad shoulders braced against the wind.

It was frighteningly easy to let her imagination take over when it came to this man. She was drawn to the mystery surrounding him. In some ways she found it intriguing. In others, disturbing. Why did he seem to have no ties with anyone? What did he do that he moved around with so little in his possession? And where had he been going to have come to such an isolated town as Winston?

"It's been five days," she told him late one evening. "You have to wake up." She preferred not to think about the steps that would become necessary if he failed to regain consciousness and the state and the courts took over. "Tell me about where you've been. Tell me what you like to fly. I know you fly airplanes. Are they little ones, Mitchell? Are they big jets?"

She slipped her hand over his, loath to give up. The phenomenon defied explanation, but it was almost as if she could feel the struggle in him. As if she had some instinctive knowledge of him that made her know he didn't want her to leave him alone. To know, too, that he needed her to help him come back, to help him hang on.

He needed her. If for no other reason than she was all he had, she knew he needed her. That was all the reason Jamie needed herself to continue talking to him, cajoling, encouraging. If only he could let her know that he heard.

To Jamie there was nothing unusual about the way she stroked his hand or smoothed his hair back from his brow. She touched people all the time, offering reassurance in what could sometimes be foreign and frightening situations. The touch of a hand could often calm anxiety where logic and scientific explanation could not. That simple human contact could be very powerful medicine.

The blips on the screen above his bed made little mountains and valleys with a line of iridescent green. Jamie watched it, wondering at the strength of the heart that maintained such a steady rhythm—then held her breath when, having just told him she'd have to go soon, she saw his heart rate increase.

"Mitchell?" Her glance darted to his face. "Mitchell, can you hear me?"

Nothing. Beneath the bandage on his forehead, nothing moved. His features remained still, rugged even in repose. But his hand. With her fingers resting lightly on his, she felt the movement. It wasn't much, but he definitely inched his thumb toward hers.

A call button was clipped to the sheet at the top of the bed opposite where she stood. Her heart pounding, she reached across to signal for assistance. Dr. Moody needed to know this. But she didn't want to leave, in case Mitchell awakened further.

The bed had been raised slightly and the railings were up, so Jamie had to stand on tiptoe to reach over him. As she did, her braid fell forward, brushing the sheet covering his shoulder. Stretched across him, one hand on the button and the other still holding his, she heard him draw in a deep breath. Then she heard him moan. The sound was faint and low and as sweet to her as a baby's first cry.

"Easy," she told him, depressing the button that illuminated the appropriate room light on a panel at the nurses' station. "It's all right."

She started to pull back, stilling halfway when she thought she heard him speak.

"Say it again," she urged, not moving at all so the rustle of her clothing wouldn't interfere.

As if checking to see if his lips would work, the tip of his tongue touched the corner of his mouth. Lemon-flavored glycerine swabs had been used to keep his lips from cracking, but his mouth was dry. She was sure he wanted water.

That wasn't what he wanted at all. Leaning over him, one hand holding his and the other braced by his head, she heard him whisper.

"Want to make love?"

His voice sounded thick and rusty from disuse, but there was no mistaking what he'd asked. Looking down at his beautiful, battered face, his eyes still closed against the light, she couldn't help but admire the guy's spirit.

"I like a man with a sense of humor," she returned, smiling to herself. "But you'd better save your strength. Don't try to talk."

"I'm not kidding, lady. The way you smell drives me crazy."

Jamie pulled back, more than a little surprised at how his words made her feel. She'd received her share of passes from male patients before. None of them serious and all easily dismissed. But Mitchell's words jolted her more than she cared to admit.

Oddly pleased with his questionable compliment, and perplexed at herself for feeling that way, she gave his hand a squeeze. "I'm glad you're back." An instant later, her glance swept the monitors to be sure his blood pressure wasn't doing anything dangerous.

"Where've I been?"

"How about I tell you where you *are?* You're in the hospital in Winston. Arizona," she added as Pam Whitney hustled through the door.

Pam and Jamie had never worked together, but Pam's reputation for being brisk seemed well earned. Within seconds, the tall woman was at the side of the bed, her carefully composed features betraying inquiry only by the arch of one eyebrow.

Jamie started to speak, to tell her that her patient had regained consciousness. Mitchell's moan made it unnecessary. At the low, pain-filled sound, the women's glances jerked from each other to the bed. Pam registered mild surprise at his change in condition. Jamie, her expression no less unremarkable, flinched inwardly at his pain.

He had tried to lift his head—and immediately become aware of why that hadn't been a good idea.

It had been important that Mitch's response to stimuli not be suppressed. Therefore, he hadn't been given anything for the pain of his broken bones, contusions and surgical wounds. With the return of consciousness, the beating his body had taken now fully registered. His dark features twisted, his jaw growing rigid as nerves sent their agonizing messages to his brain.

His voice was decidedly weak, but the expletive he uttered was easily understood. Jamie thought the slow "Aw, damn" he exhaled between his clenched teeth quite appropriate. Awakening from the self-manufactured sedation of a coma to such distress, at the very least entitled a man to swear a little.

Pam had been in the room only seconds. That was all the time she needed to know what had to be done.

Jamie knew, too, but she wasn't thinking about drugs and tests and protocols. Had she been charged with his medical care, she'd have been busy implementing procedures. But she was at his side only because she'd wanted to be. She thought about what she *could* do to help, and came up with nothing. It was a familiar feeling. She'd fallen short so often that in some areas of her life she'd simply stopped trying.

"We'll see what we can get you for pain. Hold on, Mitchell," she urged, and felt his fingers slip between hers.

Jamie found the strength in his hand surprising. It felt as if the thin bones in her fingers would break as he squeezed, doing what she'd all but begged him to do so many times before. She squeezed right back, letting him know he could hold on as tightly as he needed as she tried to absorb his pain.

Sweat popped out on his forehead and beneath his eyes. A cool washcloth wasn't handy. She started to reach for a tissue to dab the dampness away. His raspy voice stopped her.

"Don't call me Mitchell." Another expletive, this one stronger in form but weaker in delivery. "God. I feel like I hit a freaking wall."

She thought about telling him that, for all practical purposes, he had. Instead, she tried to make him concentrate on something else. "Tell me what to call you, then. If you don't like Mitchell, would you prefer Mr. Kincaid?" That was, after all, what she should be calling a patient. She'd just become so accustomed to using his first name these past several days that the name had slipped out.

"Not if you want me to answer." Even raw pain couldn't seem to cover the faint touch of cynicism in his tone. "It's just Mitch."

She *had* liked Mitchell better, but she opted for another subject—one of more immediate import. "We haven't notified anyone that you're here. Who can we call for you?"

His eyes opened. Blinking against the light, he closed them before he could focus on anything. A moment later, his nostrils flaring, he drew a deep breath and seemed to concentrate on slowly releasing it.

"Do you want me to call your wife?" she persisted when several moments later he still hadn't answered her earlier question.

"Don't have one."

"How about your parents, then? A brother, a sister?"

She refused to be relieved that he didn't have a wife. Instead she waited for him to respond, aching a little at how much the effort was costing him. His brow was already furrowed with pain. Concentration etched those lines deeper.

"The guy who hired me."

"What about him?"

"He needs to know I'm here."

"How do we reach him?"

His hand tightened around hers again, his voice growing ragged. "Chopper service. Name's Mallory, or Maloney. Something like that."

For a moment she had no idea what to make of what he'd said. Then she remembered a local company that offered, among other services, helicopter tours of the Grand Canyon. Jamie was about to ask if he meant Red Malloy, the gruff and grizzled owner of the nearly defunct Red Rock Airlines, when Pam came back, hypodermic syringe in hand.

"This won't do more than take the edge off, Mr. Kincaid," she said, pulling a chain above the bed to add more light. "But it'll help. Dr. Moody doesn't want you to have anything stronger until he can assess your neurological functions." After running a swab over a rubber stopper in his IV line, she injected the medication. "I caught him in the middle of dinner, but he's on his way. Mr. Kincaid?" she asked, looking from his grip on Jamie's hand to the empathy in her colleague's eyes. "Do you know where you are?"

"In hell," came his tight reply.

Mitch thought he heard someone laugh, the woman holding his hand maybe, but he wasn't sure. It could as easily have been the other one. The sound was too subdued to tell. All he knew for certain was that had someone asked him to describe the place he'd just mentioned, he could now do so with unerring accuracy. Right down to the horrific burning that seemed to fill his entire midsection. His whole body felt like one giant bruise. Even his lungs ached, more it seemed whenever he breathed, which proved necessary every five seconds or so. He'd known pain before, but nothing like this. Nothing like this mind-numbing haze that made rational thought little more than a dim memory.

Only one thing kept him from believing he'd finally cut it too close and entered the unearthly realm some had said he was destined to ultimately discover. They didn't have angels in hell. Certainly not one with a voice as soothing as a cool breeze on a hot summer day and a touch so gentle it could calm the most agitated soul.

He knew that touch somehow, felt intimately familiar with it, though he knew that was impossible. He didn't know anyone in this town. No one. Yet he knew the voice. The one that had called him Mitchell.

The other voice, the one that now wanted him to recite his name and birth date, had a higher pitch, a more strident quality.

He'd yet to fully open his eyes. He'd tried, because he wanted to see the woman who held his hand, but the light hurt too much and his head was already pounding. So he kept them closed and put up with the conversation taking place over him, telling the woman with the voice of an angel that Red Malloy was the right name when she asked him about it, but letting the conversation go because his head was hurting too much now for him to worry about why contacting him had been so important.

A few minutes later his eyes were being opened for him and some guy with cold hands was shining a penlight into first one then the other and asking him to move fingers and toes, count backward and name presidents. He must have given the right answers because the guy with the icy fingers kept muttering, "Good. Good."

Mitch didn't have the energy to tell the doctor that his brain wasn't broken or otherwise damaged—though his lack of brains had been questioned on more than one occasion. He knew who he was, where he was, and exactly what had happened to put him here. He could even remember how fast he'd been going when he'd swerved to avoid the tumbleweed blowing across the road and hit a patch of loose gravel. The last thing he remembered was seeing a bunch of writing on a huge boulder and thinking he was about to make scrap metal out of his new motorcycle. But about all he could do after several minutes of poking and prodding was mutter, "Hurts," when asked how it felt when something sharp was stuck into his heel.

"No more," he finally asked, finding even his throat sore.

He wanted them all to leave. He wanted to sleep, to find some escape from the pain. And he finally did. But somewhere in the back of his mind, he wished the angel had stayed.

Maybe she had, he thought when the metallic clank of breakfast trays being pulled from the heating cart in the hall awakened him.

Opening his eyes, Mitch looked past his suspended leg and saw a slender woman in baggy surgical scrubs standing in the doorway.

"I hope I didn't wake you."

She hadn't. He'd merely been dozing since some redheaded nurse who'd done her basic training under General Patton hustled in an hour ago. She'd cranked his bed up, filled a washbasin and proceeded to flip back the sheet, talking all the time about how "we" would feel better once "we" had "our" bath. He didn't know how most people felt about it, but he didn't trust anyone who talked in the plural. He was also dead certain that what was under the sheet was not community property.

He moved his head to see better, carefully because movement tended to cause pain, and watched the woman enter the room. Silently she moved to the side of his bed, letting her fingers rest lightly on the metal railings that made him feel as if he were sleeping in a cage.

The scent of jasmine drifted toward him. Light. Familiar. Disturbing. He felt his body react with each breath he drew, tightening, hardening. It had come as no small relief when he'd realized that certain rather important parts of his body had remained unimpaired by his accident. He found it equally disconcerting that this one particular woman should so easily elicit the effect. If he remembered correctly, he'd even propositioned her when he'd awakened to find her leaning over him.

"I won't ask how you feel," she said. "No offense, but I can see that by just looking at you. You do look better, though."

"I'm sure that's a relative comparison."

"True. But relative to how I've seen you, you definitely don't look as bad as you did for a while."

She had a smile like sunshine. Not the intense burning kind, but the gentle sun of a spring day. Healing. Rejuvenating. The word *kind* came to mind—not a word he tended to associate with most females—and he found himself adding to the other impressions he already had of her.

He'd recognized her voice the instant he'd heard it. Odd, but had he tried to picture her, he'd have thought her to have pale blond hair, blue eyes and a china-like delicacy to her features. A living Botticelli angel.

Instead, the woman who smelled like springtime had hair the color of burnt taffy pulled back in a long, intricate braid, and the lanky, leggy look of a young colt. A hint of freckles, probably lighter than they'd been in her youth, dusted the bridge of her nose and her clear skin was the color of honey.

She wasn't sexy by any means, but something about her spoke of sensuality. She liked to touch. He knew that because he remembered her touching him.

His glance moved from her face to the shapeless blue scrub shirt she wore. He tried to imagine the shape of her breasts. They were small, undefined beneath the loose material, but the gentle roundness would fit comfortably in his hand. Her hips were small, too, but again the baggy scrubs made it impossible to do anything but guess at their shape.

Realizing what he was doing, he jerked his glance to the name tag above the pocket of her shirt. The white letters on the black background identified her as J. Withers, R.N.

He cleared his throat. "What does the *J* stand for?"

"Jamie."

"That's short for what?"

For the first time, he noticed what he'd missed before— the hint of fragility in her eyes, a guardedness that lay beneath the warmth. She hadn't even noticed the little side trip he'd taken between her face and her name tag. For that, he was enormously grateful.

She laughed, the sound light and musical, and in his mind, forgiving.

"James. I was supposed to have been a boy. I have a message for you," she went on, easily moving the subject away from herself. "I called Red Malloy. He'd like to come by this afternoon if you're up to seeing him."

When Jamie had called him last night, Red had been in the process of going through a stack of aviation weeklies looking to replace the pilot he'd hired but who hadn't shown up. She'd told him he was the only person Mitch Kincaid had asked to have called, then asked if he knew of any family the hospital could contact.

Red knew of no one. He'd never even met Mitch. He'd hired him on the recommendation of a friend who knew someone who'd flown with him a couple of years ago. A roundabout way of finding an employee to be sure, but Red trusted the grapevine. It seemed that airmen knew who they wanted to fly with and who they didn't; who could be trusted, and who the hotshots were. Word was that Mitch Kincaid was the man for the jobs with the bigger risks and that he wasn't dead yet.

She supposed that to be a cryptic way of saying he was good, but he hadn't missed death by much this time. And he hadn't even left the ground.

Mitch's left arm was encumbered by an IV board. Raising his free hand, he gingerly rubbed his forehead. When he brushed the edge of the bandage running from his left eyebrow straight up to his hairline, he went still, his features shadowing as if he'd just remembered the injury was there.

He lowered his hand. "I need to know what to tell him."

"What do you mean?"

A touch of impatience flashed in his eyes—blue eyes that were every bit as compelling as she'd thought they might be. "How long am I going to be here? How long before the leg heals? When can I go to work? He hired me to fly for him and I'd like to be able to tell him when I can start."

The man obviously didn't appreciate the extent of his injuries.

"Your doctor will have to tell you that." Since it was early it was possible that Dr. Moody hadn't been in yet this morning. She knew he hadn't mentioned a prognosis to his patient last night. "He'll be in soon."

"*You* tell me. You know, don't you?"

"That's not my place." She refused to admit that she did know. If his quick impatience was any indication, what he would soon hear wasn't going to set very well. "I'm not even assigned to this unit."

"Then what are you doing here?"

It occurred to her that she might have liked him better comatose. "I came by to give you the message from Mr. Malloy," she returned reasonably. "What do you want me to tell him?"

There was a distinct pinch to his mouth. An indication of exasperation possibly, but Jamie was more inclined to think it from pain. His eyes were clouded with it, his movements conservative to avoid causing more.

Without thinking, she uncurled her fingers from the rail and started to touch the back of his hand. It lay in a fist on the white sheet near his hip, only inches below hers.

The instant she realized what she was doing, she pulled back. Why she did that, she couldn't say for sure. When he'd been unconscious, she hadn't thought twice about taking his hand or brushing the hair from his brow. Now, though, it didn't feel as natural as it had all the times she'd touched him before. He was conscious. The rules had changed and she no longer had the right.

Taking a step back, she stuffed both hands into her pockets. She'd never hesitated to reassure a patient before. "How long since you've been given something for the pain?"

The gentleness of her question made Mitch feel even worse than he already did. Either she was gracious enough to offer the excuse, or she instinctively knew the reason for his abruptness. One thing she couldn't do was guess at his panic. The thought that he might not be able to function as he had, that he might be permanently incapacitated...

He wouldn't even allow himself to complete the thought. "I don't know." He drew a deep, unsteady breath, and slowly released it. "Sometime last night."

The pain had made him edgy, but the sedatives made his mind weird and he hated the floaty, detached way they made him feel. He needed to be able to think. But when his head was clear, he was too aware of the pain. He needed to focus on something outside himself. The mind was powerful. Concentration could increase that power once distractions were tuned out and an object to focus on was found. There wasn't anything in the place where he could center his concentration—except on her, and he doubted that mentally disrobing Jamie Withers, R.N., would solve his problem.

He looked around for something else. The room he occupied was truly Spartan. Now that much of the machinery he'd been hooked up to had been wheeled out, all that remained was his bed, a single chair and a tray table.

"About Malloy," he said, already hating the four off-white walls. "Ask him if he can come by this afternoon." If the doctor was coming by soon, Mitch would know what he needed to know by the time he saw the guy. "And Jamie," he added, "I really appreciate you calling him for me."

Her smile came back, soft and forgiving. "No problem."

"One more thing?"

She'd started to turn. As she looked back, he noticed the light catch the shades of wheat and honey in her hair.

"Is there any way I can get a room with a window?"

She was about to tell him she would see what she could do when Dr. Moody, wearing a fresh—and therefore only *semi*rumpled—lab coat, came in brandishing Mitch's chart. The doctor took it upon himself to tell Mitch that he needed to stay in the room where he was so the staff could keep an eye on him.

Jamie saw the disappointment in Mitch's expression. "You'll let me know what Malloy says?" he asked as she started for the door.

His smile wasn't much, tempered as it was by his discomfort, but it held the potential of being downright sexy. Without thinking, Jamie touched her hand to the pulse at the base of her throat. "I will," she said, and left before the doctor began explaining Mitch's injuries and giving him his best estimate of how long he'd need to heal.

Jamie learned later that she'd been right. He didn't take the prognosis well.

Chapter Six

Jamie didn't see Mitch until late that afternoon. She finally reached Red Malloy but Mitch was asleep when she went to deliver the message. She'd decided to leave a message with Raye Anne when the soft ping of a patient's call signal sounded and his room number lit on the panel at the nurses' station.

So he was awake. And according to Raye Anne, who answered the call, he wanted to see Jamie.

"Why didn't you come in?" he asked when she appeared in his doorway.

"I thought you were sleeping." Her brow furrowed. He hadn't opened his eyes when she'd come in a minute ago. She was sure of that. "How did you even know I was here?"

"I smelled your perfume."

She hesitated. "I'm not wearing any."

"I still knew it was you. You smell like jasmine or wild-flowers or something."

What he'd probably noticed was the scent of her herbal shampoo.

The way you smell drives me crazy. She remembered the words he'd spoken yesterday. They were hardly subtle, and watching him watch her, she found their impact now even more unnerving. No man had ever said anything like that to her.

Mitch obviously found his comments unremarkable. "I'm glad you're here," she heard him say and she could only wonder at how the hardness of his expression prevented him from looking as if he meant it.

Mitch did mean it, though. He didn't know why, but he felt better when she was around. Her presence somehow lifted the shadows. Or at least pushed them far enough into the corners that he could forget they were there. It would be nice if she could chase a few of those shadows for him now.

Despite Mitch's attempt at a smile, the bleakness in his expression was evident. "Your Dr. Moody doesn't pull any punches, does he?"

"What did he tell you?"

Mitch tipped his head, his eyes narrowing as if to get a clearer picture of her. As he did, he couldn't help but wonder how her thick and shining hair would look unbound and spilling over her slender shoulders. Its texture, he somehow knew, would feel like silk in his hands. "Do they teach you that in nursing school? Find out what the patient knows first, so you don't give anything away?"

She gave him a shrug and a smile. "It's the first course we take," she teased. "What can I say?"

He would get no further until he told her what she wanted to know. And since something about the woman made her far more dangerous than she looked, he dutifully itemized his injuries.

"He told me that I have two cracked ribs, stitches in my head, pins in my leg, which was broken in two places, and a couple of internal organs that took a bit of a beating. Apparently I'd lost a lot of blood and also had a concussion that, along with all the rest of it, kept me out for five days. Did I miss anything?"

"During the five days? Or in your inventory?"

"In the inventory."

She shook her head. "I think that about covers it."

A harder edge slipped into his voice. "He also said that it's going to take months of therapy before I can walk and then I'll probably have to use a cane. I don't have months to spend trying to get back on my feet, and I certainly have no intention of leaning on a damn stick to get around."

She didn't doubt his conviction. What she doubted was his grasp of his own limitations. The man was flat on his back in a hospital bed, one leg elevated by a pulley and most of his nourishment coming through an IV because his system wasn't yet up to steak and eggs. Yet he sounded very much as if he were willing to give this small inconvenience only a couple of days to take care of itself.

"Whether or not you think you have the time isn't going to change how long it's going to take for you to heal. Considering the shape you were in when you were brought to emergency, you're lucky you even have the chance to walk."

The look he gave her was level and amazingly calm for the tension in his expression. "Don't you mean I'm lucky to be alive? That's what Moody said. That I'm lucky I didn't break my neck considering the impact." His jaw hardened, making his words quieter, more ominous. "Maybe just being alive is good enough for some people."

Jamie said nothing. Crossing her arms over her uniform, she stood quietly at the side of his bed trying to discern the emotions in his brooding expression. What she saw in his unwavering gaze was not the conviction he was trying for. This wasn't self-pity, or a bid for sympathy. In his eyes she saw fear. It was masked somewhat by the anger that often followed news such as he'd been given by Dr. Moody, but that fear was there—along with a lot of uncertainty. It was clear enough to her that he didn't know how to deal with any of it.

She wouldn't tell him that what he was feeling was normal under the circumstances. Right now he wouldn't care that a lot of other people in his circumstances had felt those same emotions, suffered the same anxieties. He had to work through this his own way. So she concentrated on the other traits she recognized in him. The stubbornness in the set of his jaw; the hint of challenge, as if he dared her to tell him he was going to have to settle for less than he'd always had.

"Why isn't it enough?" she asked, finding that she very much wanted to know what drove this man.

Her quiet question turned his eyes surprisingly hard. Caught by the power in that deep, steely blue, she hugged her arms a little tighter.

"Because people stagnate when they settle for less than what they want. I won't settle. I never have and I have no intention of starting now. It's all or nothing. No half measures. I'd rather be on the edge than anywhere else. That's where I feel alive. And if some physical limitation makes it impossible for me to do the things I've always done, then I should have hit that rock a little harder."

She didn't back down from his quiet vehemence. She arranged her expression so it would betray nothing but a willingness to listen. Yet beneath the practiced facade she felt a tug of apprehension. His attitude hinted at what could be more serious problems. But even as she noted what he'd said, she reminded herself of how well she knew the strength of his will. All those times she'd sat with him, she was sure she'd felt him struggling to surface. He'd fought too hard to come back to give up now.

"What kind of things are you talking about? Do you mean with your flying?"

"That's part of it." He looked toward the featureless wall, seeming defeated when he found nothing beyond it to see. "Flying is as much a means to an end as an end in itself to me. I'm talking about watching a sunrise from a mountaintop. Feeling the wind holding you up in a ten-thousand-foot free-fall. Playing tag with a stingray, or exploring a wreck at the bottom of the sea." His glance returned to her, catching her with its intensity. "Do you understand what I mean?"

She wanted to. Very badly. "You've done those things?"

"Yeah," he muttered as if such endeavors weren't so unusual. "But I want to do more. A lot more."

"Why?" What, she wondered, made a person want to risk his neck jumping out of a plane or diving in the ocean?

"I told you," he said simply. "I like the feeling."

"Of having survived?"

He smiled at her tone. "Of being on the edge."

"What does your family think of what you do?"

The smile faded. "I don't have a family."

He closed up right in front of her. Had he been on his feet, she was sure he would have walked away. Immobile in the bed, all he could do was turn his head on the pillow and face away from her. Raising his hand, he drew a deep breath and rubbed at his right temple. "What did Red Malloy say?" he asked, his tone utterly lifeless. "Is he coming?"

"That's what I came here to tell you. He'll be here in about an hour. Mitchell . . . Mitch," she immediately corrected, unable to let him dismiss what they'd been speaking about. "I'm sorry."

Curling her fingers over his forearm, she felt him tense. Her first instinct was to pull back, to protect herself, though she had no idea where such a thought had come from. Her need to keep him from blocking her out kept her right where she was. "I was only thinking of how the people who care about you might feel about what you do. I was just trying to understand. I didn't mean to intrude."

The apology in her voice drew him back. Trying to ignore the steady ache in his head, he looked from where her soft hand lay on his arm to the quiet concern in her eyes. She seemed to understand far more than she realized.

Had her uniform not reminded him that as a nurse it was her job to be understanding, he would have turned his hand over in hers and brought her fingers to his lips. The gesture might have struck some as gallant—which he definitely was not—or old-fashioned—which he certainly wasn't, either. But it was what the expression in her eyes made him think of doing. How long had it been since a woman had looked at him as if she really cared about how he felt?

"Every other person who's come in here has asked about my family. If it's not because they're wanting to call someone for me, it's because they need names for their records. I'll tell you what I've told them. My parents are dead. I'm an only child. My parents had no brothers or sisters, either. I have no wife, no ex-wife and no fiancée. There is no one."

And that was exactly the way he wanted it. With relationships came responsibilities and obligations and the right of others to make demands. Just the thought of someone having such control over him could make him panic.

"No girlfriend?" she asked, hoping she sounded teasing even though she thought it incredibly sad that he should truly be so alone. She might not be especially close to her family, but at least she knew they were there.

"No girlfriend," he confirmed, responding to her smile. "No woman in her right mind would want me. At least, that's what I've been told."

A warm knot centered in her stomach when she felt the full impact of his smile. Stepping back, she crossed her arms, very aware of the speculation in his eyes as they moved over her loose scrubs. "So," she began, disconcerted to know how easily she could be rattled by him. "Since you don't have to worry about family criticizing what you do, I guess that pretty much leaves you free to go wherever you want. Why Winston, though? There isn't all that much here."

The quality of his speculation underwent a subtle shift. For a moment he'd wondered if she'd been fishing, trying to find out just how unattached he was. Now his interest shifted to the way she'd posed her statement. There had been a hint of defense in it, as if she were intimately familiar with familial criticism. God knew he'd encountered enough of it himself to recognize the scars it left.

"Does *your* family not approve of what you do?" he asked.

She'd been studying the scuff marks on the tiles beside his bed. The question brought her head up. Meeting his unnervingly steady gaze, she immediately returned her attention to the little black streaks. "There's nothing wrong with being a nurse."

"I didn't say there was." He moved his head on the pillow, inching his chin down so he could see her eyes. "But someone obviously did."

Her defensiveness, subtle as it had been, surprised Jamie. It had been a long time since the old argument had even mattered. "My parents just thought that if I wanted to go into medicine, I should be a doctor."

"Lots of parents like the idea of having a doctor in the family."

"We already had one," she said, and let the matter go because she didn't like thinking about how she'd failed to measure up. "You didn't say why you'd come to Winston."

To Mitch it seemed there might be more than just her career that met with her family's disfavor. Or maybe he was just reading his own lousy experience into her evasion. He had never been particularly insightful where others were concerned. With this gentle woman, though, he had the feeling she'd taken the criticisms to heart, believed them, let them control her. He had taken the criticism and thrown it right back. That freedom hadn't been without a price.

"I came because of the Grand Canyon," he told her, then saw her smile when he said he'd been thinking about it since the first time he'd seen it the summer he turned nineteen.

He'd spent that summer white-water rafting on the Colorado, the river that had carved the Canyon over the millennia. He'd been wanting to come back for a long time. Then, about a month ago, he'd heard about an outfit in Winston that needed a helicopter pilot for the summer tourist season.

As Jamie listened to him, oblivious to the low-keyed sounds of staff being paged and hushed conversations filtering in from the long corridor, she began to see the picture her imagination had created of Mitch merge with the man he really was. Reality was proving more formidable, more compelling than the fantasy.

While she could appreciate some of the more necessary risks people faced in life, she couldn't begin to relate to the mentality that thrived on putting oneself in physical jeopardy. That seemed to be exactly the type of man Mitch was, too. Red Malloy had been having trouble finding a pilot because flights through the Canyon had such a high percentage of crashes that the FAA had begun investigating the reasons. The risk had appealed to Mitch and he felt the wind currents affected by the unusual topography and such would be a challenge to his skills.

Those skills had apparently been tested quite thoroughly. He'd flown drilling equipment for an oil company through sandstorms in Saudi Arabia. And he'd spent three summers flying teams of scientists and their equipment around the Antarctic. Even in summer, the weather at the bottom of the earth had allowed only tiny windows of time to make the trip from Argentina to the Antarctic Peninsula, the shortest route from land to land. Mitch said that, as often as not, they had taken off in the clear and set down in a storm.

But as much as he enjoyed the flying, he told her, the side benefits of the jobs were what he enjoyed the most. The jobs in the Antarctic had eventually allowed him to spend time in Australia where he'd dived along the Great Barrier Reef. And he'd taken the job in Saudi Arabia because, aside from the pay being good, it wasn't far from Pakistan, and the world's second-highest mountain was there. He hadn't tackled Everest. Yet. But he would, and when he said it Jamie found it hard to doubt his conviction.

As he talked, it seemed to Jamie that, in the past fourteen years, he'd climbed up, skied down, flown over and dived under some of the most difficult terrain on earth. And everywhere he'd gone, he'd come across other men equally bent on pursuing such pastimes. Some of those men he'd known for a long time, like the two buddies he climbed with whenever the three of them could make their schedules coincide. Others he'd meet on a job and, like soldiers who forged fast and fleeting friendships, never see again once one of them moved on.

Though he didn't say as much, it was clear that when he moved on, he did so alone. As he'd done when he'd come to Winston.

Jamie had the feeling that he didn't believe in strings, or loose ends.

She had reached that conclusion when she heard voices behind her. The female voice drifted off with fading footsteps. The one remaining sounded like a frog croaking from the bottom of a well.

"Excuse me? This Mitch Kincaid's room?"

In the doorway stood a leprechaun of a man, wearing a yellow T-shirt stretched tight over his paunch and a pair of jeans that needed hitching up. They called him Red for the obvious reason, though there was almost enough gray in his curly, copper-colored hair to forsake the nickname. From beneath bushy gray eyebrows, his pale eyes narrowed as he came toward Jamie.

"I know you," he said with his hand outstretched. "I've seen you over at the nursing home. My wife's mother is there. Clairesse Whitaker?"

She smiled when she said she remembered Mrs. Whitaker. Seeming pleased that she recalled having seen him, too, he gave her hand an extra shake so firm it was all she could do not to wince.

"You're the lady who brings the cookies."

"What kind of cookies?" Mitch wanted to know.

Jamie started to reply. It was Red who answered.

"You name it. Chocolate chip. Peanut butter. Oatmeal. Little whitish ones with cinnamon on 'em."

"Snickerdoodles," Jamie supplied.

"Yeah, them," Red said, looking back at the brawny man in the bed. "Elaine's mom likes those best."

He stepped a little closer, seeming to know it was impolite to stare but unable to help himself. Mitch's leg wasn't suspended at the moment, but the heavy brace that covered his left leg from hip to toes lay exposed on the pillows propped under it. With the hospital gown and sheet covering the rest of him, the bandages on Mitch's torso were hidden. The bruises on his face and the eight stitches on his forehead, now that the bandages there had been removed, were plainly visible.

The cookies were forgotten.

"Red Malloy." He extended his hand, accepting Mitch's with more caution than he had Jamie's. The caution proved unnecessary. Mitch's handshake was firm. "Understand you did battle with a boulder. If this is the shape you're in, I hate to think of what happened to your car."

"It was a motorcycle."

One gray eyebrow arched. "Oh, yeah? What were you riding?"

Mitch named something that sounded very ominous and ended with numbers like the caliber of a bullet.

Apparently the model deserved respect. Red whistled between his teeth and shook his head. "Man. That's too bad. Nice piece of machinery."

"Yeah. It was brand new."

Red looked truly sympathetic, obviously more comfortable commiserating over a chunk of metal than over the condition of the man who'd been riding it. Red was sorry Mitch had been hurt, but lamenting the demise of the bike was his way of conveying that concern.

When Red mentioned that he also owned a small auto repair shop and had a mechanic who was absolutely gifted when it came to rebuilding anything on wheels, Jamie started backing toward the door. With her brothers, she'd become quite aware of how unnecessary a female was to the conversation once anything mechanical became the topic. It was a sort of male bonding thing that no amount of technical knowledge on a woman's part could overcome. Not, Jamie thought as she watched Red straddle the chair by Mitch's bed, that most women could get too excited over a camshaft or fuel injector or whatever it was she heard Mitch mention as she waved goodbye at the door.

He gave her a smile—and kept right on talking.

It was silly of her to take that smile to heart. But she did, knowing that it meant nothing and letting herself enjoy the oddly giddy feeling it gave her, anyway. There was a definite recklessness about Mitch, and as inexplicable as it was to her, she was drawn by his blatant disregard for danger. It was as strangely seductive as the man himself.

As she started down the hallway, she admitted that she'd been fascinated by the places he'd been, the things he'd accomplished. She'd found it intriguing, too, that he hadn't taken any pleasure in recounting what he'd done. At first he'd spoken of his pursuits only to make her understand what it was that he refused to relinquish. Then he'd elaborated only because of the questions she'd asked, prodding him to go on when he probably would have fallen silent. It was almost as if, once he'd achieved something, it meant nothing. All that counted was pursuing the next exploit, the next goal.

That made her all the more curious. Most people enjoyed, in some way, the knowledge of their accomplishments. Many—to the infinite boredom of their friends and unsuspecting acquaintances—rested on those laurels. It was clear enough that Mitch would rather concentrate on what he wanted to do *next*. In general this was a good attitude, but Jamie couldn't admire it in him because of what he chose to do. In some ways, he seemed almost driven. Possibly by something even he didn't understand.

A shrill "Oh, Jamie! Wait!" as she passed the gift shop brought her up short.

Two wild tufts of straight gray hair poked out of Agatha Spencer's bun as the rail-thin lady hustled into the hall. The head of the hospital auxiliary never did anything at normal speed. She talked as if she were an old forty-five record being played on seventy-eight speed.

"You remember my little Roxy, don't you?" she asked and went on before Jamie could so much as nod. "Well, my sister's sixtieth birthday is next week and her children are having a big party for her there in St. George and if I don't go I'll be the only family not there. But Agnes, she's my sister, you know, is allergic to dogs and she'd just spend the whole weekend being stuffed up and itchy if I had to take my darling little Roxy. But I can't leave her locked up in a room over there and I'm just so afraid to leave her at the kennel. She's never been in a kennel before and the experience could upset her whole little system. You know, she just loved it when you took her in for me when my husband and I went to Idaho last—"

"Would you like me to watch her, Agatha?"

"Oh, would you?"

The question was posed as if the thought had come as a total surprise. Suppressing a grin for the woman's performance, Jamie mumbled, "Sure. When are you leaving?"

"In the morning. I already checked the nursing schedule. Martha lets me peek at it, you know, and I noticed that you're off for the next two days. It'll work out just perfect. I'll bring her and her toys by about eight in the morning. Well, gotta run."

Agatha, looking pleased, hustled back behind her counter. Jamie stood there for a moment, frowning. She didn't mind baby-sitting the little dog. She'd done it before and the poodle really was kind of cute. The problem was that Agatha had just reminded her that she had the next two days off. That meant she wouldn't see Mitch.

She wondered if she should go tell him. Then decided that would be silly. Just because she'd become a little attached to him in the past week didn't mean anything. He'd been unconscious most of that time, so as far as he was concerned now that he was awake, she was just another nurse. Whether she was there or not probably wouldn't even matter to him.

Jamie knew that a patient's desire to recover quickly sometimes could be as much of a detriment as an asset. Once Mitch had come to, it hadn't taken her long to suspect that his determination would be equaled only by his stubbornness. Within days, the entire staff was in agreement. The general consensus was that the coma he'd been in had probably been nature's way of making him stay put in order for his body to start healing. Once he was awake, he was worse than a child when it came to being bored.

The doctor ordered him to be up à couple of times a day, but because movement was so awkward with his leg braced, a trapeze was suspended above his bed so he could help swing himself into his wheelchair. Part of the problem there was that once he was mobile he could rarely be found in his room. When it came time for medications or a meal, the nurses would have to track him down to the solarium with its small library and big-screen television—which he invariably tuned to the channel running outdoor and wildlife programs. If he couldn't be found there, it was because he'd slipped past the nurses' station to the visitors' waiting room with its long bank of windows looking out to the east.

Within a week he was spending more time out of his bed than in it.

Within two weeks he was using the trapeze as a make-shift exercise machine, doing heaven only knew how many reps of pull-ups, which would leave him glistening with sweat and breathing heavily from the exertion.

Doris was first to find him in that alarming condition. When she had, she'd been certain he'd spiked a fever due to an infection, which was a logical conclusion given the nature and extent of his injuries. But once she'd realized what he'd been doing, she decided not to be upset with him because the activity did have the advantage of keeping him in his room. What Jamie couldn't understand was how he was able to manage the pull-ups with two cracked ribs. Even with arms like iron, which they'd have had to be to support his considerable weight, the pain would have stopped him. Dr. Moody said to leave him be—which is exactly what Jamie did the afternoon she walked into his room with an aviation magazine he had asked for.

Mitch had been moved from the windowless single room to a two-bed unit at the end of the hall. He didn't have a roommate yet and, as Jamie stopped by the vacant bed nearest the door, she heard the groan of metal against metal and the slow exhalation of air. The beige privacy curtain was drawn to conceal him from the doorway, but Jamie could see his reflection in the mirror above the washbasin. His bed was raised to a sitting position and he'd taken off his hospital gown, leaving only a sheet covering him to his waist and exposing the white tape around his ribs. His hands gripped the metal bar hanging from the chain over his bed.

Though he would have had to look into the mirror himself to see her standing there, his concentration was so absolute that he didn't notice her. His eyes were fixed on the window opposite his bed, his breathing deep and controlled. It was almost as if he were in a trance as he slowly pulled himself up, the force of his will equaling the force of muscles bulging beneath the mahogany sheen of his bare arms and chest. Lowering himself just as slowly, he allowed those tense muscles to relax only long enough to release a deep breath before the cords on his forearms tightened and he began again. Over and over he repeated the motions, his jaw tense with purpose and his body damp from the effort. Even from where she stood, unashamedly staring at his reflection, she could see the tension rippling through him.

That power was almost a tangible thing. Raw, masculine, sensuous. There was a primitive sort of beauty about him, a beauty made more compelling by the shaded bruises and stark white bandage. The wounds gave him vulnerability. The sheer strength in his body gave him command.

Dear God, she thought. To be held by a man like that.

Jamie swallowed against the thickness in her throat. Mitch may have felt compelled to push his physical endurance to the limit, but she didn't. She'd had all she could take.

Jamie didn't give Mitch the magazine. She left it with Raye Anne to give to him later and went home to clean out a cupboard she'd neglected for the past couple of years. But the sensation of heat in the pit of her stomach stayed with her until late that evening when she finally fell asleep in the middle of the late show while trying very hard not to think that she might be more attracted to Mitchell Kincaid than was truly prudent or wise.

That attraction was obvious to no one but her. Even Martha, who tended to zero in on that sort of thing, said only how nice it was that she'd befriended the man and suggested that Jamie bring him some of her cookies the next time she baked.

For the most part, Jamie's visits to him were prompted by some small request he'd made of her the last time she'd stopped by—as with the magazines he'd asked for and the return of his knapsack and shaving kit. But she did stop by on occasion just to see how he was doing. He never seemed very anxious for her to leave and Jamie was beginning to feel that, somehow, they were becoming friends.

Jamie hadn't realized how strong that friendship was until one evening nearly a month after Mitch had been admitted.

She'd just left work and in forty minutes she was supposed to meet Stan to go over the program for safety day at the elementary school. That meant she had time either to shower or to eat. Not to do both. With her hand and part of her head buried in her tote bag as she walked across the parking lot digging out her keys, she opted for the shower. Stan could buy her a taco.

That decision made, she withdrew her keys, took a deep breath and looked up at the sky. It was almost sunset, her favorite time of day, and the fading sun bathed everything in a dusty desert pink. The sky would have been prettier had there been clouds to reflect the color, but she thought the

evening beautiful anyway—as long as she looked out beyond the field and not at the uninspiring back side of the
hospital.

The rear of the hospital visible from the employees'
parking lot was a stark beige structure whose architectural
austerity was interrupted occasionally by galvanized air-
conditioning and heating ducts. There were no public en-
trances through the back of the building, only emergency
exits and service ports. Right now the building looked almost abandoned—except for someone at the far end of the
low, sprawling building. She noticed the movement just as
she started to give her car door the extra-hard jerk necessary to open it.

A man in a wheelchair was sitting just outside the gray
metal door.

She wondered if a patient had become confused and gone
through the wrong door. The only way off the small landing was down a short flight of steps, so Jamie tossed her bag
through the open car window and headed at a jog past the
nearly empty parking lot. Her pace slowed the instant she
saw who it was, her approach becoming almost cautious.

"Mitch? What are you doing out here?"

At the sound of her voice he turned, his face devoid of
expression. He watched her until she stopped at the bottom
of the steps. Then, with his elbow on the arm of the chair,
he hooked his thumb under his chin, pressed his knuckle to
his mouth and looked away. His focus settled somewhere
beyond the field of scrub grass and wildflowers. A purple
mesa rose in the distance, its outline glowing golden pink
from the sun sliding behind it. He seemed to be looking
there, but she couldn't tell for sure.

"What's the matter?" Slowly she ascended the steps and
leaned her hip against the rail when she reached the top one.
He was wearing one of the blue-and-white pin-striped hospital robes. A light white blanket lay over his lap, covering

part of his extended leg. His other foot, bare and high-arched, he'd propped against the rail as he might had he been sitting in a deck chair watching the sunset.

It was all too easy for her to picture him away from this place.

She had the feeling that was what he was doing, too. "Cabin fever?" she offered when several seconds passed and he'd said nothing.

"You might say that."

"How long have you been out here?"

He shrugged, the motion betraying weariness more than indifference. "I don't know. Not long. All I do know is that if I have to spend one more day in there I'm going to go out of my mind."

Cabin fever, she silently confirmed. "How much longer does Dr. Moody think you'll have to stay?"

"Two or three more days."

She hated wishing it could be longer. "That's not so bad, then."

The look he gave her was tolerant at best.

Wondering where he'd go when he did leave, not wanting to ask because with him looking at her that way he might see that she was going to miss him terribly, she glanced toward the door. "Does anyone know you're out here?"

The look in his eyes remained the same, which told her clearly that he hadn't told anyone. He'd simply felt the need to escape and had before anyone he would have told could stop him.

"I'm afraid it's against hospital policy for a patient to be outside the facility without a member of the staff present."

"You're staff."

She matched his droll expression. "You know what I mean."

"I'm not going back in there." The cords in his neck tightened as his jaw clenched. "Not right now. I just want to sit out here for a while and breathe air that doesn't smell like it's been disinfected.''

He turned away then, the faint breeze teasing the ends of his dark hair. Both of his forearms now rested on the arms of the wheelchair. Jamie noticed the tendons stand out on the backs of his hands as he squeezed the edges. The tension lacking in his voice was evident in his grip. The man was a time bomb simply waiting for the last tick to explode.

The rivets on her acid-washed jeans made a scraping sound against the metal as she pushed herself away.

''Don't go.'' The quiet desolation in his expression slipped into his voice. ''Jamie. Please. Stay and talk with me so I don't have to think.''

It wasn't easy for him to ask that of her. He seldom asked anything of anyone, requesting or accepting help only with things impossible to accomplish himself. What he asked of her now was such a little thing, really. A few minutes of her time.

He obviously hadn't known it, but he hadn't had to ask.

''I was only going to tell your nurse where you are and to make a phone call.'' She didn't think Stan would mind if she was a little late. ''I'll be right back.''

It proved unnecessary for her to go. The gray metal door swung open just as she stepped toward it. Pam's sleekly coiffed head poked out. Her brow was drawn down, giving her the look of a perplexed Pekingese.

''There you—'' Swinging the door wider, she caught sight of Jamie. Her frown deepened. ''What's going on?''

Mitch's voice was as flat as the field he continued to stare across. ''I needed some air.''

''You can't stay out here, Mr. Kincaid. It's against hospital regulations.''

''That's what Jamie said.''

''It's okay, Pam,'' Jamie cut in. Mitch had just closed his eyes, his shoulders rising with the deep breath he drew. A man like Mitch couldn't be kept cooped up for as long as he had without something blowing. He looked ready to blow right now. "I'll bring him in in a few minutes. Would you do me a favor and call Stan Hubbard at the sheriff's office? Just tell him I'm tied up and I'll call him later."

Jamie could see Pam's reluctance. The patient was Pam's responsibility and for a moment Jamie was afraid her concerns about policy and liability might override her compassion. But she apparently shared Jamie's views about the rules. With a nod, Pam backed up. There were times when a patient's needs couldn't be met by policy, and Jamie breathed a sigh of relief when it became clear Pam didn't mind bending the rules a little.

"I'll make that call for you," she said, and the door closed with a solid thunk.

For several seconds the only sounds to be heard were the honk of a car horn from somewhere in front of the hospital and the twitter of sparrows gathering for the evening in the jacaranda trees lining the east boundary of the lot. A quiet residential neighborhood bordered the wash beyond the huge vacant field, but it was suppertime so there were no shouts from children roller-skating in the streets or playing hopscotch on the sidewalks.

"I don't want to interfere with your plans."

"You're not," she returned, too concerned with Mitch's frame of mind to notice how carefully he was watching her.

When she stepped in front of him she noticed only that he looked as if he didn't believe her. But he didn't question her decision to stay. And he didn't give her a chance to change her mind.

Chapter Seven

"Talk to me, Jamie."

The plea in Mitch's quietly spoken words drew Jamie nearer. She lowered herself beside his chair, bringing her eye level with his broad chest. Banishing the errant memory of those solid muscles straining with exertion, her glance swept past the dark hair visible at the neck of his robe to the ridged line of his jaw. When she met his eyes, she thought she'd never seen anyone look so lost.

She was sure he'd have hated knowing that. "What do you want to talk about?"

"Anything that has nothing to do with this hospital. Tell me about this town." He looked from her to the plains stretching uninterrupted toward the mesas. "What makes you stay? You said before, there's not much here."

With the tip of her finger she traced across the metal ring outside the wheel on his chair. A smile, soft and encouraging, touched her mouth. "We have the Canyon. You said yourself that's what brought you back."

"The Canyon is miles away. I mean the town itself." Though he didn't sound impatient, his jaw clenched. "Is this the only place you've lived since you left Los Angeles?" *Talk to me so I don't have to think.*

Jamie knew that the topic of conversation didn't matter. What he really wanted was an escape from his fears and frustrations. Wanting very much to provide that escape if she could, she told him it was, though from the distant look in his eyes she was certain she could have said she spent winters in Siberia and it wouldn't have mattered to him. She mentioned, too, that she stayed because she'd made friends here. In Winston she felt accepted. Necessary. Useful. But she kept that to herself. She mentioned only that she liked the size of the town—small enough to make a person feel she belonged, but big enough that not everybody knew your business.

She remained crouched beside his chair, her hand on its wheel for balance. He continued to stare toward the horizon, his thoughts so concealed that she wondered if he'd even heard her.

She was thinking of telling him there was plenty to do, if one knew where to look. But there wasn't much in the way of the excitement he seemed to seek, so she said nothing and watched the breeze tug at his dark hair. He wore it swept back straight from his face, hanging free to his shoulders. The style gave him a vaguely savage look that Jamie found incredibly disturbing.

Almost as disturbing as the look in his deep blue eyes when he finally drew his glance to her. It settled dark and intent upon her upturned face.

It was impossible to know what he saw as he held her eyes with his, or what manner of regret shadowed his rugged features as he shoved his fingers through his hair and released an unsteady breath. She thought only that if she looked away, he would know she was affected by him in ways that were probably better left unexplored. But by not looking from him, she was being bound somehow and that was a little frightening, too. A man like Mitch couldn't ever want all the things she no longer let herself dream about. And such a man, one drawn to adventure and the call of exotic places, a man who seemed content to have no one special in his life, wouldn't ever want someone as settled and ordinary as Jamie Withers.

"Tell me why you left L.A."

The quiet command surprised her. So did the way he studied her. Boldly. As if he felt that fragile bond, too, and wasn't at all sure why it was there.

"I found a job here," she said, aware of his gaze settling on her mouth.

"I'm sure a nurse could get a job just about anywhere. Something else had to bring you here. This place isn't exactly on any main roads."

His glance skimmed down her throat, his expression far more approving of her T-shirt than it ever had been of the scrubs he usually saw her wear. The approval, though, was gone with the quick clench of his jaw, replaced with a familiar distance she found much less unnerving.

"Did you know someone from here?" he asked, and she knew from his tone that he very much needed her to keep talking.

"If you want to know how I found the position, it was posted on the employee bulletin board at L.A. General under travel opportunities. I was going through a phase where I wanted to see the world. Or at least the part between our borders," she clarified, since she believed in realistic goals. "I arrived here thinking I'd stay a year, then try Alaska or Vermont. But I got here and found what I was looking for. There was no reason to keep going."

"What were you looking for?"

That was easy. "Space. I'd always wanted to live in a place where people weren't living on top of one another. My parents were both professors at the university and the housing was nice, but with five kids it was pretty cozy. Then there was just the congestion of living in a big city."

There was more to it than that. She had constantly craved the solitude she could never find. She'd longed for room to breathe, and found it in the wide-open vistas of the desert. There were other things she'd probably craved, too. Such as attention, approval.

Remembering that Mitch was an only child, she thought how different it must have been for him. She didn't comment, though. He had tended to get defensive when his parents were mentioned and she'd wondered on occasion if he was still grieving for them. She knew only that they'd both passed away within the past three years, and even though she wished she knew more about him, she put her curiosity aside. Mitch was looking for a little peace of his own right now and he wouldn't find it if she brought up something he didn't want to discuss.

She watched him studying her. They may have come from completely different backgrounds, but she was certain he understood her need for surrounding herself with such space. What she didn't expect was that he would understand so much.

"Is this far enough for you?"

"What do you mean?"

"Are you far enough from your family here?"

For the briefest instant she considered denying what was apparently so obvious to him. The direction of his gaze wouldn't allow the dishonesty. Her motives were as clear to him as they'd been to her four years ago.

"I love my family," she needed to preface. She did truly love them all, even if she didn't like the way they made her feel. "But we aren't especially close. My brothers and sisters are all very successful, very competitive and very well married. Their lives are quite busy."

"And you don't fit in?"

The question wasn't a question at all. More of a statement that required no response for him to know how very right he was.

With a hesitant laugh she drew back, amazed at his perception and a little shaken by it. "Not with a physicist, two lawyers and a surgeon." She didn't mention one of the lawyers was also a model. Catherine had earned extra money in law school doing bathing-suit layouts. Her parents hadn't liked that at all, but Catherine, like every other member of the family with the exception of Jamie, was very headstrong.

If she hadn't borne such a strong resemblance to her father, she'd have sworn she'd been adopted.

Seeking distance, and with it perspective, she leaned against the silver railing. Her hands at the sides of her hips gripped the smooth metal. She wanted to take Mitch's mind off his circumstances, but not necessarily at her own expense. Her shortcomings were the last thing on earth she wanted to discuss.

Despite her easy smile, she felt exposed. "What else do you want to know about Winston?"

"Are we changing the subject?"

"Please."

Mitch would have preferred to continue their discussion. He didn't like the fact that she felt as if she didn't measure up to her family. It sounded to him as if she lacked the aggression they thought she should have; that she had chosen a career not in keeping with the family's standards. She'd indicated that her siblings were all married, too. Maybe her parents even had a problem with her still being single, or with her living so far from their idea of civilization. He wouldn't push her, though. If anyone understood how a family could manipulate its own, he did.

A change of subject probably wouldn't be such a bad idea. He tipped his head toward the massive rises of limestone that had claimed so much of his attention. "Those mesas out there. Do they have names?"

Gratefully she released the breath she'd held.

"They're called the Widowed Sisters," she told him, certain the panorama must come as a relief to him after having spent nearly three weeks cooped up inside. He would require the outdoors for sustenance as much as he would oxygen to breath. "The one to the north is White Flower. The Navajo named her that because of the white striations along her rim. The other is Weeping Dove." She turned more toward the horizon, letting the gentle evening breeze carry away the strands of hair that had loosened from her braid. "At certain points on the Dove's eastern face, the wind makes the saddest sound as it blows through the formations along the base. You can't always hear it, but when you do, it's kind of eerie. Like one would imagine a weeping dove might sound."

"You've heard it?"

"Lots of times." She would hear it and wonder what loss made the dove ache so. "It's beautiful up there. Especially this time of day. There's a trail of sorts that leads through the boulders to a ridge perfect for watching the sun set. It's an easy climb," she added, but stopped herself before saying how much she thought he'd like the view. He was in no condition for a climb, easy or otherwise, and the last thing she wanted was to remind him of what he couldn't do.

Mitch didn't feel her constraint. What he felt was the tension beginning to ease in his shoulders and the demanding urge to hit something starting to fade. "Go on," he urged. "Describe it to me. Tell me what you see when you're up there."

She'd noticed a while ago that the edge had left his tone. As she began to tell him of the colors and textures in the rocks and about the delicate shades of wildflowers that blanketed the plateau in the spring, she noticed, too, that he seemed to find comfort in simply listening to her. It was as if he really needed her to be with him right now and Jamie, though she knew it wasn't wise, was drawn by that need. It touched her much as had his whispered request when he'd reached for her hand the day he'd been brought in. So she told him about the glorious sunsets she'd seen from her ledge and after a while she began to suspect that he found peace in sunsets, too. That was why it was so easy for her to tell him how she would often go there when she needed to restore a little balance to her life. She'd never spoken of such a thing to anyone else.

"Every once in a while you see something really awful here," she said quietly, referring to the emergency unit. "It helps to have a place where you can be surrounded by silence. Or if there are sounds, only the ones from nature. There's just something about listening to the wind and watching the colors in the rocks change as the sun goes down..."

She couldn't describe the feeling, so she ended her sentence with a shrug and let her words trail off. The sun had set now, leaving only a pale gray twilight that would soon give way to darkness. Already the evening star was glowing brightly in the ombré blue sky.

In that fading light, Mitch studied her profile. An aura of gentleness seemed to surround her and he found himself wondering how she could possess something so fragile when she'd no doubt seen so much suffering. Life normally tended to harden people. Yet there was nothing hard or cynical about her. Beneath the gentleness was a kind of yearning, something most people wouldn't notice unless they'd felt it themselves. He'd felt it often enough to recognize it—and to learn how to ignore it. After ignoring it long enough, the feeling had eventually died. Or so he'd thought until he'd found himself with nothing to do but think.

Not liking the path of those encroaching thoughts, he let his glance roam over the shades of wheat and honey woven in her hair. He understood what she hadn't found the words to convey. He'd often sought the restorative power in nature for himself; more so lately than he had in a long time. But he knew what she was talking about and he was getting better every day at using his concentration on that power to overcome his pain. A wizened and wise old Tibetan monk had once told him his resentment would never allow him to achieve the purity of spirit necessary for total mastery of himself, but what he had learned of the discipline had helped him through some tough situations. It was helping him now. Mitch's motives were far from religious. His purpose was strictly personal. Being his own master was all that he wanted and he'd do whatever was necessary to achieve that mastery... and to protect it.

As she turned to smile at him, he thought it interesting that she should seek the same solace as he did. But he said nothing about it. There was something vaguely threatening about having someone that close to his thoughts.

Jamie saw him withdraw the moment she looked over at him. The distance in his expression seemed to confirm what she'd already feared. She was boring him silly.

The halogen lights flanking the back parking lot began flickering to life. The one above the door behind Mitch gave an irritated buzz before throwing its harsh light in a circle around them.

It was with some relief that they felt the quiet intimacy ruined. "I should take you back now," she told him. "Before Pam comes looking for you again."

His response was nothing more than the clench of his jaw as his hands fell to the wheels and he turned his chair toward the door, his leg pointed straight ahead. She pulled the heavy metal door open and watched him roll inside.

"Will you be all right?"

"I can get back on my own."

"That's not what I meant."

He stopped to glance back over his shoulder, the bright overhead lights in the white-tiled hallway making his black hair gleam silver and blue.

He didn't answer her question. He just gave her a smile that deepened the creases by his beautifully shaped mouth and made her heart do an utterly stupid little flip. "Thanks, Jamie," was all he said, then left her leaning against the door.

She'd wanted to know if he'd be all right. That she'd even asked made him feel better. Concentrating on that, he turned down the corridor to his room, hating the smells, the sounds and the very sight of the aseptic environment. Thinking about Jamie, about how her concern touched him, he was allowed a little longer reprieve from the thoughts that usually plagued him. He'd found himself turning to thoughts of her often in an attempt to avoid considering what he didn't want to think about. Unfortunately, the nature of those thoughts tended to produce an entirely different sort of frustration.

If there was any feeling with which Mitch was intimately familiar, it was frustration—in all its forms and guises. Dr. Thompson, the orthopedist who'd put the pins in Mitch's fractured leg, came by to see him almost as often as did Dr. Moody. Each time, he also made sure Mitch understood it could be months before he would be able to walk. He could begin therapy in a few weeks, but until then there wasn't anything Mitch could do toward his recovery other than rest.

Mitch hadn't liked the sound of that at all. So Mitch, on crutches now, found his way to the therapy department to see for himself if he couldn't start doing some sort of exercise sooner. Jamie heard about his visit from Dr. Moody when he asked if he could have a word with her and motioned her into the cramped little office he used at the hospital.

"Just move those journals," the doctor said, waving his hand vaguely toward the stack of magazines in the chair across from the cluttered desk. "I want to talk to you about Mitchell Kincaid."

With her hands full of the heavy journals, Jamie hesitated. Seeing an empty spot on the floor by a model of the human skeleton, she put the magazines there and returned to the chair. She didn't sit, though. "What about him?"

"Go on. Sit. Sit." He did so himself, lowering himself into the large chair behind the desk where he began polishing his glasses. When he saw that she'd done what he asked, he leaned back himself. "Mr. Kincaid is absolutely determined to cut his recovery time. He was down in physical therapy this morning asking Barney to give him isometric exercises and trying to find out where he could get ankle weights. I know you'll recall what happened when he tried to put more weight on his leg than it would bear last week." Sliding his glasses up his nose, he peered over the top of them until she nodded. "I thought you might, since I heard that you gave him a bit of a lecture when you learned of it."

"I didn't *lecture* him, doctor. I just told him that he'd need full mobility of his knee if he wanted to climb again and that pushing himself at this point would do more harm than good. I'm sorry if you feel I overstepped—"

"Don't apologize. It's what he needs to hear. The point is that he listens to you. He seems to trust you."

Dr. Moody paused as if he'd just said something quite significant and was waiting for her to see its import. Jamie knew that, in many ways, Mitch *did* trust her. She also knew that he didn't necessarily want to. Among so many strangers, however, he didn't seem to have much choice. Red, sharing Mitch's love of anything that would go over sixty miles an hour, had come by a few times to see him. But Red had a wife and two businesses to run and his time was limited. She was the only other person Mitch really talked with about anything other than his medical needs.

Dr. Moody's point, however, escaped her.

"Do you want me to talk to him about something?"

"Not exactly." Another pause. "I've been considering Mr. Kincaid's situation. He doesn't need to be hospitalized any longer, but I'm a little wary of releasing him. My first concern was travel. I told him I wouldn't recommend his traveling any distance at this time and he didn't find that to be a problem. Apparently, he has no home to travel *to*." Several charts lay in front of him. Pulling one toward him, he opened it. "He needs to be close to a medical facility because he will be needing therapy soon. As you know, the nature and extent of his injuries warrants a close eye for the next several months. He had no problem with that. When I asked where he'd go if I did discharge him, he said he'd probably stay at the motel he'd checked into when he first arrived."

His mouth puckered as he considered Mitch's plans. "I don't find that acceptable. And an extended care facility," he added dryly, "is out of the question. He needs to be in a place where he can live as close to normally as possible."

"Normal for Mitchell Kincaid isn't quite what it is for the rest of us."

"I've gathered that his life was rather active prior to his accident. That's what is making his recuperation so difficult." Papers rattled as he closed the chart. "I remember your having a young lady living with you for a while. I hear from Martha that the girl is gone now. I wonder if you'd be interested in renting that room again?"

Jamie's eyebrows rose. The doctor's lowered.

"I realize Mr. Kincaid wouldn't be an ordinary tenant," he said, as if the thought hadn't already occurred to Jamie. "And if you're not interested in renting to a patient, I'll understand. But I do hope you'll consider it. If you're willing to take him in, please speak to him in the morning."

Even if the telephone hadn't rung just then, Jamie knew the conversation was over. Receiving a dismissing nod to confirm the conclusion, she left the office contemplating the doctor's gift for understatement. She thought it was matched only by his lack of perception. Mitch would indeed be anything but an ordinary tenant. But that wasn't the problem. The problem was that she'd stopped thinking of him as a patient long ago.

I do hope you'll consider it.

A few hours later, Jamie was on her knees by a pile of weeds on her walkway, doing exactly as the good doctor had asked. Thinking about his request. The rational part of her—the part that knew Mitch to be a loner, a man who had no ties and wanted none—said to let the matter go. Another part of her, the feminine, nurturing, caring part—the part that knew he had no home—said let him have the room.

With that mental war raging, Jamie wiped the dampness from her forehead with the back of her hand and sank back on her heels. Even at its late-afternoon angle, the April sun was warm on her back. The pansies she'd planted where the weeds had been seemed to sympathize, wilting a little themselves in the heat of the high desert spring.

Don't let go.

Her frown deepened as the memory came back to her, and she stuck her trowel in the ground.

Ignoring the itchy feel of damp grass seeping through the knees of her jeans, she sifted the red-brown dirt through her fingers. Working with the earth usually made it possible for her to forget everything else. It was her therapy, the thing she did when she couldn't otherwise clear her mind of what troubled it. The feel of the earth, the satisfaction of tending, nurturing, seeing her efforts produce. The beauty. She normally found pleasure in it all. Not today.

Talk to me, Jamie.

How could she clear her mind to make a logical decision when her memory kept interfering?

"You're doing it again, Jamie."

At the sound of her neighbor's voice, Jamie's head came up. Agitation was immediately masked by a smile. Standing over a small pile of uprooted weeds on the cracked sidewalk, her fists on the hips of her very short shorts, was her next-door neighbor, Barb Robinson. Pretty and petite, with the kind of angelic face that drew men like magnets, Jamie considered the frank and forthright mother of two to be everything she was not. The only reason she could stand her was that she was a terrific friend.

Swiping back the strands of hair tickling her cheek, she watched Barb step over the wilted pile of vegetation. Most thirty-three-year-old women wouldn't wear barrettes shaped like teddy bears, but that's exactly what held Barb's auburn curls back from her scowl.

"What am I doing?"

"Making me look bad. Jerry's going to see these flowers and start bugging me about planting some. I can't do flowers yet. I still have the Christmas decorations to put away." Her pert little nose wrinkled in disgust. "At least I got the damn things down."

"Mommy!" An equally disgusted sound, this one sharp with shock, came from behind Barb. "You used a bad word. Daddy said—"

"I know what daddy said," Barb cut in, cutting off the six-year-old version of herself as the little girl bounced up the walk. "I'm working on it."

Apology, along with a touch of irritation at herself—and possibly her husband—shadowed her expression. The frown softened. Clasped to the child's middle was a large, rather bedraggled toy bunny. "You're supposed to be picking up the toys in your room. What are you doing out here?"

The little girl shrugged in the exaggerated way children have that brings their shoulders to their ears. "Nothin'. I just wanted to see if Jamie can fix Pete."

"What's wrong with Pete?"

Solemnly the little girl held out her stuffed friend. One plush pink ear dangled a little more than it should. "He got caught under my bed. When I pulled him out, he ripped."

Her mom reached for it. "I can fix that, honey."

Tammy snatched it back. "His ear's broke. He needs a nurse."

It was apparent enough that while a mommy could fix torn clothing and such, it took more specialized care for a favorite bunny. The bunny wasn't simply torn. He was hurt. And Jamie, because she was a nurse, could make it better.

Jamie turned her smile to the ground as she stood and brushed her hands off on her jeans. "He needs a little surgery, huh?"

With a very somber nod, Tammy held Pete out again.

Ever so carefully, as if it were as real as the child's concern, Jamie took the bunny in her arms. "He's going to be fine, Tammy. Now you go do what your mom told you to do and I'll have Pete back to you by bedtime."

The recent loss of a front tooth was evident in Tammy's grin. With an obedient "Okay, Jamie," the little girl skipped across the lawn, skirted a tricycle and baseball bat abandoned by the front porch and entered her own house with the slam of the screen door.

A bright blue ball dislodged by the vibration was still bouncing down the Robinsons' front steps when Barb turned her bewildered expression back to Jamie. "How do you do that? I have to beg, plead, bribe or threaten to get them to do anything. You ask and it's 'Okay, Jamie.'"

Barb was exaggerating. Tammy and her brother, T.J., didn't *always* do everything she asked. "I guess it's because I'm not their mother."

"Well, you should be somebody's mom. You've got a lot more patience for the calling than I do. Have you ever considered adoption?"

Barb didn't expect a response, especially since the reference was to her own children. The question was simply a teasing commentary, but it struck a chord deep inside Jamie. She tended to ignore such twinges and, normally, she'd have let the comment go. The pensiveness she couldn't seem to shake wouldn't let her.

"Actually," she said with a little half laugh, "I have."

The quality of Barb's frown underwent a subtle change as she crossed her arms over the howling coyote on her shirt. Jamie had spoken so offhandedly that it had taken a moment for her to realize she wasn't kidding. "Do we need to talk about this?"

From somewhere down the street came the sound of supper dishes being washed and the distant shouts of children playing. Instead of finding comfort in the homey sounds, today they increased her restlessness. "Don't pay any attention to me." With a smile for her friend's concern, Jamie dismissed the idea she'd only fleetingly entertained. "It's just been one of those days."

Understanding, underscored by accusation, was suddenly evident in Barb's expression. "You've been hanging around the nursery at the hospital again, haven't you? You know how you get when you're around those babies.''

"I haven't been in the nursery. As far as I know we haven't had a baby born all week.''

That made Barb hesitate. She'd known Jamie for a long time. Long enough to know that it took a lot to get Jamie down.

Her eyes narrowed. "Well, something's wrong,'' she announced, her scrutiny taking in the shadowed expression in her friend's eyes. It was as rare as rain in the desert for the warmth to be missing from Jamie's smile. More unusual still to see her so pensive. "Did something terrible happen at work today?''

Some days in emergency were definitely worse than others. Barb obviously realized that, though Jamie seldom shared many of the details. As willing as she was to listen to others, she wasn't inclined to talk about her own concerns or frustrations. She much preferred to pretend they didn't matter; that by not considering them, they somehow didn't exist.

Old habits were very hard to break. But there were some concerns that wouldn't allow themselves to be ignored.

"There's a patient at the hospital I'm kind of worried about.''

"You mean worried as in might not make it?''

"Oh, he'll make it,'' Jamie said, realizing she must have looked more troubled than she'd thought. "In fact, he's being discharged soon.''

"Then why are you worried?''

Jamie glanced down at the bunny she held so tightly. "Because he doesn't have anywhere to go.''

Looking a little uncertain, Barb glanced toward Jamie's tidy white ranch-style house with its charcoal trim and its flowerpots by the door and the white Priscilla curtains on the front windows. The windows along the side were for a bath and bedroom, and the curtains there had been freshly washed and starched. Barb had seen Jamie rehanging them just last week.

"What are you thinking about doing? Jamie?" Barb prodded when her friend didn't look up from the ratty old bunny with the missing whiskers. "Are you thinking about taking him in?"

"Dr. Moody asked me if I would."

"Who is the guy?"

Answering her question was unavoidable. Barb would just keep nagging at her until she did. So Jamie told Barb that Mitch Kincaid was a pilot who'd come to Winston to work for Red Malloy, but who'd been injured in an accident that prevented him from doing so. For a while, anyway. Except for her and Red, he didn't know anyone in town. And, yes, she was thinking of offering him a place to stay while he recuperated.

"Does the doctor know him very well?"

She had the feeling no one really knew Mitch. "Not especially."

"What about the owner of the helicopter place?"

"He'd never met Mitch before he came to Winston."

"Then do you think having him move in with you is very wise? I mean, what do *you* know about him? He could be some depraved maniac and there you'd be all alone in that house at night."

It was nice to know that someone's imagination was more active than Martha's. "He's not a depraved maniac," she said flatly, and would have teased Barb for reading too many thrillers had the woman not looked genuinely concerned. "Mitch is a very... nice man," she decided to say, though she didn't think she'd ever really thought of him as "nice" before. Compelling, intriguing and mysterious were words far more suited to him. But those descriptions, while certainly more accurate, would only raise questions Jamie didn't want to answer.

When Barb crossed her arms and shifted her weight to one leg as if settling in for the duration, Jamie knew she'd have to answer them anyway.

"What's going on here, Jamie?"

"Nothing's going on. We've become friends. Sort of. I don't even know if he'll want the room from me."

"Do you want him to stay?"

Leave it to Barb to ask the one question Jamie didn't want to answer. The truth was that she hated the thought of saying goodbye to Mitch. She savored the anticipation of seeing him as much as she did the time they shared together, and though he never said or did anything to make her think he was interested in anything other than the strange sort of friendship that had developed between them, she spent her nights creating impossible fantasies.

There was no danger of confusing those fantasies with reality. Like dreams, they faded in the harsh light of day. Her own dreams had begun to fade long ago, which is why she filled her life with other people's children and the kinds of activities that didn't allow for many empty hours. Hours where she had nothing to do but think.

She'd often wondered why Mitch did some of the things he did. Maybe she understood better than she'd thought.

"Yes," she finally said, wondering if it was possible that his pursuit of adventure wasn't a form of escape. "I do."

A considered silence preceded Barb's next request. It was clear enough she had questions she was dying to ask, but she chose to respect the conviction in Jamie's expression that asked her not to pry any further. "Just be careful, will you?"

"I told you, the guy's okay. He can't move that fast, anyway," she added, wanting Barb to lighten up. "He's got one leg completely casted and he'll be on crutches for months. I'm sure I could outrun him."

Barb was not amused. "That's not what I mean. There are all kinds of ways to get hurt."

No one knew that better than Jamie. "He just needs a friend," she said. "And before you go warning me about getting involved, he told me himself that his track record with women is lousy. How involved could I get with a man like that?"

Fortunately, Barb didn't have time to make her face the answer to that not-so-insignificant question. Four and a half feet of mud-caked little boy came whizzing past on his bike, yelling "Hi, Ma! Hi, Jamie!" just before he came to a sliding stop on Barb's front lawn and bounded up the stairs.

"Go around back, T.J.!" Barb shouted. "I just mopped—"

The screen door slammed.

"The entry." Defeated, she turned back around. "I don't know why in the hell I bother."

Jamie grinned. "You used a bad word."

Defeat turned to a glare. "No worse than what I've heard from you when your car door won't open. I don't know how anyone can raise kids without swearing, and I think it's damned unfair of Jerry to expect me to. The only reason he has patience with them is because he's only home three nights a week." With a frown for her husband, a sales rep for the local tool and die company, she resigned herself to the inevitable. "I gotta go. T.J.'s probably got mud all over the refrigerator by now."

With that, she tromped across the lawn, only to turn back as Jamie tucked Tammy's bunny under her arm and started putting the limp weeds into her wheelbarrow to haul around back.

"Just be sure you know what you're doing, Jamie," she said, then having allowed that, followed her son's footprints into her house.

Jamie wasn't so certain she did know what she was doing. She knew only that Mitch had a way of drawing her out, of making her feel that what she said and thought really mattered to him. He also had a way of looking at her that made her feel . . . alive. As if before she'd met him, she'd merely been going through the motions. The feeling was too special to lose.

Mitch had once said that the gain from a risk was usually proportionate to how much fear one felt prior to taking it. She did have to admit to a little apprehension when she decided that, first thing tomorrow, she would talk to him about what Dr. Moody had suggested.

Chapter Eight

Jamie found Mitch in the solarium the next morning. He was leaning on his crutches, standing in front of the window looking into the atrium. Impatience made his jaw rigid as he watched a bird trapped among the foliage frantically searching the large screen atop it for an escape. Every once in a while a finch or jay would find its way into the small garden area through the tear in the top, then drive itself nuts trying to get out.

Mitch looked as if he could relate.

"Good morning."

At the sound of her voice, he turned.

"Hi," he said with the enthusiasm one might have for a root canal, and went back to watching the bird.

Jamie checked her footsteps. Maybe now wouldn't be a good time to talk to him, she thought, then told herself to stop looking for excuses. Mitch was not a morning person, and now might be the only opportunity she'd have before he was discharged this afternoon.

She tried again. "You're up awfully early."

He looked back at her, turning just enough for her to see that his robe hung open over his bare chest and that he was wearing the drawstring pajama bottoms the hospital supplied.

Quite deliberately, she raised her eyes to his. Certain examples of the male anatomy were definitely more perfect than others. "They're just now bringing over the breakfast trays from the kitchen. It looks like oatmeal and that stuff they call scrambled eggs. If I were you, I'd pass."

"Thanks for the warning." A faint smile touched his mouth, making him look even more appealing than he already did. "I'll hide out here until they take it away."

"Want me to sneak you a doughnut?"

"How about a maple bar?"

"No problem."

Finally, he smiled.

Jamie moved closer. Her uncertainty about what she was doing had her heart beating a little faster and her palms damp. Or maybe it was his smile that had caused the little surge of adrenaline. The reason didn't matter. She was going to mention Dr. Moody's idea. That was all. Then leave him to think about it. There was no reason to feel so anxious.

Not unless he accepted.

Joining him by the window, she pretended great interest in the leaves of a particularly healthy ficus. "Dr. Moody said he's letting you out of here today."

Mitch looked back to the jay. It had perched high on a palm branch seeming, for the moment, resigned to its fate.

Oddly, resignation was what she heard in Mitch's voice, too. She'd have thought he'd sound a little happier about the prospect of leaving the place he very nearly hated.

"Yeah," he muttered. "Reluctantly, I think. I've never heard of a doctor who asked so many questions about what a person would do after he was discharged. He sounded as if he didn't think I could manage on my own. Or like he thought I might not take care of myself. I've been taking care of myself for years and since I can't *do* anything, it would be a little difficult to get into trouble."

"I think you might be underestimating yourself."

The same droll look he'd gotten from Dr. Moody was on Jamie's face. Both seemed to know him better than he'd thought.

Mitch, unwilling to admit or deny anything, simply smiled at her conclusion.

"He said you plan on going to a motel."

"Seemed logical," he said with a shrug. "Since I'm grounded for a while, I figured I could go stir-crazy in a motel here as well as anywhere else."

She liked that he could make light of his situation. On the surface he seemed no more concerned about having no place in particular to go than he would have been with the current trends in women's fashion. But Jamie, unnervingly attuned to him at times, didn't miss the dispiritedness he was so quick to cover with his disarming smile.

"Would you like an alternative?"

"Such as?"

"Renting a room from me." She made herself look at him then, needing to see his reaction. "I have an extra room that I've rented out before. It has its own bath and a separate outside entrance. It's yours if you want it. At least you'd have meals and some space to move around in. There's a yard and a park across the street, too," she added, then shut up because she was afraid she sounded as if she was trying to sell him on the idea and she wasn't so sure she was sold on it herself.

His sudden silence was unnerving. The way he watched her, even more so. She thought for a moment that it was speculation making him narrow his eyes as he searched her face, but she really had no idea what he was thinking as his smile faded completely. His eyes remained on hers as he drew a deep breath. There was something he wanted to say, she was sure, but either he wasn't comfortable with the thought or he didn't know how to phrase it.

The muffled sounds of voices and of trays clanking drifted through the closed double doors.

"Thanks, Jamie," he finally said. "But I don't think that would be a very good idea. If you wouldn't mind, though, I could use a ride to the motel."

She didn't allow herself to consider the quick pang of disappointment she felt. All she let Mitch see was her easy acceptance of his decision. Telling him that the ride wouldn't be a problem, that she'd be off at three-thirty, she added that she'd better get to work before Martha put out an APB on her.

Now that he'd turned her down, she was free to admit that she'd really wanted him to accept.

That afternoon Mitch and one of the hospital orderlies were ready and waiting for Jamie by the potted palms near the hospital's main entrance. The young man responsible for seeing Mitch safely off the premises gave her a lazy nod as she approached. She returned it with a smile and glanced at Mitch in the wheelchair.

He was wearing a yellow T-shirt that made him look very tan despite the weeks he'd spent inside, and a pair of jeans that someone had split up the left inseam to accommodate his brace. On the floor beside him was the leather duffel that had been rescued from the motel he was returning to and he held his crutches in his right hand with the rubber tips resting on the gleaming tile floor.

When she met his eyes she was smiling, a bright, easy smile that took an unimaginable amount of effort to produce. "Ready?" she asked, though the question was obviously unnecessary.

"You sure you don't mind doing this?"

"I wouldn't have offered if I did."

She had such an easy way about her that Mitch almost immediately felt an easing of the agitation he'd struggled with all day. It was always like that with her, he thought. When she was around, he didn't feel quite so anxious, quite so... angry. He'd let himself acknowledge the phenomenon before. He acknowledged it again now—then let the admission go in favor of concentrating on being out of confinement when the orderly pushed him through the yawning double doors.

The expression "free at last" came to mind when he drew in a lungful of clean, fresh air. But to his disappointment, thinking about the months stretching ahead of him, he didn't feel nearly so free as he'd thought he would.

Jamie had brought her car—a vintage sky blue Mustang that Mitch thought might have been built around the year she was born—up to the front entrance. With the help of the orderly, Mitch maneuvered into the passenger seat while Jamie flung the duffel bag and her pink tote into the back. As soon as Mitch was settled, the young man headed back in with the wheelchair. He'd just disappeared inside when Mitch heard a loud thump on the driver's side door and Jamie's muffled "Damn" through the two-inch open space at the top of her window.

The thump came again.

"What's the matter?" he called, leaning over to see if he could see her.

Her bland "Nothing" preceded another thump and another curse as she yanked on the handle. Seconds later the door opened and she slid inside, stuck the keys into the ignition and shifted into first.

"What was that all about?"

"Oh, the door just sticks sometimes. It's been that way for a year."

"Why don't you get it fixed?"

"The same reason I haven't fixed the radio. I never think about it when it's convenient to take it to a garage and when I do have the time, something else comes up. Actually," she admitted, giving up the excuses, "I procrastinate. Ready?"

It occurred to him then that he'd never noticed how truly lovely her eyes were. Maybe it was because he'd never been quite this close to her. Always before, she'd been at arm's length. Although somewhere in his subconscious was a vague memory of her being much nearer, of her hand soothing his brow, of her sweet breath feathering against his cheek as she spoke in a voice so exquisitely soft that the sound itself was a caress.

It was possible, of course, that what he recalled was only a dream. But he wasn't dreaming now. He was close enough to see the flecks of topaz in her amber eyes and to count the thick individual lashes surrounding them. She had such expressive eyes. He had seen them filled with compassion, concern, caring. He had seen them alight, too, with laughter, pleasure and the gentle smile that never failed to ease him somehow. Unexpectedly, he would find a hint of shyness there, or a sad and weary wisdom. He'd never thought about how much could be learned about a person just by watching her eyes. Or maybe he'd just never taken the time before.

The possibility existed, too, that he'd never wanted to know anyone that well until she'd become part of his life.

The thought was nebulous, replaced with feelings he could identify with more easily as he concentrated on the more physical aspects of her appeal. The fine grain of her skin made it look very soft, very touchable, and as his glance moved past the gentle part of her mouth, he noticed that the smooth skin visible between the lapels of her olive-colored blouse looked very touchable, too.

A faint knot formed deep in his midsection when he breathed in her scent. He leaned back, unprepared for its effect when combined with an attraction he didn't trust. Whatever *need* he felt for her, he was sure, stemmed only from the situation that no longer existed now that he was out of the hospital. The *want* was purely physical.

His voice sounded strained when he finally responded to the question she'd asked nearly a minute ago. Telling her he was ready, he added that he was going to the Hi Desert Motel on the east end of town.

Jamie, her throat feeling as if she'd just swallowed cotton balls, kept her eyes straight ahead. The air had a faintly electric feel to it, agitating a restlessness she couldn't quite explain. The feeling had something to do with the way he'd looked at her, as if he were seeing something in her she didn't even know existed. But, she supposed, too, that the feeling could be from lack of nerve. She wanted badly to ask him again if he'd consider staying with her. But she knew she wouldn't. Even as she turned onto the street that would take her within two blocks of her house, she knew she wouldn't take such a risk. Being turned down once was enough.

"Do you need anything before we get there?" Passing the turn to her house, feeling somehow relieved now that she had, she motioned vaguely down Paiute Boulevard, Winston's main street. "There's a shopping center up here if you want me to stop. Or, maybe," she suggested, feeling braver now that she could afford to, "you'd like to drive around for a few minutes. Or stop at a park for a while."

"The park," he returned, jumping on the idea. He was going from four hospital walls to four motel-room walls.

The thought already had him climbing them. "If you've got the time."

There was a park right across the street from her house, a very nice one with a baseball diamond and a duck pond and an ice-cream man who circled it on hot summer afternoons. But she headed to the one on the opposite end of town because it was nearer where he was staying. On the way, they drove past the Hi Desert and she watched his jaw clench as it passed from view. It was a pretty uninviting place. A single row of rooms with metal lawn chairs and tables on a patch of lawn out front. The view from the back was of a parking lot for a strip center housing a pet groomer, a florist, a travel agency and a small restaurant that changed hands with predictable regularity. This year it offered Chinese food. Last year it had been Italian. The view from the front of the motel, across the two-lane, dirt-aproned highway, was of a car-repair shop and the municipal storage lot.

Inspiring it was not.

"Are you hungry?" she asked, since it was nearing suppertime and she couldn't help wondering how he was ever going to feed himself. The Chinese place was close enough that someone from there could run over with takeout if he called. And the local Dairy Queen was around the corner, provided he was up to a two-block walk on crutches. But neither was big on fresh fruits and vegetables and he needed to eat well to heal.

She reminded him of that as she pulled into the park, hoping she didn't sound like the hospital's nutritionist as she did.

He responded with a vague "I'll manage," and seemed to pull inside himself as the car rolled to a stop on the gravel parking strip.

The flatness in his voice matched the fatigue in his expression. Watching him carefully, concerned as much about his mental state as his physical one, she reached for the keys to cut the engine. "Do you want to get out? We could sit at that picnic table over there."

He shook his head, opting to sit in the car with the windows down as he watched four teenaged boys chase a soccer ball. Farther down, a father and his young daughter were tossing a Frisbee to a beautiful golden collie. "I'm just procrastinating," he said, using her excuse. "I can do that right here."

She knew exactly what he was avoiding. "You don't *want* to go to the motel, do you?"

She'd seen the way he'd tensed when they'd passed the forlorn-looking building. As someone who very much needed the comfort of familiar surroundings, she could only imagine how she would feel were she in his position. A little lost. Apprehensive, maybe. Sad. And when a person didn't feel well, those feelings would only be magnified.

Mitch, however, was the kind of man who would rather choke on those feelings than admit them.

"Not exactly," he said, and tried to smile.

Jamie looked away, too aware of the lifelessness in his eyes to be fooled by his smile. There was pain in this man, buried deep and probably barely recognizable to him. But she'd noticed before how his smiles never touched his eyes. She had seen cynicism, bitterness, a touch of fear and even, surprisingly, a hint of awareness there, but she'd never seen pleasure.

What she recognized now was a kind of resignation—or, possibly, defeat.

The knotted sensation was back in her stomach again.

A piece of lint clung to the knee of her khaki slacks. Picking it off, she rolled it between her fingers, flicked it out the open window and drew a deep breath. As faithfully as she avoided such situations, she could never have imagined herself deliberately risking rejection. He'd already turned her down once, but she couldn't stand the thought of him recuperating all alone.

"Mitch..."

"Jamie..."

"You first," she graciously offered, and watched the furrows in his brows deepen when he glanced away to study the tabs on his metal brace.

He seemed to have had second thoughts about what he wanted to say.

The shouts of the boys drifted toward them, the only sounds in the stillness. Not even the wispy leaves on the nearby paloverde trees moved, the breeze seeming to hold its breath as Mitch kept his glance turned from her, considering.

He truly didn't know how to begin. Seeing her had been the only thing that had made the past few weeks bearable, but he couldn't tell her that. She had often been his source of escape when the unthinkable—that he might not fully recover, that he might not fly again—had threatened to overtake his thoughts. He couldn't tell her that, either. He had no problem with the glib phrases that women seemed all too eager to hear. He wasn't necessarily proud of that ability, but he did know the right buttons to push. Jamie had made him realize that he didn't know how to be honest about what he felt deep inside, where feelings really counted. With that kind of honesty came vulnerability, and he'd rather deal with the devil himself than give anyone a hold on him. That was why he'd turned down the offer she'd made to him this morning. She'd suggested something beyond what he'd expected of her and the first thing he'd done was back away.

The need to pull back was as strong as ever, but he knew he wasn't being fair to Jamie by adding her to all the others he'd shut out. She wasn't demanding anything of him. She never had. All she'd ever asked of him was that he not give up on himself. She had been his friend when he'd badly needed one and she was still being one. That was all she had offered this morning, too—her friendship and a place to recover. God knew he could use both.

"Is that room you mentioned still available?"

She hesitated, sounding unsure. Of herself? She wasn't certain. Of him? Quite probably. "It is if you want it."

"I do." Very badly, but he didn't think it necessary to tell her that. Seeing her gesture for the gift it was, he did think it only fair to warn her that he might be around for a while—and to assure her that he wouldn't abuse her generosity. "The orthopedist wouldn't commit to how long I'd need therapy. It sounds like it'll be a while, but once he releases me I'll be leaving. I've got to be out of here by the end of September at the latest. The oil company I worked for wants me in Houston, October first."

Four months, Jamie figured. Or five. "Fine" was all she said, though her heart was suddenly beating a little faster.

"What do you charge for rent?"

She'd have given him the room for nothing. But, taking his businesslike lead, she gave him the figure she'd charged the teacher who'd moved out in December. It was much less than he'd be paying at the motel.

"I'll pay double to take care of the board."

"That won't be necessary."

"It will be when you see your grocery bill."

He was a big man. No doubt he did eat a lot. When he felt good, anyway. "If that's what you want."

He gave her a nod. The motion didn't admit much. Certainly it didn't let her know how very much he wanted what she offered. At one time, he'd have let the inadequacy stand. With this woman, it wasn't enough.

"I really appreciate this," he told her and wearily rubbed at the headache threatening near the scar on his forehead. "Thanks."

Jamie didn't trust herself to say anything. She merely matched his nod and started the car so she could get him home. In the past several minutes, his fatigue had begun to show, and as he laid his head back on the seat and closed his eyes she thought only of the rest he needed. It was easier to think about his care than to consider that the man who had haunted her nights would now be sleeping in her house.

It didn't take long to drive back through town and turn into the quiet residential neighborhood where Jamie lived. Mitch lifted his head and straightened when she turned the corner, more in an attempt to find a comfortable position than because he sensed they were nearing their destination. Clamping his hand over the back of his neck, he rotated his head to relieve the stiffness. Then he shifted in the seat, trying to adjust the position of a leg weighted down by a metal brace.

Giving up on comfort, he turned his interest to her house when they pulled into the driveway in front of her attached garage.

Painted white, with charcoal shutters and red geraniums blossoming in large clay pots by the front door, the house sat on a postage-stamp-size lawn. A narrow front porch ran the length of the house, and the walkway leading from its two steps to the sidewalk was flanked on either side with a row of yellow marigolds. A paloverde tree at the far end of the house spread its filtering shade over the driveway of the house next door. Under it lay a toy sword and a decapitated doll.

"Nice neighborhood," he muttered dryly, though he really did find it quite nice as he extracted himself from the car, propped himself up on his crutches and glanced around.

Just as Jamie had said, there was a park across the street. Its neat lawn was a cool contrast to the shades of the desert displayed in the crushed cinder jogging path and rosy beige rock in the landscaped areas. A baseball diamond, complete with kids in the middle of a game, was on the far corner.

Jamie came around the back of the car. "Go on up," he heard her say as her head disappeared inside the passenger door. He saw her push the seat forward and reach into the back for his duffel. What had his attention, however, was the enticing curve of her backside as she leaned forward. "I'll be right there."

Thinking it better to start moving than to stand there staring at the way her pants molded the incredible length of her legs, he pointed his crutches toward the sidewalk and started toward the porch. It goaded him that she should have to carry his heavy bag, but there was no way he could do it. It was awkward enough trying to get around with his leg sticking out in front of him and his palms and armpits being rubbed raw by the hard rubber pads of the crutches. But what bothered him the most was how easily he tired. Though the doctors had warned him that it would take time for his strength to return, he found it monumentally irritating that he had so little energy.

Unfortunately, when that irritation was coupled with the discomfort of an aching side, leg and head, his mood left much to be desired.

The telephone was ringing as Jamie opened the front door. Carrying his duffel bag in one hand and her bright pink tote over her shoulder, she swept through an archway off to her right the moment he cleared the threshold. The screen door had barely closed behind him when he heard her bright "Hello?" A moment later her head popped around the corner of the arch and she motioned for him to come in to where she was. Through the archway, he could see a white table and chairs and the corner of a stove. The room she'd entered was obviously the kitchen.

He stood in the living room, in no great rush to interrupt her call, and used her absence to take a look around. As he did, he couldn't help feeling grateful all over again for her offer. None of the hospital's austerity was here, or the plastic symmetry he'd have found at the motel. This was a real home.

There was a comfortable look about the fat cushions on the pale blue sofa and the throw pillows in coral and peach and mauve piled on it. The colors were of a desert sunset. They were even reflected in a print of one such sunset hanging above the white brick fireplace. Looking at that picture, he remembered when she'd told him of the peace she found in watching the setting sun. That evening, listening to her, he'd almost felt a hint of that peace himself. It wasn't a familiar feeling at all, but he knew enough to recognize the sense of ease it brought. Oddly, standing here in her home, he could feel it again. He couldn't put his finger on the reason for the phenomenon, but he thought it might have something to do with the atmosphere Jamie had managed to create for herself.

She chose to surround herself with delicate colors, soft textures and living things. Two ferns flanked the fireplace, a lush vine draped over its mantel and something with little pink buds sat on a small stand beside the room's only chair. Nothing in the room was expensive. In fact, the coffee table, which held a stack of magazines, a basket of yarn and a small vase of yellow flowers, was actually an old steamer trunk that had been painted white. The only wood in the room was the bleached oak bookcase between two white-curtained windows. Its polished surfaces were full of books and bushy green plants. The room was uncomplicated, feminine and smelled faintly of cinnamon and the potpourris she had on the mantel.

"Oh, I really don't mind," he heard her saying as he glanced down at the floor. An Indian print rug in pale pastels lay on the white tile floor. Aiming his crutches around it so he wouldn't trip, he followed the sound of her voice.

"I've got Tuesday off, if you want to do it then. The morning would be best," she added as he moved past her.

Mitch stopped beside the gleaming white counter, frowning at the beige mushroom-shaped canisters growing out of it, then looked back at Jamie. She had her back to him, the phone cradled against her shoulder, and was looking at a calendar that already appeared fairly full.

When she turned back around, listening intently to whoever was on the other end of the line, he motioned toward the sink.

Jamie pointed to the cabinet to his left, assuming it was a glass he was after, and waited for Stan to check his calendar to see if Tuesday was all right with him for safety day at the elementary school. They'd been trying for a week to get it scheduled. As she listened to pages being turned on the other end of the line, she watched Mitch rest his right crutch against his side, take a glass from the cabinet and turn on the faucet. His motions, restricted somewhat by having to maneuver with the crutches, seemed almost weary. That tiredness showed, too, when he raised the glass to take a long swallow of water.

It wasn't his fatigue she was thinking about. With his head tipped back as he drained the glass, she found herself staring at the muscular cords in his neck. Watching those muscles work as he swallowed, his eyes closed as the water quenched his thirst, she couldn't help but think how very physical he was. Everything he did seemed underscored by his maleness. And having him here, in the confined spaces of her home, suddenly seemed more of a threat than a solution. His presence filled the room, making the space she'd once thought cozy and comfortable seem far too intimate.

She was still staring when he lowered the glass to refill it and caught her watching him. No expression marked his features. He simply held her gaze with the unnerving intensity of his own. It was almost as if he knew what she had just realized and was waiting for her to decide how to deal with it.

A half-dozen very long seconds passed before she was able to look away. By the time she did, Stan had said her name twice. Tuesday was fine with him, he told her when he again had her attention, and she confirmed the time she'd meet him, dutifully entering it on her calendar. The conversation ended when she told Stan that she'd see him soon, and she tried to ignore the odd knot in the pit of her stomach when, hanging up the phone, her glance strayed back toward Mitch.

With his left hand gripping his crutch for balance, the other crutch rested just under his arm. He leaned forward to set the glass on the counter. As he did, the loose crutch started to fall.

Jamie dove for it just as Mitch straightened to catch it himself. Jamie caught the crutch, but Mitch's elbow barely missed the side of her head when he turned. Grabbing her arm to keep from knocking her over, he pulled her upright.

The motion brought her to within an inch of his rock-hard body. She was so close she could feel the heat of it penetrate her shirt. The feeling was nothing compared to what she felt when she raised her eyes from the solid wall of his chest.

It looked as if he'd been about to say something—to ask if she was all right. He said nothing. His eyes locked on hers and she saw his nostrils flare slightly as he drew a deep breath. Her own breath locked itself in her lungs as his gaze darkened, slowly roaming her face and coming to rest on her mouth.

Feeling scorched by his touch, branded by his eyes, she tried to shy back, but she felt powerless to move, even though his grip on her arm had loosened considerably. He held her there more by the power of his will than any physical restraint. Realizing that only magnified the threat. She didn't fear him. She feared herself. She knew enough about this man to know she could easily get in over her head.

"Is Stan your boyfriend?"

The question threw her. "Uh, no," she muttered, commending herself for sounding so utterly unintelligent. "I don't have . . . Stan's just a friend."

For reasons Mitch didn't care to explore, he was relieved. But mostly he was aware of the guileless way she held his eyes. The woman didn't seem to know how transparent she was. She was scared, yet she wasn't going to back away. She was attracted, yet she wasn't going to do a damn thing about it. The awareness between them was definitely there. Real. Powerful. Taunting. He could see it in the softening of her expression; hear it in the altered pattern of her breathing. He could even feel it in the suppleness of her skin where he touched her so lightly. It would take no effort at all to pull her to him, to feel that softness against his hard, aching body.

But he wouldn't take advantage of her. Not when she was being so generous to him. Jamie was the kind of woman who needed promises; the gentle, nurturing sort he'd always avoided. Mitch didn't make promises. And she was too good a woman—too good a friend—to risk alienating with little white lies.

His hand fell and the wall went up.

"Where do you want me?"

Confusion swept her lovely face. "Want you?"

"My room," he clarified, annoyed with himself for nearly blowing the only decent living arrangement he had. "Where is it?"

Two bright spots of color sat high on her cheeks as she stepped back. Looking quickly from him, she indicated a doorway behind her. "At the end of that hall." Clearing her throat, she moved toward the pantry. "I'll take your things in as soon as I've fixed you some dinner."

"I'm not hungry."

"You have to eat. If you don't keep your strength up—"

"I don't need a mother, Jamie," he cut in, and could have bitten his tongue when he realized how curt he'd sounded. He was irritated with himself. Not with her. She was nothing like his mother had been. "I'm sorry," he told her, really meaning it. "I'm just tired. All I want to do right now is go to sleep."

Her response was nothing more than a subdued nod. Picking up his duffel from where she'd left it on the floor by the telephone, she led the way down the short hall to a room that had been added on as mother-in-law quarters by the previous owners. As she'd told him before, the room had its own bath and a separate entry from the patio out back.

He heard her mention those amenities again as she pointed them out, but he actually noticed little about the room, other than it was of a decent size, very neat and that it had a bed. It was to the bed that he headed, easing down on it with an awkwardness that was becoming all too familiar.

"Will you be all right?" she asked, looking as if she didn't want to pose the question but couldn't help it.

"I'll be fine."

Having put his duffel bag on the dresser, she backed toward the door at his terse response and stood with her hand on the knob. After a moment's hesitation, she pulled the door shut with a soft click.

The only thought that registered after Mitch had lifted his leg onto the downturned bed and laid his head on the pillow was that the sheets smelled like fresh air and sunshine. Within seconds he was asleep.

Chapter Nine

Jamie never had been very good at confrontations. Professionally she could handle just about anything. When it came to her personal life, it seemed she was just a coward at heart. Rather than face a problem, she'd ignore it or avoid it or treat it with some vague hope that it would eventually go away. Sometimes the tactic worked. It wouldn't this time. The problem was living right under her roof.

Twenty-four hours of sidestepping each other had pretty much proved to Jamie that her relationship with Mitch just wasn't the same as it had been while he'd been a patient in the hospital. The companionship they had established was no longer anywhere in evidence. It had taken a hike late yesterday afternoon as they'd stood at her kitchen sink. For a few nerve-shattering moments, she thought he'd been about to touch her. She'd even had the audacity to pray that he would, suspecting even as she did that God had no time for such foolish requests. When he hadn't touched her, when instead he'd seemed angry with her for being so close, the quality of their fragile friendship had undergone some indefinable change. What existed between them now was a polite caution that only increased the odd restlessness Jamie had begun to feel and made Mitch so edgy that the following evening they'd scarcely said a dozen words to each other that weren't absolutely necessary.

She'd tried ignoring him, but that hadn't worked. Now she was avoiding him.

Mitch had gone to his room just before nine, and the light under the door had gone out just after eleven. Jamie noticed because, unable to sleep, she'd waited for him to turn it off before she'd come back into the kitchen. She didn't expect to see him again tonight. She was therefore finally free to bake. The task wasn't a necessity. It was simply something she did when the weather or the time of day made it impossible for her to work in her garden to unwind. She also baked when she couldn't sleep, which was why the people she worked with were sometimes treated to fresh cinnamon rolls or cookies.

She'd been baking a lot more since she'd met Mitch.

Collecting a mixing bowl, measuring cup and a cake mix from various cabinets, she also thought about throwing something together for tomorrow's dinner. After Mitch's remark about not needing a mother, she'd been very careful with comments about what he ate or when he ate it. This morning she'd simply left cereal and fruit out on the counter, and this evening she'd made a casserole and a salad to which he was invited to help himself, if he wanted any. He'd cleaned up both. She also mentioned that she'd stop at the grocery store for anything special he'd like if he'd leave her a list. So far, he hadn't noted a single item on the piece of paper she'd stuck on the fridge with a plastic magnet shaped like an ice-cream cone.

Quite deliberately she'd refrained from asking if he was taking his medication and vitamins. He hadn't hired her as his nurse and she didn't want him telling her as much. He didn't need a nurse. He didn't need anyone to take care of him. He'd been taking care of himself for years, she distinctly recalled him saying. All he wanted from her was his room and board.

That, she reminded herself, was all she'd offered him, anyway.

She pulled two pans from a lower cupboard, quietly, so as not to wake him, even though what she really felt like doing was slamming them on the counter. She envied him his sleep, mostly because he was robbing her of her own, and found herself wondering if he slept very much during the day. She had no idea what he'd done while she was at work. Both last night and this evening he'd spent alone on her front porch watching the children across the street in the park until they were called in to bed. He'd then gone to bed himself. It seemed he was doing his level best to stay out of her way. Just as Jamie was trying to stay out of his.

"What are you doing?"

At the sound of his voice, Jamie whirled around, clutching a muffin tin to her stomach. It was stupid to feel guilty. But for some reason, standing there in her own kitchen, wearing a perfectly modest, if not a little short, cotton sleep shirt, she did.

"Baking," came her quietly defensive reply.

He moved from the shadows of the doorway, the tips of his crutches making muffled thuds on the white tiles. All he wore were tan denims, the left leg of which had been split up the inseam like his blue jeans. Barefoot and shirtless, leaning against the crutches and with his hair looking as if he'd spent more than a few minutes tossing and turning, he looked far more appealing than any man had a right to look. Big. Powerful. Alarmingly male.

"At this hour?"

Still clutching the baking tin, she shrugged. She'd intended the motion to be dismissing. All it did was remind her that she wasn't wearing a bra. With the tin snug against her middle, the movement pulled the thin pink fabric tighter over her breasts.

She'd never been well endowed; in fact, she was rather self-conscious about having less than many fourteen-year-olds. She wondered if Mitch found her lacking as his glance skimmed the length of her slender frame and came to rest on the gentle swells. Her skin heated at the thought. But oddly, not with embarrassment. What she saw in his eyes actually seemed to be approval as his glance lingered then wandered back to her legs.

Maybe it was the late hour, or the stillness in the room, or the fact that their respective attire would have been more suited for two people more intimate with each other than they were. Whatever it was, Jamie knew that standing there staring at each other wasn't a particularly wise thing to do.

"I'm sorry if I woke you." Setting the pan on the counter, she turned away, conscious of how the soft fabric of her nightshirt moved against her shoulder blades. The two eggs she'd taken from the refrigerator sat by the mixing bowl. She cracked them both into the bowl, fished out a bit of shell, then started rummaging through cupboards in search of paper muffin cups. "I was trying to be quiet."

"I wasn't asleep."

"Oh."

"You never answered me."

She heard him move closer and her hand crumpled the package she'd been looking for. "I didn't?"

"No. You didn't."

The thuds stopped, but she didn't turn around. She knew he was leaning against the counter by the sink, his eyes on her back. She could almost feel his gaze moving down her spine.

"I asked why you were doing this so late."

The package ripped when she pulled too hard on the tab. Not only had she crushed the paper container, now it wouldn't close as it was supposed to. "Because I couldn't sleep. I've never seen any point in lying there getting frustrated when I could be doing something. I like to bake. So when I can't sleep, that's what I do."

Mitch had been lying in bed feeling frustrated himself. He had the feeling, though, that they weren't talking about quite the same thing.

Hesitation marked his tone. It was the opening he needed. God knew he was lousy at initiating this kind of conversation, but he had to do something to ease the strained atmosphere. He didn't want her to regret taking him in. "Why couldn't you sleep?"

It would have been easiest to say that she just wasn't tired. The circles under her eyes wouldn't support the assertion, though. She never had been able to lie very well. Rather than being dishonest, she said nothing and returned to the task he'd interrupted. Adding water and oil to the bowl, she then dumped in the cake mix. It was hard to tell if it was his presence or simple lack of concentration that caused her to do everything backward tonight.

She'd forgotten to turn on the oven.

The question she hadn't answered was abandoned in favor of another. "Can I help?"

At his quiet request, Jamie's hand fell from the oven knob and she finally turned to face him. Some problems, it seemed, refused to be ignored.

He was studying her legs, seeming inordinately occupied with the shape of her calves and slender thighs. His glance jerked up when he realized she knew exactly what he was doing. "I can't sleep, either," he admitted.

For the first time since he set foot in her house, he smiled. It wasn't much of one, for all the caution in it. It was enough, though, he hoped, to let her know that he was willing to try to get past the awkwardness if she would just give him the chance. The only way she could give him that chance was to stop avoiding him.

He had to stop avoiding her, too. He knew he'd been doing it, and he knew exactly why. When they'd left the hospital, the rules had changed. The protective nurse-patient definitions with their built-in proprieties didn't apply anymore. Here, she was simply a very compelling, sweet-smelling woman with legs that made him ache just thinking about how they'd feel wrapped around him, and he was a normal, red-blooded male whose hormones were still in excellent working condition despite the beating his body had taken. By avoiding her, he avoided temptation. But avoiding her was creating problems, too—especially since she chose to deal with problems the same way he did. By not confronting them. Two people who didn't talk weren't ever going to solve anything.

He also thought it would help his frustration level enormously if he could find some way to keep himself occupied.

That was why, a few minutes later, as he settled himself at the table to line muffin tins with paper liners and spoon batter into them while Jamie made frosting, he asked if she had any tools in her garage.

"I have a hammer and a screwdriver," she told him, adding vanilla to powdered sugar in another bowl while the scent of baking chocolate filled the room. "What do you need them for?"

"I already found the screwdriver in the drawer over there. But what about a ratchet and socket set? And some pliers." He licked dark batter from his index finger, then stuck it back into the bowl to get a blob he'd missed. "I'll fix the door of your car." He studied the batter on his finger, enjoying the process of licking the bowl in a way that made her wonder if he'd never done it before. "I took your coffeepot apart this morning. You don't have to boil coffee on your stove now."

Apparently he hadn't liked the bitter brew any better than she had. "I don't?"

"Nope." With a vaguely satisfied look, he pushed the cleaned bowl aside. "The pot just needed a new plug. I took one off the old iron I found in a box in your laundry room. I'd have fixed that, but the heating element is shot and I saw you had a newer one, anyway. If you've got anything else like that around here that you want me to take care of, just let me know."

Jamie was no fool. If Mitch wanted to play handyman, she was more than willing to let him. After all, he needed something to do and she did have a number of projects she'd promised herself she'd stop putting off one of these days. There was the slow-running drain in her bathroom—he could lie flat on his back to do that one—and the lawn mower her neighbor said needed a new starter but that she'd been making work by squirting ether into the engine because the only time she remembered it was broken was when she needed to use it. They were little jobs she didn't know how to do herself, but which wouldn't require any real physical effort for Mitch. Exactly the sort of activity he needed.

The prospect of having something definite to do the next day seemed to remove more of the stress from Mitch's features. By the time the cupcakes were frosted most of the strain had left the atmosphere, too. Conversation turned quiet, companionable again, and the only tension remaining was of a kind neither one of them was willing to mention—Mitch because he was trying very hard to think of her as he might a sister, had he had one, and Jamie because she was sure that if he was attracted to her at all, it was only because she was all that was available at the moment. She didn't fault him for that. She was simply going to keep it all in perspective now that they'd gotten beyond the initial awkwardness of living in the same space.

All she had to do now was make sure her nosy next-door neighbor didn't go jumping to any conclusions.

Three days after Mitch moved in, Jamie was taking out the trash when she heard Barb call to her across the low shrubs dividing their backyards. From her stoop, Barb hollered for Jamie to stay put while she dumped the load of laundry in her arms and practically flew out her back door, leaving the lid on her washer up and the machine chugging soapsuds onto her floor.

"I see you decided to do it," Barb said, coming through the gap worn in the hedge.

With the garbage-can lid in one hand, pushing back a loose strand of her freshly braided hair with the other, Jamie frowned at her neighbor. Having had only half a cup of coffee so far this morning, Jamie wasn't quite prepared for her friend's way of starting a conversation. The woman inevitably began somewhere in the middle, and while she knew what she was talking about, rarely did anyone else.

The lid was replaced with a clank. "Do what?"

Her voice low and conspiratorial, the auburn-haired busybody nodded toward Jamie's house. "Took in Dr. Moody's patient. Lindsey Candless and I saw him sitting on your front porch the other night. And I must admit he's definitely easy on the eyes. But is it working out all right?"

Jamie knew what Barb was getting at. She was still worried about the man's character, which was nice, she supposed. But that wasn't what Jamie was concerned about. "Lindsey?" she said. Lindsey had one of the biggest mouths in the neighborhood.

"You don't need to worry about her. I told her who he was and why he's staying with you. She thought it sounded like something you'd do." Having dismissed Jamie's obvious concern, she pushed her hands into the pockets of her orange terry romper. "You're the only person I know who could have a hunk like that move in with her and make it look respectable."

"Thanks," Jamie muttered. "I think."

"So, is it working out okay?"

"So far," was all Jamie could think to say before she caught Barb's glance skimming over the old football jersey and cutoffs she wore.

Barb's expression turned hopeful. "You're not working today?"

"It's my day off."

"Great! You want to help me paint my bathroom?"

The question was barely out when Jamie's screen door groaned open. Barb straightened abruptly.

"I told you I'd take it out," Mitch said, then stopped, still frowning, when he saw that Jamie wasn't alone.

Leaning against the can, she crossed her arms over the large red forty-two on her white shirt. "And I told you there was no need for you to wrestle with it. You dried the dishes. Barb," she said, not wishing to continue the discussion she and Mitch had been having over who was responsible for which chores in front of her very interested neighbor, "this is Mitch Kincaid."

Mitch pushed the screen open farther with his crutch and filled the doorway with his decidedly imposing frame. To her credit, Barb did try to be discreet as she smiled and extended her hand. From the quick way Barb looked him over, silently approving the fit of his jeans and white cotton T-shirt, Jamie knew her friend was still reserving judgment.

"Mom?" came a small, soft voice from across the hedge.

Tammy, still sleepy eyed and wearing a frilly nightgown, came stumbling out the Robinsons' back door, Pete the Rabbit in tow.

"I'm over here," her mother called.

Dragging her toy bunny by the ear, she entered the hole in the shrubs, shuffled across the lawn and stopped beside her mother. "I'm hungry."

"I'll be home in a minute. Go on in and get dressed."

"I wanna have breakfast with Jamie."

"She has company."

Jamie opened her mouth, but Mitch beat her to it. "I'm not company."

Tammy hadn't seen Mitch in the doorway. Now, peeking around her mother's leg, she looked from the man darkening Jamie's threshold to her mother and back to Mitch again.

"Are you the chunk my mom told Bethany's mom about?"

"The chunk?" Mitch repeated, then realized what she meant just as he saw Jamie press her fingers to her forehead and, grinning, glance at the ground. He cleared his throat, trying not to choke on his smile. "I don't know. You'll have to ask her."

"Yes," Barb hissed to her daughter. "He is. Now go home."

"But I wanna eat at Jamie's. I haven't got to eat with her for a whole week."

"You had dinner over here the other night."

"That was different." Hauling her stuffed bunny up by his ear, she tucked him under her arm. "She was making Pete better and I had to keep her company."

"Pete?" came the deep voice from the doorway.

"Her bunny," Barb replied, arching her eyebrows at Jamie. *He was sure quick to pick that up,* the motion seemed to say.

Jamie ignored her. "Let her stay, Barb. I'll send her home after she's had a bowl of cereal. She's still got half a box to finish."

Mitch, seeming more interested than Jamie would have thought he'd be in the conversation, suddenly cut in. "That explains it."

"Explains what?" both women asked.

"I couldn't figure out why a grown woman would have cereal shaped like little bears in her cabinet."

"She's probably got ninjas in there, too." Pushing her fingers through her auburn curls, Barb smiled. "That's what T.J. likes. He's my other one. And why I'm already going gray," she added as the child in question poked his head out their back door.

"Mom?" he hollered at the top of his lungs.

"What?" Barb shot back, obviously having long passed the stage where a mother yearns for that first "Ma-ma" from her offspring's mouth.

T.J.'s voice lowered a couple of decibels. "There's suds coming out of the washing machine. They're all over the floor. Can I make pancakes?"

"No!" With a curse as she remembered the washer lid, Barb took off at a trot, her frazzled "Nice to meet you, Mitch" trailing after her.

"Nice to meet you, too," he said to the space where she'd stood, and warily eyed the six-year-old staring back at him. "I think I'll go work on your lawn mower," he said to Jamie and, careful not to bang his brace against the door as he maneuvered down the single step, he left the two females to their own devices.

Jamie scarcely saw him the remainder of the day. Mitch was still in the garage when she left for the grocery store and the cleaners an hour later, and he was in his room with the door closed when she returned. He slept until suppertime, still unhappy with the amount of rest he required, but giving in to it because he really had no choice. Jamie spent the afternoon helping Barb paint her bathroom and that night Tammy came back to watch an old movie on television with Jamie and Mitch before Jamie sent the child home and turned in early because she had to be up at six the next morning to go to work.

The routine was pretty much as it would have been for Jamie on any other of her days off. She knew she couldn't say the same for Mitch. He wasn't saying how he felt about his living arrangement. But she suspected he felt a little better being occupied, especially since he was able to help her out. She was providing the environment he needed to heal and he was catching her up on all the little projects she'd neglected.

Since she didn't have the tools he needed to fix her car door, Mitch called Red, who was nice enough to stop by and lend him both the tools and a hand. Mitch would have put in a new radio for her, too, but Jamie didn't want to buy a new one, so hers simply stayed broken. She was used to singing to herself as she drove, anyway.

He managed to stretch the car-door project out for an entire Sunday afternoon, seeming to enjoy Red's company as much as actually doing something with his hands. Over the course of the next week he also fixed the timer on her dryer, recaulked the kitchen sink and fixed a drippy faucet. Then, when all the minor stuff was done, he took apart her stereo and rewired it so he could hook it up to the VCR he had sent over from the local electronics store.

He was making himself at home and Jamie, though she was normally very protective of her space, didn't mind at all. The student teacher had used the kitchen, but kept to her own room when she was there. Not Mitch. Jamie felt his presence everywhere—in the living room where he'd leave a book or magazine he was reading, or the dining room where he often worked at the table because the light was better there than in the kitchen. She even felt his presence in her bedroom, though he'd never so much as set foot in the short hallway leading to it. She would lie in her bed at night imagining him standing on the other side of the door, her heart pounding as the door swung open and he came to stand beside her bed. She could visualize him so easily, his beautiful, scarred body stretching out over hers and easing the ache she felt every time he looked at her.

As she had long ago discovered, Jamie was much better off when she didn't think about herself or what she wanted. Entertaining such fantasies only led to frustration, and Mitch frustrated her enough as it was.

She wanted him to be comfortable in her home. She wanted him to be happy, too, mostly because she had the feeling he'd never really been that way. There was a deep sadness in him that he couldn't quite overcome, though he did a remarkable job of pretending it wasn't there. She would notice it most when she would find him sitting on the front porch watching the children play in the park across the street. He reminded her of a little boy himself at those times, much as he had the night he'd licked the batter from the bowl at her kitchen table. A little boy who'd never had a childhood. That was silly, of course. Everyone had a childhood, be it good, bad or unremarkable. But what made her wonder about his youth had something to do with the curiosity in his expression, as if he couldn't quite understand what the kids were doing because playing as they did wasn't anything he'd ever done himself. They would run and shout and tumble and some of the bigger boys, the twelve- and thirteen-year-olds, would set up cones in the street and play hockey on their rollerblades.

The children seemed to fascinate him. It was an arm's-length fascination, though. When actually faced with two and a half feet of outspoken six-year-old, he was decidedly reticent. Whenever Tammy came over, Mitch kept as wary

an eye on her as she did on him. The little girl was intimi-
dated as much by his size as his scowl—which was actually
nothing more than a frown of incomprehension. He had no
idea children were so literal.

Her brother, T.J., on the other hand, regarded Mitch with
something just short of awe. After the inquisitive nine-year-
old learned that Mitch flew planes—something Jamie told
him while doling out cupcakes to the neighborhood kids—
T.J. found every conceivable excuse to hang around. T.J.'s
first passion was baseball, but his second was airplanes and
he had a collection of plastic models that he would have
given his Bart Simpson T-shirt to show Mitch.

The offer was hesitantly made by T.J. late one afternoon
as Mitch sat on the front porch. The little boy, his blond hair
covered by a blue baseball cap with its brim covering his
neck, stood at the end of Jamie's walkway. He'd screwed up
his courage and extended the offer, hoping to sweeten it by
adding, "I've got a MIG and an F-15, too. They're really
neat."

Mitch gave the boy a weak smile. "Maybe some other
time."

Jamie was sure Mitch didn't see the dejection in the
child's eyes as T.J. backed away with a muttered "Sure."
Mitch didn't like to talk about planes and flying. At least he
hadn't in a while, though if he spoke with Red about it she
didn't know. She knew only that he never mentioned it to
her, and his silence made her all the more certain that he was
trying to cope with the possibility that he might not ever be
able to fly again.

From where she stood behind the screen door, Jamie
watched Mitch after T.J. had gone home. Mitch was sitting
on the top step, his right foot planted on the next one down
and his casted leg stretched out and resting on the walk. The
dejection she'd seen in T.J.'s eyes was no greater than that
revealed in the slope of Mitch's broad shoulders.

The screen door groaned as Jamie stepped out onto the gray, painted boards of the porch. A moment later she sat down beside him on the step. It had been several days since he'd had any kind of project to tackle and time was beginning to weigh a little too heavily. "I think you hurt his feelings."

Mitch continued staring at a caterpillar inching its way up the bottom step. The poor little critter had a long way to go to reach the top. "I didn't mean to."

"He thinks you're pretty special, you know."

Mitch turned toward her, uncomprehending. He'd only seen the kid twice. Both times, the boy had just stood and stared. "He does? Why?"

"Because of who you are."

"A washed-up pilot?"

So that *was* the problem.

Reaching down with a twig, she gave the caterpillar a boost. "I think that conclusion is a little premature," she said without censure. He was entitled to how he felt. "I was thinking more of a man who's done things kids only dream about. You might not think what you've done is all that extraordinary, but I know a little boy who'd love to hear about what it was like to fly in the Antarctic or climb a mountain in Nepal. Actually, I know several of them. An entire Cub-Scout troop, in fact."

He had a very uncomfortable feeling about the way she was watching him. The woman was about as subtle as a tank. "You may be able to do that stuff," he said flatly, thinking of the safety program she'd done with the sheriff last week, "but I don't know the first thing about kids. I wouldn't know how to talk to them. Hell," he muttered, thinking about the kid next door. Had he ever been that young? That innocent? "I don't even know how to apologize to T.J."

"Maybe words wouldn't be necessary. You might try pitching grounders to him. The Wildcats have a game coming up Saturday and I know he could use the practice."

A softball, one of many she tended to find in her front yard, lay in the bush beside the porch. With a smile, she held it out to him.

There was no answering smile in his eyes. He looked from the ball to her and back again. When he raised his eyes a second time, she saw the hesitation there. Reluctantly he reached for the ball, then sat staring at it, running his thumb over the seam. "I'm not much of a pitcher."

"It'll come back to you."

For a moment he said nothing. His expression as closed as she'd ever seen it, he gave a derisive snort. "It probably would . . . if I'd ever done it. I never played baseball." He'd never played football, or basketball, either, though the exclusive private school he'd been sent to had been known for the soundness of its athletic programs. It had been an excellent academic facility, too, which is why he'd been sent there. But he'd felt like a freak when he'd had to spend his P.E. time in the library. "My parents were what you might call overly protective," he said in a tone so casual he might have been discussing the weather. "I wasn't allowed to participate in anything where I might get hurt."

Her quiet "Why?" carried genuine interest and as so many times before, he found himself needing the solace she offered. So he told her as succinctly as he could about how his parents had wanted a child so badly that by the time he came along they had treated him as if he were made of glass. He was spoiled and pampered and given every possession imaginable.

They'd also treated him as if he didn't possess a brain.

They'd completely dominated his life. His activities, his friends, anything that influenced him had to meet with their approval. They even chose a university and major for him.

But that was where their control was lost. Their obsessive protectiveness led to his rebellion when he entered college, which was why he dropped out and joined his friend on the Colorado that year so long ago. But what Mitch didn't tell Jamie was that he'd had little contact with them for years afterward. She already knew they were both dead and he saw no point in mentioning what had happened the last time he'd seen them. Especially the last time he'd seen his father. He could still too easily remember the bitter recriminations—and recall the hollow feeling in his heart when he'd learned of his death six months later.

He told her only that there was a lot he hadn't gotten to do as a kid. And just by looking at her, he knew she'd already figured out that he liked to fly planes and climb mountains because of what had once been forbidden him.

He knew himself that well—that, in the beginning, rebellion and the need for independence had made him set out to prove he could do anything he put his mind to. What he didn't understand was what continued to drive him now.

One big drawback to being laid up was the amount of time he had available to think. He'd done everything short of counting the leaves on the trees across the street to avoid considering the course of events that had led him to this point in his life. Yet here he was again, doing exactly that. God knew he'd give just about anything to keep his mind occupied with something—anything—else.

Jamie, in that quiet, accepting way of hers, seemed to know that, too.

She laid her hand over his forearm, her touch soft, reassuring.

"Maybe it's time you learned to play, then," she said. "I'll go get T.J. Okay?"

He could have said no. After all, she did give him time to respond before she interrupted his silence with a decisive "Good," and gave his arm a pat. A moment later she'd left to tell T.J. to bring his bat and mitt. The boy must have been sitting on his front porch. Mitch heard her tell him that Mr. Kincaid was going to meet him across the street to pitch grounders.

Even as Mitch watched her sweet little backside as she retreated into the house a minute later, he wanted to wring her neck. The last thing he wanted to do was hobble across the street and throw balls to a kid he didn't know. Seeing T.J.'s eager, expectant face when he appeared on the lawn, he also knew it was exactly what he needed to do just then.

As it turned out, Mitch was a pretty good pitcher. Good enough for T.J. and the other boys who ultimately joined them, anyway. The nine-year-old members of the Winston Wildcats weren't all that demanding. Anyone willing to be patient with them would do, as he discovered a few afternoons later when Billy Marston—T.J.'s buddy from three blocks over and the team's second baseman—showed up with his father.

Billy's dad, the manager of the grocery store that sponsored the team, was the team's coach. Though he didn't come right out and say so, he'd come to check out the stranger hanging around the park with his boys. His son had told him that the man lived with Jamie Withers, the lady who lived next door to T.J. and gave all the kids cookies. Sam Marston already knew of Jamie through his son's den mother. She helped out on the Scouts' hikes once in awhile and he remembered her as the nurse on duty at emergency when Billy had tried playing Superman by jumping off the roof into their Dough-Boy pool and broken his arm. *She* seemed nice enough, and though his wife questioned the principles of a woman who would live with a man without benefit of matrimony, he normally wouldn't have thought it anyone's business if she took up with some guy no one knew anything about. He tended to leave moralizing to his wife, their preacher and the ladies frequenting his produce section. He did, however, care about what influenced his son and the boys on his team.

As soon as he found out that Mitch was only renting a room from Jamie while he waited for his leg to heal and his doctor to release him so he could go to work for Red Malloy, he mentally dismissed his wife's concerns. His own were set aside, too, when he noticed how sympathetic the man was to a couple of the smaller boys who'd never played before. The guy wouldn't put undue pressure on the kids as some of the parents did, and Sam gamely mentioned that he could sure use an assistant coach. Would Mitch be interested in signing on?

It didn't matter to him that Mitch was on crutches, or that he knew nothing about Little League. He was breathing and that was qualification enough. Feeling oddly pleased with the offer, Mitch said he'd think about it, even though he knew he had to turn it down.

"Why?" Jamie asked when Mitch mentioned Sam Marston's request that evening. "I think it's a great idea. Half the kids on that team don't have any male figure in their lives. You'd be good for them."

Mitch watched her over the skillet he was drying. She was good for him, too. No one had ever said anything like that to him before.

He wasn't about to let the compliment go to his head, though.

"I told you before that I don't know anything about baseball." Male pride hadn't allowed him to admit as much to Marston. Odd that he hadn't thought twice about mentioning it to Jamie. "How could I possibly help coach? I don't know the rules or the signals or how to help a kid untangle his feet to run bases. And I sure as hell can't get out there and show them how to hit a ball."

Jamie was washing dishes. He was drying them. The skillet he'd just run the towel over hit the counter a little harder than he'd intended.

As calm as he was agitated, Jamie rinsed a lid and set it in the drainer. "You could do just what you've been doing. Helping them with their batting by getting the ball over the plate. Encouraging them. Being there for them." Water gurgled in the sink as she pulled the plug and gave her hands a shake to rid them of suds. Her eyes held a hint of challenge, along with a smile. "What else have you got to do?"

He had no answer for that and she knew it. She also seemed aware that there was more bothering him than a lack of knowledge of the game.

"Nobody will expect a guy in a brace to be shagging balls, Mitch. And you can't be expected to know signals because each team makes up their own." Taking the towel from him, she dried her hands and handed the towel back. Her voice was quiet, her eyes knowing. "That's not what's really bothering you, though, is it?"

It was impossible for Jamie to believe that a man who would risk his neck in a free-fall would be afraid to take on this minor challenge. His lack of knowledge about a game wasn't holding him back. It had to be something else. From the stubborn set of his jaw, she had the feeling that whatever it was made him feel vaguely threatened. Mitch wasn't a man who threatened easily, either.

"There's nothing bothering me," he muttered, and turned away when he realized they both knew he was lying. Something *was* bugging him, but it was easier to deny its existence than face up to it. Besides, how much sense did it make to feel uneasy simply because he'd really begun to like it here?

Chapter Ten

In the past fifteen years, Mitch couldn't recall a single place where he'd stayed more than eighteen months. The most time he'd spent anywhere had been in Saudi Arabia, and there only because he'd gone back twice, since the money was so good. He also couldn't recall having been grounded for as long as he had been now. Before meeting up with that boulder, the longest he'd been out of commission was two weeks. He'd pulled a hamstring skiing and spent his recovery time losing his salary playing pool. At least he hadn't been bored. The only other time he'd been down, he'd sprained his wrist badly enough that the oil company's flight doctor had pulled him off the schedule for a week. He'd jumped a cargo flight to Bangkok and killed six days there getting into more trouble than he cared to remember.

There wasn't much trouble to get into living under Jamie's roof, but at least time didn't drag as much as it had in the beginning. Within six weeks of his leaving the hospital,

Mitch noticed that his physical stamina had improved remarkably and he no longer slept away the afternoons as he had at first. Having those extra hours alone each day might have done him in, had it not been for Jamie.

Mitch had never been one to spend much thought on consequences or outcomes. Not when it came to himself. All his adult life, he'd done pretty much what he wanted to do, figuring that whatever happened simply happened and there was no sense wasting energy on "what if." He'd been a fly-by-the-seat-of-his-pants kind of guy. He enjoyed the adventure of it, the excitement of not knowing exactly what to expect—or where he would end up next. He followed the wind not because it sounded romantic, but because the movement allowed a constant source of distractions. And maybe, mostly, because he didn't have anywhere in particular to go.

He'd thought about that a lot lately. And the more he thought, the more grateful he felt to Jamie for the sanctuary she'd offered him. She'd never know how grateful he was for the reprieve. If it hadn't been for her, he'd be over at the Hi Desert Motel working crossword puzzles, staring at a television set and quietly going out of his mind. Because of her, he had things to do, to look forward to. Granted, what he now did to keep himself occupied would never have occurred to him in the past, much less held any interest. But he had to admit he was finding pleasure in the activities.

It had been over three months since his accident. The full leg brace had been replaced with a lighter one to stabilize his knee, and his physical therapy had finally started. No longer leaning on crutches, sometimes using a cane, Mitch now spent the mornings in Jamie's garage nailing together portable booths for the Fourth-of-July celebrations coming up in a couple of weeks. She'd roped him into the chore the evening she'd come home from a meeting disgusted with somebody named Elbert Auerback for changing his mind about building them. She'd said she'd do it herself if she had a power saw and Mitch believed she'd actually try, even though she admitted to not knowing a thing about power tools or carpentry. She was willing to take on just about anything and everyone seemed to know it. So instead of letting her risk a limb on a saw or having her put together a structure resembling the Leaning Tower of Pisa, Mitch said he'd ask Red if he could run the boards through the saw at his shop and he'd put them together himself.

He couldn't help but wonder when she smiled at him, her eyes as warm as sunshine, if that wasn't what she'd had in mind all along. When she smiled that way, he'd find himself agreeing to the darnedest things. He'd actually helped her plant her tomato starts, though most of his attention had been on her legs as she'd sat in the dirt patting the delicate stems in place. And he'd caved in on the coaching issue because she'd made him realize it was something he really wanted to do. To his surprise, he really cared about that bunch of uncoordinated little kids.

What he wouldn't let himself consider was how he really felt about Jamie. He knew he cared about her. But he didn't let himself examine the quality of that feeling too closely. He simply went from one day to the next, doing what he could to keep from thinking about what he *couldn't* do, and accepted the circumstances for what they were. Temporary.

The temporary nature of their relationship was something Jamie wasn't likely to forget. She was reminded of it every time she saw Mitch watch a jet streak across the bright desert sky. His frustration was almost tangible to her at those times, his desire to be behind the controls of a plane or a helicopter so strong that she couldn't help but feel it herself. September, when he'd said he would be leaving, would suddenly seem that much closer. And whenever she thought of Mitch leaving, she would begin to crave the peace she found up on her ledge. She hadn't been to the mesa in a long time, even though she needed that peace as much as ever. Jamie had finally managed to explain that contradiction to herself by deciding she must be a masochist. Why else would she want so badly to be around someone who was going to leave nothing but an empty space in her life once he'd gone?

She thought it best not to answer that as she pulled into her driveway late one sultry afternoon. Thinking about Mitch wasn't helping her frame of mind. It had been one of those days that Martha would describe as living hell, and Jamie was trying very hard to occupy her mind with more calming thought. Coming home to the periwinkles that had replaced the geraniums because of the heat and the neat lawn with its patches of crabgrass was exactly what she needed. Or it would have been had Mitch's presence not affected its tranquillity. Instead of feeling relieved of the day's burdens when she arrived home, she now met an unsettling mixture of anticipation and anxiety.

It was very hard to deny that she was falling in love with him.

Lately, Mitch had been working in the garage when Jamie arrived home from work. He wasn't there today, though. The overhead door was closed and it would be up if he was inside, to catch what little breeze there was. Heading around the house, stopping by the garden to check her tomatoes and cantaloupes, she wondered if the gathering heat had driven him indoors. The temperature hovered somewhere around a toasty ninety-four degrees. Great for growing melons, but a bit on the draining side for most humans. It was only late June. It could easily get hotter.

Thinking about the weather helped. Until she found Mitch. He was in the kitchen. Nothing so extraordinary about that, except that he was wearing nothing more than a towel and a frown. The frown she barely noticed. What immediately caught her attention was the heavy blue terry cloth hanging low on his hips. It was wrapped snugly enough to mold his tight buttocks, but not so tightly that she didn't worry about it slipping off when he turned at the sound of her coming through the back door.

Jamie's step slowed considerably. Mitch stood beside the row of drawers near the sink, dripping water on the floor and creating little puddles under his bare feet. Without so much as a blink, his glance made a cursory sweep over the blue chambray shirt and white shorts she wore, then darted to the clock on the stove. He seemed surprised at the time.

"I thought I'd be ready before you got home." He turned back to the drawer, frowning as he pushed the items in it around.

"Ready? For what?"

"I finished sanding the booths," he said, which explained why he'd showered so late in the afternoon. He'd been sanding yesterday, too, and gotten sawdust everywhere. "They're ready to be painted, so I thought I'd go to the hardware store and pick up some brushes and stuff." His frown deepened. "Where are the scissors?"

She didn't mean to stare; tried not to, in fact. But there was something quite compelling about the water droplets running down the groove of his spine to be absorbed by that dangerously low-slung towel. His shoulders glistened with beads of moisture, the muscles in his broad back rippling with his movements.

"They're in the sewing basket." Setting her tote on the table, she let her glance sweep downward. He wasn't wearing the knee brace at the moment and she noticed how careful he was to keep his weight on his right leg. On his left, she could clearly see the long, cherry pink scars crisscrossing his knee and the side of his thigh. They looked angry and painful, though not nearly so painful as they once had. "What are you going to do with them?"

"Actually, now that you're here, you could do it." With a flick of his wrist he shut the drawer. Two steps—one with a slight limp—and he sat on the corner of the bleached oak trestle table, sort of straddling it but leaving his feet touching the floor. To be sure he wouldn't knock it over, he pushed the bowl of carnations toward the other end. "I need a haircut."

"You were going to do that yourself?"

"It's not that difficult. Just cut it straight across here." He motioned to the lower back of his neck. "It'll be easier for you to get it straight than for me."

She could suggest that he go to a barber. They did have one in Winston, along with a unisex salon that would be happy to give him a trim. But the thought of being that close to him, of having an excuse to touch him, made her overlook that bit of practical common sense.

The sewing kit was by the sofa. Retrieving the scissors from it, she returned to stand a couple of feet in front of him. He still straddled the corner of the table and, in that position, she was eye level with him. "I don't think I can do it with you sitting there."

"Fine," he returned agreeably enough. "Where do you want me?"

She glanced around the room. A chair would be too low and she didn't have a bar stool. There was a short stepladder in the garage that would be about perfect, but it would take longer to get it and bring it back than it would to cut the curls away. She assumed the curling was what he didn't like.

She looked at him again. He had his wet hair combed straight back from his face, slicked tight to his head so that one clean cut across the back of his neck was all that was necessary to rid it of the length he didn't want.

The thought was dangerous, disturbing—and one she'd had many times before. But today, still trying to put the events at work behind her, it was awfully difficult to let the memory go. As she stood there while he waited for her to respond, she remembered the nights she'd sat next to his bed stroking his hair from his forehead, hoping to comfort him. He hadn't even been aware she was there. What she wouldn't give to have someone soothe her that way right now. Just hold her...

She cleared her throat and stepped back. "Maybe if you stood up."

For a moment she thought he might be hesitating because he didn't want to stand. He just sat there looking at her, his face devoid of expression and his eyes searching hers. She had no idea what he saw as half a dozen seconds passed. She knew only that she felt oddly relieved when he finally planted his palms at his sides, pushed himself up and turned around.

Moving closer, eyeing the dark hair curling against his skin, she drew a deep breath. That breath brought with it the clean scent of his soap and something that was unmistakably Mitchell.

Mitchell.

She hadn't thought of him as Mitchell since shortly after he'd asked her not to call him that.

To her dismay, her hand was shaking when she raised the scissors.

"About an inch?" she asked.

"Yeah. That ought to do."

It didn't take but a minute—after she'd remembered to pull over the trash basket and get a towel to lay over his shoulders—to clip through the dark hair at his nape and even it up. When she pronounced it done, she stepped around in front of him and, scissors still in hand, critically eyed her work from that angle.

"Looks even to me," she told him and started to take the towel off his shoulders so he wouldn't get hair all over the floor.

He caught her wrist. "What about right here?"

He turned his head a little, indicating a spot behind his ear.

She lowered her arm, wondering if he was even aware of how slow he was to let go of her, and tried to concentrate on whatever it was he wanted her to check. "It looks okay to me."

"You sure? I don't want it curling up."

The dark strands of his hair were beginning to dry, so they weren't lying quite as flat as before. To be certain they wouldn't be tempted to curl, she smoothed his nape with the pads of her fingers. As she did, the palm of her hand skimmed his neck. At the same moment he turned toward her.

In reality it was all of two seconds. In the surreal time created by her constant awareness of him, it seemed like forever before she realized that she was standing in front of him with her hand curved over the side of his neck—and that he wasn't moving.

Her hand fell and she looked away. "I think it's okay," she told him and made herself smile as she took the towel from his shoulders. Deliberately she ignored the precarious hold of the one slung around his hips. "Now, if you'll get dressed, I'll run you over to the hardware store."

"You don't have to do that. Sam's going to take me after dinner." He paused, his jaw clenching as he watched her ball up the towel. "I don't want to keep imposing on you."

"You're not."

The look he gave her was most indulgent. "You're already dropping me off three mornings a week for my physical therapy, and you've taken me for my appointments at the clinic twice now. You even took me to get new jeans...."

"You needed them. You'd sliced up the legs on both your other pairs to get them over the other brace."

"I'm not saying I didn't need them. I'm saying you don't need to run me around for little things like paint."

"It's not like I'm keeping count, Mitch."

"Well, maybe I am." An edge had unexpectedly crept into his voice. Jamie heard the irritation and shrank from it. She knew he hated feeling as dependent on her as he did at times. He'd never said so. He hadn't had to. "Thanks for the haircut."

Mitch took the scissors from her, thinking to put them away before he went back to his room. His irritation was with himself, not at her. Well, not directly at her, anyway. Usually he was more careful. But living with her, sharing meals and chores, having spent weeks thinking about her all day, and trying not to think about her all night, was all beginning to exact its toll. It had been stupid to ask her to cut his hair, but he knew exactly why he'd done it. He'd wanted her to touch him—and she'd been very careful not to.

"Mitch?"

The sound of his name was as tentative as the look on her face when he looked back at her.

"You're not imposing on me. I like doing things for you."

He should let it go. If he was smart he would. But she did things for everyone; giving much and giving easily. Doing something for him wasn't so extraordinary. "Why?"

So much for smart. The question was out before he'd even realized how important it was that he know. It hung between them, suspended like an invisible, ticking bomb.

"Do I have to have a reason?"

Yes, he wanted to shout. He didn't want to be just like everyone else to her. But as he stood there considering the thought, wondering what it was he did want and not too comfortable with the answers that came to mind, he saw the vulnerability in her expression. He'd caught a glimpse of it earlier, but he hadn't considered why it might be there. He'd been thinking only of how he could lose himself in her eyes, in her.

"Not if you don't want to give me one," he told her, backing down because she didn't look up to dealing with an idiot right now. Maybe he'd sucked up too much sawdust in her garage. Or maybe little Eddie Cuttler had done some damage when the only ball he'd hit all season had whacked Mitch in the head. If he'd been paying attention at all, he'd have noticed something was wrong. "Are you all right?"

She nodded and tried to smile. "I'm fine."

"You don't lie very well."

"I guess I'll have to practice more."

"Bad day?"

She gave a shrug. The motion had about as much enthusiasm as her smile.

That lack of energy convinced Mitch that he'd diagnosed the problem. He also knew she wouldn't want to talk about whatever had happened at the hospital. She seemed to deal with unpleasantness best by working it out in her garden or getting everyone fat on her baking. She would rid herself of the negative by focusing on something positive and eventually her perspective would be restored. It had taken him a while to realize that about her, but once he had, he respected the process. He envied it a little, too.

With a sigh, she pushed back the strands of hair escaping from her thick braid. "I'll get dinner started. You're probably hungry."

He stayed back, watching her turn on the faucet to wash her hands before pulling the refrigerator door open. She closed it without having done anything more than stare at the top shelf.

He dropped the scissors in the drawer. Jamie always took care of everyone else. Who, Mitch wondered, ever took care of her?

"Why don't I get dinner tonight?"

"You?"

"Sure." He tried to look offended, though what he really felt was concern. "I can cook. Well, heat things, anyway. We've got canned stuff. And I can burn steaks as well as you can."

A knowing light entered her eyes. It removed a bit of the sadness, but the strange quiet in her remained. "If you're looking for something to do to keep yourself occupied, you can wash the lettuce for me."

She was only an arm's length away. Looking very soft as she smiled that sad smile. He knew of a better way to keep himself occupied. But it wasn't himself he was thinking of at the moment. "The lettuce can wait." He laid his hand on her shoulder. "Come here."

She felt the pressure of his hand drawing her closer, then felt his arms cross her back as he pulled her to him. His hand covered the back of her head, the gentle strength of it holding her to him. "You looked like you could use this."

The scent of soap and spice clung to his skin. With her cheek pressed to his bare chest, she breathed it in and felt her insides knot.

"I just can't seem to get the day out of my mind." It seemed necessary that she explain so he wouldn't know there were so many other reasons she wanted this. "I'm sorry."

"What happened?" he asked, wanting very much to listen if she was willing to talk. How many times had she listened when he'd felt that there wasn't a soul in the world who cared enough to listen to him?

"Burns," was all she said.

All he could think to say was "Oh, Jamie" before he pressed his lips to the top of her head. He didn't think about what he was doing. He just did it. It felt good to hold her. Right in ways he couldn't have imagined.

She saw so much, gave so much. Yet as easily as she offered comfort, as she had to him and no doubt hundreds of others, she wasn't comfortable receiving it. He'd felt her tense when he'd drawn her nearer and she sounded embarrassed now when she tried to pull back.

"Sorry about this," she mumbled, but he wouldn't let her go.

"Don't be. I''m just returning the favor. You did it for me."

Jamie felt herself go still as his fingers flexed against her back. She'd spent hours at his side. What did he recall of them? "I never held you."

"You held my hand."

From the tone of his voice, she'd thought he would be smiling. Looking up at him, she discovered that he wasn't. His face was devoid of expression, his eyes dark and intent upon hers.

"I didn't know you remembered."

"I remember a lot of things. Impressions mostly. But I knew you were there."

He'd never told her that before. The knowledge pleased her, even as it made her feel vulnerable in ways she hadn't until now. She'd shared things with him in his silence that she might not have told him under other circumstances. Silly things, really, and nothing that mattered in the overall scheme of things. Was that why she felt he knew her so well at times?

Dear God, was that why it felt so right to be in his arms?

The moment he'd touched her, warmth had gathered in her stomach. It now seemed to radiate through her, taunting nerves and driving all thought but of him from her mind. She felt too much being this close to him. Sweet, forbidden feelings that had nothing to do with the gratitude he expressed. Her hands lay in fists on his chest. What would he do if she were to spread them over those hard muscles and sink her fingers into the thick swirls of soft dark hair? If she only knew what he was offering.

The same thought crossed Mitch's mind. He really had so little to offer her. Certainly, he could give no promises. But these past months, he'd trusted her with more of himself than he had any woman—and he'd never even kissed her.

Don't do it, Mitch warned himself. Let her go.

That was exactly what he should do. He really had been thinking only of what she might need when he'd reached for her, and he wanted to feel good about the small selfless act. Feeling good about himself had been a rather infrequent occurrence in his life. If he were to take advantage of the situation he'd created, he wouldn't feel right at all.

But how she felt in his arms. And how she looked as he scanned her upturned face. Before the surge of nobility ebbed completely, he gave her the chance to pull away.

A strand of hair clung to her cheek, golden like the lights in her hazel eyes. He pushed it aside with his finger, his body tensing as the feel of her soft cheek hinted at the softness beneath her clothes. His body hardened further when he heard her faint intake of breath, and he drew his touch to her jaw. When she didn't move, he slipped his hand behind her neck.

"I think I'm going to regret this," he said and eased her forward.

His lips brushed hers. Again. Once more. The friction was unbearably light, but it created the quick, lightning heat of a match set to dry tinder.

A shiver raced through her at the contact. The touch of his lips was so gentle it nearly brought tears to her eyes. But the sweetness of it was forgotten in the next few moments. Curving her arms around his neck, Jamie let him pull her fully against him. His mouth settled warm and full over hers.

Swallowing a moan, she leaned into him, allowing the access he sought. It didn't occur to her to question the wisdom of what she was doing. She knew only that she'd wanted this for a very long time. He'd awakened yearnings within her the moment he'd stepped into her life. Vague, indefinable needs that she hadn't wanted to consider because there was so little hope of fulfilling them. Now, in his arms, she felt those yearnings break free.

"Jamie," he whispered, drugging her with the feel of his harder, coarser body against her softer one. Letting his hands slide down the curve of her spine, he urged her closer. With her hips nestled to him, he pushed forward, taking her deeper with his kiss and turning her blood to steam.

His hand pushed under her shirt.

She stilled, startled by the intrusion, but he let his hand fall before she could tell him it was all right, that she wanted his touch, that she needed it as much as she did the very air she breathed.

But it was too late. Already the pressure of his mouth on hers had gentled. A few moments later he pushed her head to his chest, holding her there as if he needed to keep her safe. From him. From herself. Beneath her ear, she heard the beat of his heart racing like an over-revved engine.

Her own was no steadier.

"I shouldn't have done that." He felt his chest rise with his deeply drawn breath. "I really shouldn't have done that."

She lifted her head, warned by the conviction in his tone.

The hunger she'd felt in his kiss remained in his eyes. But there was something else there, too. A certain distance, and definitely displeasure.

Confused by the change in him, she eased out of his arms.

He started to reach for her when she stepped back. Then thought better of it. If he kissed her again, it would be that much harder to let her go. "I think I'd better go get dressed."

His towel had loosened considerably. Casually securing the end at his waist, he turned away. His leg wasn't the only thing throbbing as he headed into his room.

Sinking against the counter, Jamie watched his door close behind him. His words had left her as shaken as his kiss, but even as unsteady as she felt, she was sure she knew what he meant. He wanted her, and the admission made her heart leap. But he didn't want to want her. He'd even said he'd probably regret kissing her before he'd done it—and she, having heard the warning, had simply melted in his arms.

She'd known all along that she cared more for him than she should. Unfortunately, now that she knew what it felt like to be held by him, the ache he caused inside her was that much worse.

She really didn't need this.

Taking her gardening gloves from the shelf in the laundry room, she decided to go pull weeds. They didn't usually eat dinner for another hour, anyway.

Mitch came looking for her five minutes later. She was crouched on the ground between two head-high rows of corn, pulling the few bits of grass that had escaped her attention last weekend. She could see that he'd pulled on a pair of cutoffs and put on his knee brace. Other than tennis shoes, he hadn't bothered with anything else. No socks. No shirt. She glimpsed all that from the corner of her eye, not looking up.

"What do you want me to do?" he prefaced.

Carefully, she picked a ladybug from a long leaf and let it fly. "Do?"

"For dinner. I said I'd cook."

"You don't have to do that."

"I want to. You said something about lettuce. You just want a salad, or what?"

Salad. He'd pulled the emotional rug out from under her just minutes ago and he wanted to talk about a salad. "I can do it."

"So can I. Jamie," he said flatly, "would you please look at me?"

Defiance was something new to her, but that's what she felt when she set her jaw and bent her head back. He had his hands on his hips and out here, in the sunlight, the fading bruises on his shoulder and chest looked a little green.

He didn't seem satisfied. "How about standing up? I can't squat down there."

Without a word she brushed the dirt from her hands and stood. "Better?"

He'd blown it. There was no doubt in Mitch's mind that what he'd done in the kitchen had a direct correlation to the temperature level out here. It might have been ninety-plus degrees but there was a definite chill in the air.

"It would be if you'd stop acting like this. Would it help if I apologize?"

"You have nothing to apologize for. Just forget it, okay?"

"I just don't want you angry with me."

"I'm not angry."

He tipped her chin up with his finger. He'd seen something in her eyes a moment ago. A flicker of hurt. He knew he'd put it there.

"Yes, you are. Or at least you are with yourself. Don't be," he whispered and brushed his lips over hers. "You're the best thing that's happened to me in a long time, Jamie. I just don't want to mess anything up."

That was the closest he could come to telling her how he felt—especially since he wasn't so sure what it was he did feel. Whatever it was had gotten all mixed up with gratitude, need and desire and he wasn't sure he trusted the feeling at all. All he knew for certain was it felt like more than just plain lust. Though, at the moment, he'd have to admit that was a hefty percentage of what occupied his thoughts.

They'd have to talk about that. Soon. Now that he knew the taste of her, how she felt in his arms, he wanted her more than he'd thought possible.

In stunned silence Jamie stared up at him, scarcely aware of the creak in the gate when it opened. His hand fell as the gate slammed back into its latch and a moment later she was staring at the back of Mitch's head. His body prevented her from seeing who had just arrived.

She'd expected it to be T.J. or Tammy. Instead, she heard a man's deep, raspy voice.

"Yo, Mitch," Sam Marston called as he followed the stepping stones past the white metal storage shed and on to the garden. "Nobody answered the bell. With all the windows open, I figured somebody was home."

He sauntered over, acknowledging Jamie when she stepped from behind Mitch by pushing his red baseball cap back by the brim.

"Mighty fine garden you got here, Ms. Withers." With an approving nod, he looked down the row of corn, then back to his assistant coach. "I have to run uptown for the wife before supper. Thought maybe you'd like to come with me now, then we won't have to make a second trip. We can pick up the league stats on the way. Paul's dad just finished them up."

Mitch laid his hand flat on his chest, rubbing it absently. It was clear enough to Jamie that he hadn't finished his conversation with her, but he didn't want to turn down the offer. "Sure. Just let me get a shirt. We need anything from the store?" he asked Jamie.

"Nothing that I can think of," she returned, and saw him watch her drop her fingers from where they'd pressed to her mouth.

She wasn't sure, but she thought she caught a hint of a smile in his eyes. "I'll stop at the Colonel and pick up chicken for dinner."

Mitch was nothing if not determined. She'd known that about him from the moment she'd met him. Knowing some things just weren't worth arguing about, she mumbled, "Fine."

"You don't mind, do you, Sam?"

Sam didn't. They'd be driving right past the place, anyway. All they'd have to do was swing into the drive-through.

With that agreed, Sam did the semilift with his hat again to say goodbye and Mitch gave her a look that held as much uncertainty as it did promise. A moment later they were walking away. Sam, the salt-of-the-earth type whose love of good cooking and an occasional beer had put a bit of a belly on him, and Mitch, tall, solid as a rock and limping because he wasn't using his cane. She could hear them talking about getting stencils for the lettering on the booths. Sam was going to help Mitch with the painting and Red was going to come by with his pickup truck to haul them to the fairgrounds Wednesday morning. The conversation faded when they reached the door.

Mitch held out the screen for Sam to go in ahead of him and turned back to Jamie.

"We'll take the chicken and go over to the park, okay?"

Standing there between the rows of corn, she gave him a nod and watched him disappear with the creak and slam of the door. She felt a little bewildered and terribly confused. But what she felt mostly was a faint hope that refused to be locked away in the little box where she'd stored so many other hopes and dreams.

Until now, she hadn't really realized the kind of friendship Mitch had begun to establish with Sam. It was easy to see that they were pretty comfortable with each other. Mitch got along well with Red, too, and the older man had taken to stopping by after he'd dropped his wife off at the nursing home on Sunday afternoons. He obviously liked Mitch's company, and all the kids in the neighborhood thought Mitch was "an awesome dude."

Whether he knew it or not, he was becoming part of the community. And the more a part of it he'd become, the more settled he seemed to be.

Was it possible, she dared wonder, that he might be thinking about staying?

She didn't have the courage to ask him herself. But that faint hope received a major boost the night of the Fourth of July.

Chapter Eleven

The Fourth of July was Winston's day to celebrate. Not only was it a national holiday, but its founder, Jedediah Winston, had staked claim for the settlement on that day in 1888. The town worked hard to make it the high point of the year and it seemed every citizen in the county turned out onto its streets.

The day began with a pancake breakfast at the VFW hall. Then the parade started from the high school football field, winding under the red-white-and-blue banners draped over Paiute Boulevard to the fairgrounds. There the school band dispersed to man the 4-H and Honors-Club booths. It seemed every organization, club and society had a booth, including the local church auxiliaries. The Presbyterian women had handcrafts and the Lutherans sold pie by the slice. The Knights of Columbus served spicy German sausages and sponsored a beer garden, which the teenagers devised ingenious plots to infiltrate. A local day-care center had their staff painting clown faces on children for free. The town coffers even popped to bring in a carnival, and local talent was featured hourly in the park across from the town hall.

Because traffic had been rerouted, Jamie had to take a circuitous drive to the fairgrounds that afternoon. She'd worked her regular seven-to-three-thirty shift, so she'd missed the parade. But the festivities had even come to emergency in the form of burns from a firecracker, a nasty cut from a broken bottle and a splintered collarbone when someone tripped over a wire running from the Ringtoss tent. As she followed the signals of the parking attendants guiding traffic through the dust in the dirt parking lot, she could only imagine what the evening and night shifts would see.

Thoughts of work fled as the sounds from the fairgrounds filled the air. Mitch was already there, working the Little-League dunk tank, and he'd asked her to stop by before she took her shift serving up ice cream with the Cub Scouts. She'd promised the den mother she'd take over for a couple of hours. Now she wished she hadn't. She'd have much rather spent that time watching Mitch. It was hard to believe that Sam had actually talked him into sitting in the tank himself.

Jamie knew she was smiling as she made her way past the ticket stand and stepped into the rainbow colors of the carnival. But the thought of seeing Mitch also brought the reminder of what would happen when she did, and the smile faded. There had been no repeat of the incident in the kitchen, but Jamie knew from the way Mitch watched her that he, too, clearly remembered the impact of the kisses they'd shared. Now they wove cautious circles around each other, neither willing to make the first move and neither willing to forget what they'd felt in each other's arms.

Above the music of the calliope Jamie heard a woman shout her name. A hand poked out of the crowd. With so many people swarming about, it was difficult to tell who the waving arm belonged to until Barb stepped out of the throng, pulling Tammy behind her. The little girl, her pigtails tied with red ribbons to match her playsuit, was thoroughly occupied with a huge cone of sticky pink cotton candy.

Her mom looked disgusted. "Have you seen T.J., Jamie? I've been looking all over for him."

"I just got here. Is he lost?"

"Probably more like hiding. I'm sure he's around somewhere. Tammy's getting tired and I wanted to take her home. Mind helping me find him?"

"Of course not," she said automatically. "I need to be at the Cub-Scout booth in ten minutes, though. And I'd like to run by and see Mitch." She wanted to tell him what time she got off in case Sam couldn't give him a ride. "Maybe if we split up..."

Barb snapped her fingers. "That's where he is!"

Without any explanation the woman turned, daughter in tow, and headed into the crowd. As suddenly as she'd started, she stopped, glanced over her shoulder and frowned. "Aren't you coming?" she asked, then charged forward again.

She went straight to the dunk tank.

Sure enough, there was T.J., along with most of the rest of the Wildcats and a bunch of other kids Jamie didn't recognize. She wasn't paying much attention to the cheering boys, though. Her attention was riveted on the man behind the netting. Mitch, wearing soggy cutoffs and a very wet shirt, sat with his legs dangling over the edge of a platform set across the top of a Plexiglas tank. Someone had gotten lucky. He was absolutely drenched.

Crossing her arms over the stripes on her navy-and-white T-shirt, Jamie quashed her smile and tried not to laugh. Mitch was trading good-natured taunts with the boy doing an exaggerated windup just before throwing the ball toward the bull's-eye. The ball missed, hitting the plywood frame around the tank with a solid thud. Unhappy that his coach was still upright, the freckle-faced pitcher slammed his hat to the ground.

"Try it again, Darrel," she heard Mitch call. "Keep your focus on the bull's-eye and sink me. It's getting awful hot up here."

Mitch was a natural with the kids. Patient. Easygoing. Firm when he needed to be. Jamie had noticed his ability with them before, when she'd seen him in the park across from her house during practice. This was the first time, though, she'd seen him in action this close. It did her heart good to see him so clearly enjoying himself.

It did something else to her heart when he noticed her standing there.

The grin slowly left his face, his expression softening as his glance strayed from the top of her shiny braid to the sandals on her feet.

He hadn't touched her since that last brief kiss in her garden. But standing there, in the middle of hundreds of milling people, his visual caress seemed almost a physical thing.

A moment later the grin replaced itself and he raised his hand toward her.

"So that's how it is," came the voice at her elbow.

She'd all but forgotten Barb. "How what is?" she asked, though she knew perfectly well what her too-observant friend was talking about. "There's T.J. right over there. Up front, by the tank."

"I see him." Barb's voice was droll, her expression clearly inquisitive. "You can't fool me, Jamie. I saw that look. And you're blushing."

Her cheeks did feel rather warm. "It's just the heat. It must be close to a hundred out here."

"What look, Mommy?" Tammy whined through a mouthful of cotton candy.

"Never mind," both women replied in unison.

Barb glanced back to Jamie, her tone subdued as she spoke out of the side of her mouth. "We'll talk later. Here he comes."

Because Tammy was likely to repeat anything she heard, Jamie refrained from insisting there was nothing to talk about, and watched Mitch extract himself from the tank. He had to bend his knee sharply to reach the ladder and Jamie winced when she saw him do it. The motion didn't seem to bother him, though, and not for the first time she had to marvel at the man's recuperative powers. He was easily a month ahead of where anyone else who'd sustained such injuries would be. But then, Mitch was motivated, she had to remind herself. He had a personal deadline to meet. Despite the fact that he was fitting in so well here, he hadn't said a word about canceling the job he had to leave for in September.

His replacement in the tank, one of the fathers from the team, handed Mitch a towel. Mitch was rubbing his hair with it when he stopped in front of Jamie and her neighbor.

"I didn't know if you'd be coming by or not," he said to Jamie after giving Barb a nod. "You're scheduled from four o'clock to six, right?"

She told him she was. "I'm due there in a couple of minutes."

"I'll see you at six, then." With studied nonchalance, he draped the towel around his neck. "With all the food they're serving, I thought we could grab dinner here then stick around for the fireworks. Unless you've got something else going," he added, because that was always a possibility.

It hadn't occurred to her that he'd meant them to stay. Together. The idea held enormous appeal.

"No. I mean, I don't." She really wished Barb would stop watching her with that stupid smile on her face. "I'll see you at six. At the ice-cream booth."

"Can I have ice cream, Mom?"

Tammy, having long ago mastered the pleading look, turned her big brown eyes up to her mother.

"I'm not going to be up all night with a sick child. No. You may not. After we get your brother, we're going home. We'll come back tonight for the fireworks." She braced her shoulders, searching the pack of boys ahead of them for her son. "He's not going to be happy about this."

"Uh, Barb?" Since she was now looking in the other direction, Mitch tapped her on the shoulder. "I sort of promised T.J. and the rest of the kids on the team that I'd take them on the rides. Unless you really want him home, I'll keep an eye on him here."

Barb appeared as surprised as Jamie by the offer. "That'd be great. He'll just be driving me nuts at home wanting to come back, anyway. You sure you want to do this?"

"I'm sure."

"Brave man," Barb mumbled, and it was agreed then that she would meet Mitch at the booth where Jamie would be working around six to retrieve her son. Looking pleased with the reprieve, though Tammy didn't look too happy about having to go home and take a bath and a nap, Barb disappeared into the flow of other mothers and fathers towing their offspring.

"I didn't know you'd want to stay," Jamie said when she realized Mitch wasn't moving.

His eyes, dark and intent, caught hers and held. "You don't?"

"Yes. I do. Very much."

A smile entered his eyes, reminding her of how carefree he'd looked laughing with the children a few minutes ago.

"Good." Pushing his fingers through his hair, he glanced down at one of the little boys who'd just come up to him. Mitch was a big man. To the youngster he must look like a mountain. "I've got some dry clothes around here somewhere," he said to Jamie. "I'm going to change, then take my boys on a few rides. I'll see you later. Okay?"

His boys. The child at his side grinned when he heard that. But Mitch's eyes were still on Jamie. He didn't touch her. He didn't have to for her to feel a decidedly unsophisticated, probably very immature giddiness. Even surrounded by hundreds of people, he had a way of looking at her that made her feel as if she were the only person in the universe. If only he would take her in his arms again.

For the next two hours, as Jamie scooped her way through fifteen gallons of chocolate, vanilla and strawberry ice cream, the proceeds of which went to the new Scout camp, she kept trying to put that giddy feeling into perspective. She was still reminding herself what happens when a person gets her hopes up—and finding the reminder totally ineffective—when six o'clock rolled around.

The mental mechanics were abandoned along with her ice-cream scoop when her replacement arrived. But it wasn't Mitch waiting for her by the giant ice-cream cone painted on the side of the booth. It was Agatha from the hospital auxiliary hustling toward her.

"Oh, thank heavens, Jamie. I thought that was you over here." With a movement so deft she probably didn't even realize she'd done it, Agatha shoved the ever-errant strand of gray hair back into her bun. "And I'm so glad it is. I've a problem, dear, and I just know you can help me out. My volunteer for the six-to-nine shift isn't coming and I need someone over at the cake walk in just the worst way. Are you finished here?"

"Well, yes. But—"

"Oh, dear. You're working someplace else."

"No. I—"

"Oh, good," the woman cut in, obviously relieved and perfectly oblivious to the fact that Jamie might have plans that didn't include working for something or someone. Everyone who knew Jamie knew she was always willing to help. It was that assumption that already had Agatha turning around as if she expected Jamie to follow.

Agatha didn't get very far, though. The older woman, skinny as a spindle, was blocked completely by Mitch's powerful frame.

"Excuse me, young man. We're in a hurry."

Mitch's glance rested on Jamie. He'd come up behind the older woman within seconds of her arrival and had just been waiting for her to finish her conversation. "You're going somewhere?"

Jamie opened her mouth, but it was Agatha's strident voice he heard. "She's working the cake walk. If you want ice cream, that little girl in there can help you."

"I don't want ice cream." Blue eyes met hazel as he spoke. "I want Jamie."

Had the imperious little gray-haired woman bothered to pause for two seconds, she might have gotten a clue as to what was going on. Instead, dense as cement and just as unyielding, she planted her hands on her hips.

"Well, you can't have her. Jamie always helps us out when we need her." The idea that she wouldn't seemed unconscionable. "And we need her now."

"Maybe I could help out around eight," Jamie offered. "If you could find someone until then . . ."

"Jamie," Mitch muttered.

The woman's eyes narrowed on the man towering over them. "Wait a minute. I know you. You were a patient at Winston Community. I remember you from the bookmobile cart."

Mitch remembered her, too. And not fondly. The old battle-ax had kept trying to push poetry off on him.

Agatha, being Agatha, pressed on. "Certainly having been a patient at our hospital, you know what the auxiliary provides. We can't provide those services without our fundraisers. And we can't do our fund-raisers without volunteers now, can we, Jamie?"

Jamie was not allowed to respond. "Well, she's not volunteering for this." Mitch's tone was as smooth as butter, but his eyes held pure steel. "She's already put in a full day at work, then helped out here for a couple of hours. And she was up most of last night baking some of the cakes you're raffling off over there. It looks to me like you're just going to have to find someone else."

With that, he took Jamie by the elbow and, leaving Agatha blinking in disbelief, steered her out of sight.

Jamie couldn't believe what Mitch had done. Not that she wasn't grateful. Agatha was such a steamroller that she was nearly impossible to say no to. But it wasn't Mitch's decisiveness she found so revealing. It was his expression. He looked very possessive—and just a little irritated. Had it not been for what she'd just remembered, she might have asked why that irritation was there.

"Wait!" Twisting around, Jamie looked back over her shoulder. "Where's T.J.? Isn't he supposed to be with you?"

With a swiftness that was all too familiar, his manner turned casual, almost easygoing. No one else would have noticed the slight distance in it. Jamie always did, because it was what he used to keep people from getting too close.

Not even the friends he was making seemed to notice that he held so much of himself back.

She felt that protective distance now as he pushed his hands into his pockets and started walking.

"I already passed him off. Barb saw us at the bumper cars and was waiting when the ride was over."

"Us? You were riding the bumper cars?"

Her glance darted straight to his knee. He'd changed into a pale yellow polo shirt and white cotton Dockers. The outline of the brace was clearly visible under his pants.

"No, Jamie. I was watching the boys ride them. I'm not going to hurt myself," he informed her. "I know how much I can and can't do...which is more than I can say for you. Don't you know how to say no?"

He saw her frown at the question, then muttered, "Never mind" when he decided he had no business feeling as if he were being cheated by all the time she spent doing for others. She owed him nothing. He was the intruder in her life, in her world, and he had no business wanting to change anything about it. He needed to remember that.

He did feel justified in taking her away from the old bat from the hospital auxiliary, though. He'd asked for Jamie's time first. Out among all these people, he could enjoy her company away from the too-intimate confines of the house.

Telling her he was starving so she'd stop trying to figure out what his problem was, he angled to the side of the midway to avoid being plowed over by an oncoming group of teenagers, and changed course for the beer garden. As hot as it was, a cold beer sounded very appealing. Thinking about how terrific Jamie's long legs looked with the white shorts she was wearing, he thought a cold shower held a certain appeal, too.

"Hey, Kincaid. Nice job on the booths."

Acknowledging the compliment, Mitch tossed a quick smile back to a man carrying a little girl on his shoulders. The woman at the man's side waved, too.

"Who's that?" Jamie wondered aloud.

The man was a friend of Sam's. He had lent Mitch the sprayer to do the stenciling, then had stuck around to "supervise." As Mitch told her how he'd appreciated the guy's help, Jamie realized that the circle of Mitch's acquaintances had become even larger than she'd thought.

She'd just casually mentioned that when Martha, her face shaded by a bilious green visor bearing a brand of stomach antacid, spotted them and came over to see how Mitch was doing. Mitch didn't remember her from his trip through emergency, but he'd heard Jamie speak of her often enough to know who she was. Martha was still talking with them when Terese, who'd come with her, brought her two young sons over to say hello.

And so it went. As they made their way through the crowd, they ran into people Jamie knew and who Mitch knew but Jamie didn't, even joining Red and his wife for a supper of sausage and beer. And as the sun went down and the midway lights came up, Jamie tried to avoid any thought beyond the evening. Mitch seemed relaxed—more so, possibly, than she'd **ever** seen him—and it was easy to see why people were so drawn to him. Sitting back, having a beer, talking with his friends, he laughed easily and often. Every day he seemed to heal a little more; his soul as well as his body. And tonight, for the first time, she thought she might be seeing him as he'd been before she'd met him. It was hard to believe that tomorrow he'd be pacing the walls because he'd be thinking about all the things he wasn't able to do.

But that was tomorrow, and it was a fair indication of how deeply Mitch had affected her that Jamie wasn't looking beyond it. For now, the night was balmy and beautiful and something about the atmosphere made her feel strangely, enticingly free. Maybe it was the magic of a carnival, the bright lights and the glitter that hid the starker reality. Or maybe it was seeing Mitch pull out of himself that made her wish the night would never end. Whatever it was, she was going to enjoy it.

She only wished he could have gone on the rides.

Jamie had never been much on carnival rides herself. But from Mitch's expression as they wandered down the midway watching the screaming passengers fly by on various tilting, whirling and careening things, she knew he'd have been on them in a minute if it hadn't been for his leg. When it came to his leg, he wasn't taking any chances.

She suggested the Ferris wheel, but he just gave her a lopsided smile. "Don't worry about it," he said, because he knew what she was trying to do. It was uncanny how easily he could read her at times. "We'll just watch."

She should have known that particular ride would have been too tame for him, anyway. Just as she knew that he wasn't content to just watch. Mitch was not the spectator type and the fact that he couldn't participate bothered him. Rather than standing there letting him stew about it, which he was doing despite his disclaimer, Jamie tried for an alternative.

She suggested they head for the games where stuffed animals were the prizes.

The midway was alive with a cacophony of music-box sounds, shouts and conversations. Standing in front of the tentacle-armed Octopus, Jamie watched a muscle jump in Mitch's clenched jaw as he followed the undulating mechanical device. His eyes were still focused straight ahead when he reached for her hand.

"Come on," he said, and slipped his fingers through hers.

It had been a long time since she had held his hand. Too long. His grip was firm, possessive, but she was sure he'd taken her hand only to expedite their exit.

Assuming he was taking her suggestion, she fell into step beside him. His limp was more noticeable now than it had been. With all the walking he'd done today, she wasn't surprised. He should be using his cane, she thought, even though she knew he wouldn't. He hated the thing. He hated the limp even more.

They moved toward the double row of striped tents, the calls of the barkers competing with the canned calliope music they were leaving behind.

"Madam Toulous." Mitch read the gaudy green script on the sandwich board by one of the tent flaps. "Seer of pasts and futures." His smile was sardonic. "I wonder if she could tell me when I can get my life back to normal."

Jamie kept her tone deliberately light. For a lot of people, *this* was normal. "Maybe you should go ask?"

She was teasing, hoping to distract him with the absurdity of the idea.

It seemed to work. His brow drew down when he frowned and he looked at her as if she'd just misplaced her marbles. The expression made her smile. It also made her realize that if she dragged him into the tent, the silliness might alleviate his suddenly sober mood.

"Come on," she mumbled, so busy thinking about him that she forgot to consider that under other circumstances she'd have balked at the idea herself. "Let's see what she has to say."

"You ever been to one of these before?"

"No. Have you?"

The look in his eye was most indulgent. "Never."

"Chicken?"

Was she daring him? It sure sounded that way to her.

It must have sounded that way to him, too. His eyes narrowed at the challenge.

Two steps and he reached for the tent flap. There was no doubt in her mind as he tugged her forward that he was far more adventurous than she. In just about every respect. And this had been her idea.

Jamie and Mitch drew to a halt just inside the tent. Great swaths of purple and red satin were draped around the cramped space. A brass samovar sat next to a round satin-draped table. Behind the table sat a chiffon-draped Gypsy. She rose, bangles jangling as her dark eyes darted expertly over her customers before settling on their clasped hands.

"Ah," the husky-voiced woman intoned. "Lovers."

"So much for clairvoyance," Jamie muttered. "Let's go."

"Not at present," the woman quickly said, holding her hands out to her sides. "But you will be."

Mitch grinned. "This could be interesting."

He gave Jamie's hand a tug, drawing her toward a purple satin hassock with glittery gold trim. He took a green satin number and stretched his aching leg out in front of him.

Now that they were here, Jamie had no idea what to expect. Apparently, subtlety was not part of the process. The woman, whose head was covered by a transparent veil of saffron yellow with metallic gold polka dots, had hair the color of soot and appeared to have painted her eyes with the same. She held out her hand with her eyes closed.

Mitch, quick on the uptake, dropped a bill into her palm.

She opened one eye, then the other, and nodded to confirm that he'd done well. Looking straight at Jamie, she placed her hands over the glass ball on the table between them. "Don't be nervous, young woman. I won't tell him any of your secrets. He knows many of them, anyway."

Mitch's eyebrow arched at that. "I do? What?"

"Madam Toulous does not play games." The woman sounded genuinely offended. "I do not repeat what you know. Only what you don't. What have you come to discover?"

Mitch looked at Jamie.

Jamie, looking very much as if she wished he'd choose a different subject, shrugged.

"Go on," she said, relieved to see him smiling. "Ask her something."

He clearly wasn't going to ask about his leg, even though that was what had gotten them in here. The whole setup was strictly for fun and he was going to treat it as such.

"Okay," he began. "You can tell futures?"

The woman set a little gold coin in front of her glass ball. "Yes."

Not understanding what the coin was for, Jamie glanced at Mitch. He wasn't looking at her, though. He was concentrating.

"There's a team called the Wildcats," she heard him say. "They're coming up on their last game. Will they win?"

Another gold coin was placed by the first. "Yes."

Mitch looked doubtful. The Cats had won only three games all season. Three more than last year. "By how many points?"

A third coin joined the lineup. "Twenty-four."

"This is Little League baseball we're talking about."

"Two," she amended. "There. Your three questions are answered."

"That's all we get?" Jamie asked.

"Three questions, five dollars. It's on my sign. The fine print."

"I didn't see any fine print."

"It's very fine print. But legal. My son's a lawyer. You want more answers? Séance, maybe?"

Laughter bubbled in Jamie's throat as, a minute later, they stepped out into the balmy night air. As she'd stood, her foot had caught a bellows poking out by the table leg and the fortune-teller had scrambled to rearrange the satin table covering. The woman was still on her hands and knees making sure the prop wasn't visible when they'd left.

"Twenty-four points." Mitch shook his head, watching the lights dance in Jamie's eyes. "In our dreams."

Jamie stopped in front of him, still trying not to laugh out loud. "I've got to admit, I wouldn't trust her with my future."

Considering future in any sense when she smiled at him felt awfully dangerous to Mitch. Just as dangerous as pointing out that at least one of the woman's predictions had the potential to come true. The possibility that he and Jamie could become lovers was never far from his thoughts. Even now, the needs he felt for her taunted mercilessly. Being surrounded by so many people didn't diminish those needs in any way at all.

He held her only with his eyes. And as they stood there staring at each other, the air picked up a subtle charge of expectation.

Mitch had told himself he wouldn't touch her, that it would be better for both of them to leave their relationship as it was. But there was something he felt he should tell her, and without considering it he brushed his knuckles down her cheek.

"You know," he said, liking the way her expression softened with his caress, "I can't remember the last time I enjoyed a day so much."

The admission came with a smile, but it caused him a little consternation, too. Pulling his hand from her, his heart tightening when he saw her disappointment, he shoved both hands into his pockets.

Above the bright lights, even brighter ones lit the inky sky. "The fireworks have started," he said, quite unnecessarily. He cleared his throat. "Can we see them from home?"

Home. The word slipped out so easily. A little too easily, he'd have thought had he considered it.

"As flat as the land is around here, you can see them from anywhere." Jamie hesitated. "You don't want to stay here and watch?"

He didn't. He needed to get off his leg. The moment he'd sat down inside Madam Toulous's tent, he'd realized how much it was throbbing, and the damn thing was now beating like a kettledrum. As they drove home he told Jamie he thought he might have overdone it a little, and she was gracious enough to agree. She was also kind enough to fill an ice bag for him when they got to her house.

She directed him to the sofa because his leg would feel better stretched out. He didn't argue, which, as far as Jamie was concerned, could only mean he was really hurting. Mentally kicking herself for not suggesting that they leave the fairgrounds earlier, she returned from the kitchen to find him lying with his head on the arm of the couch and his forearm covering his eyes. His frame took up all four of the long blue cushions.

"You really should have used your cane," she said, snagging a mauve throw pillow and putting it under his leg. She placed the ice bag on his knee, thinking it would help more if he took off his pants. "I know you don't like it, but it would have helped."

He didn't budge. "What I should have done was ask Madam what's-her-name how much longer I was going to have to put up with this."

"As if she could tell you."

"She knew some things."

"Such as?"

"She said there was a lot I know about you."

"She said you know my secrets. I don't *have* any secrets."

"Yes, you do."

The smile left her eyes as soon as he uncovered his. But instead of letting herself think he looked so serious because of her, she chose to think the lack of humor in his expression was due to his discomfort.

She chose wrong. She knew that when she saw how carefully he weighed what he was about to say. For several very long seconds he lay there studying her. It was almost as if he were giving her a chance to leave before he mentioned what was on his mind. Or perhaps he was only giving himself a chance to change his own about saying it.

He didn't let the thoughts go. When he finally spoke, it was with the certainty of conclusions he knew couldn't be refuted. "I do know a lot about you, Jamie. If there's anything I've learned about you these past few months, it's that you underestimate yourself. You don't give yourself nearly enough credit for who you are."

The insight made her frown.

"You need other people's approval. That's why you can't say no to anyone. Isn't it? Because you want them to like you. And you're afraid they won't if you turn them down."

She didn't like this conversation. "If you can see all that, then it's not exactly a secret, is it?"

"Not that many people see it, Jamie. They're too busy taking advantage of your generosity." Her hand hung at her side. Snagging her wrist when she turned away, he pulled her down to sit on the edge of the sofa near his waist. "And you're too busy letting them to see what they're doing."

"I don't do anything I don't want to do."

"Never?"

She hesitated. "Not often," she decided, and started to get up. "Can I get you anything else?"

His hand slid over her thigh, stilling her. "Don't do that, Jamie. I'm not criticizing you. I just hate to see you selling yourself short. Think about what you want once in a while. Okay?"

What she wanted, all she'd ever wanted, was for someone to be proud of her. But such an admission would sound utterly pathetic and the last thing she wanted Mitch to feel for her was pity. She probably didn't need to admit it to him, anyway. From everything he'd just said, he might even already know.

"Okay," she whispered, wanting the protection of physical distance. His hand was splayed over her thigh. It felt hot and heavy and the sensation it caused in her stomach was much the same.

Mitch must have felt the muscles in her leg tense as she started again to rise. The pressure of his hand increased, his quiet "No" holding her in place. "I don't want you walking away upset."

"I'm not."

"That's something else I know about you."

His tone, a little wry and rather husky, drew her eyes to his face. "What is that?"

"You're a lousy liar." Slowly, as if he weren't even aware of the motion, his thumb moved against her soft skin. "I know other things about you, too."

The path of his thumb moved slightly higher, though his expression revealed nothing but the casualness in his tone. "I know you're caring and compassionate and that's another part of what makes it so hard for you to turn people down."

Raising his hand, he skimmed his fingers over her arm, tracing along her sleeve until he reached her shoulder. "I know that you like to touch."

He carried his caress to her neck. "And be touched." With his hand cupped at her nape, he drew her forward. "But I suspect you don't get held very often yourself." Soft as his whisper, his mouth brushed hers. "And I know that you're afraid sometimes."

Another kiss was feathered over her lips. "I'm afraid, too, Jamie. You scare the hell out of me."

She scared him? She was the one shaking. "How?"

He picked up her hand from where it rested on his forearm. Turning it over, he drew it down and pressed it over the bulge in his pants. She saw his nostrils flare slightly.

"That's how. I can't look at you without getting hard. Do you have any idea what it's like watching you day in and day out and trying to keep my hands off you? I feel like a damn time bomb just waiting to go off."

His eyes were accusing, pleading, and filled with frustration. Another deep breath and he moved his hand. He brought hers with it, threading their fingers together, and pulled her to his chest.

"I've never known any other woman who did that to me, Jamie." He raised his head toward hers, his last words a faint vibration against her mouth. "No one."

A groan, muffled by his kiss, bubbled in her throat. Or maybe that sound of longing was his. She couldn't tell. She knew only that he wanted her and that knowledge fed the sensations coursing through her as his hands slipped up to cradle her face. His mouth was infinitely gentle against hers, teasing, tasting, coaxing. There was no demand, no urgency beyond that building beneath the tenderness.

The tenderness had caught her unawares. She hadn't expected him to know how badly she'd ached for it.

For long, drugging moments he held her that way, memorizing the shape of her face with his fingers and the secret surfaces of her mouth with his lips and his tongue. He carried his sweet, debilitating kisses along the line of her jaw to her temple, and when he drew back slightly, his eyes were as hot as the liquid sensations simmering inside her.

"I won't take advantage of you, Jamie." Taking her by the shoulders, he set her back, then let his hands slide down her arms as he laid his head back on the arm of the sofa.

From the tightness of his expression, it was clear that the effort had cost him. "That's the only promise I can make to you."

He'd said before that he knew she was afraid. But she was afraid of nothing so much as not having this chance—even though it would change absolutely nothing. He would still be leaving. She would still remain. "I don't need promises."

"Yes, you do," he said, weariness beneath the heat. We all do, he thought. And dear God, he'd never wanted to make them so badly as he did right now. But he knew himself well enough to know he wouldn't keep the kind of promises she needed to hear. He couldn't do that to her. He wouldn't lie to her.

And Jamie wouldn't change her mind. She didn't even consider it.

She reached for the hem of her shirt.

Mitch moved his hands from her forearms when he realized what she was going to do, his gaze suddenly burning hot and hungry.

Jamie saw that hunger and with a boldness that felt far from natural to her, she raised the shirt over her head and dropped it on the floor. Her eyes closed as his hands moved back to her shoulders. A moment later, his fingers traced the straps down to the lacy fabric covering her breasts.

She drew a shuddering breath, then opened her eyes to see the heat in his. "Last chance, Jamie."

"Yours, too, Mitch."

He smiled, his gaze steady on hers as his fingers continued downward to the center clasp of her bra. A moment later, the clasp parted.

"Beautiful," he whispered and drew the straps down her arms.

She turned her head away. "Don't," he said, and sat up to brush a kiss to the corner of her mouth. "Help me."

Straightening, he tugged his shirt from the waist of his pants. Her hand trembling, she took the hem, drew it over his head and dropped it to the floor. His bare chest rippled with the movements as he lowered his arms and Jamie felt her nervousness vanish when she thought of how beautiful his scarred body looked to her.

She wanted to touch the angry red scar on his shoulders, but Mitch had reached around her back and pulled her braid over her shoulder. He slipped off the elastic band. Starting at the end, he slowly undid the thick plait, combing his fingers through her long, silken hair, loosening it, letting the light catch its golden colors. When he'd spread it over her shoulders, he leaned forward, burying his face in her neck, and pulled her against him.

Jamie felt her heart swell. Mitch had never found her lacking. He'd never made her feel inadequate. She needed very much to let him know how much that meant to her. How very much *he* meant to her. Melting against him, she knew that the risk of disappointment—of having her heart broken—was simply a risk she'd have to take. It wasn't a matter of allowing, anyway. Her heart had no choice in the matter.

"Not here." His voice was thick with desire, his features shadowed with it as he set her back and lifted himself from the sofa. Tucking her to his side, he led her to his room, not bothering with the light as he flipped back the covers and left her on the edge of his bed.

He was far more experienced than she. It had never occurred to Jamie to think otherwise, so when she heard him opening the duffel bag to get the protection they needed, she thought only of how grateful she was that he'd thought of it and refused to feel jealous because he was prepared. When he stretched out beside her a moment later and began unfastening the buttons on her shorts, she wasn't thinking of anything at all except how very much she loved him.

Loving Mitch was nothing like her imaginings. Certainly, the one fumbling experience she'd had in college hadn't prepared her for what she found in Mitch's arms. He was a gentle lover and a patient one. He took his time exploring, touching, asking what made her feel good and not settling for embarrassment when she hesitated to answer. His boldness made her bold. She kissed the scars on his shoulder and over his eye. She kissed the angry scars on his leg and drew her hands over all the places she'd remembered seeing the bruises. He seemed to know what she was doing and the expression on his face before he drew her back to him almost made her cry. In his rugged features she'd seen raw passion, but it was passion tempered with indescribable tenderness. And maybe just a little bit of wonder.

"You make me feel so good," she heard him say, and knew that was the closest he would come to expressing whatever it was he felt for her.

There was more Mitch could have told her. So much more, had he been the kind of man able to share such things. He couldn't believe how beautiful she was to him, how utterly artless. He felt soothed by her touch, even as he was inflamed by it. She gave so much, healing him deep down inside where he hadn't even known he hurt. She awakened feelings in him he didn't even know existed—the desire to protect, to possess, to cherish. He wanted to give her some small part of everything she'd taught him, of everything she was teaching him now.

The way he wanted to love her just wasn't possible. He wanted her beneath him, but his knee wouldn't accommodate that desire. So he pulled her over him, his mouth hungry, his caresses urgent, and aligned her hips with his. He heard her raggedly whisper his name as he brought them together, her body tight, his demanding, and moments later he was fighting a losing battle with his control.

Chapter Twelve

July was hot. August was hotter and there wasn't a soul in Winston who hadn't looked forward to September and the less beastly fall temperatures. Except for Jamie. She'd have gladly spent the rest of her life living in the desert sauna created by the skyrocketing temperatures and occasional afternoon thunderstorms if she could somehow slow the passage of time.

Time, though, moved inexorably forward. September arrived. School took the boys from the baseball diamonds. And Mitch found other ways to occupy himself. The boys still came around, though. Two of them especially, who didn't have fathers, and Mitch still pitched balls to them in the afternoons. The Wildcats, despite Madam Toulous's prediction, had lost their last game, but took a trophy for most improved team in the league, which Mitch told his players was all that mattered anyway. There had been a lot of talk at the awards banquet that Jamie attended with

Mitch about doing even better next year, maybe even winning—which everyone knew was only wishful thinking—but Mitch hadn't participated in those discussions. He'd skillfully avoided committing himself when asked about coaching next year.

Jamie wasn't sure why he hadn't come right out and said he wouldn't be in Winston. She'd overheard him tell Red he still planned to work for the company that had hired him to start the first of October. Yet as loath as she was to hear Mitch say he was leaving, she almost wished he *would* say it because then she wouldn't continue clinging to the hope that he might stay.

Even that nebulous hope couldn't prevent her from seeing that Mitch was distancing himself. She could feel it in subtle, indefinable ways. He would come home from having done something with Sam or Red and be strangely quiet. Or he would sit on the front porch as he had when he'd first been released from the hospital and stare out at the park as if to memorize the placement of every bush and tree. He would do the same with her, looking at her sometimes in a way that nearly made her heart break because she sensed he was struggling yet there was nothing she could do to help.

He didn't need her anymore. Certainly not the way he once had. No one was more aware of that than Jamie. Yet, when he took her in his arms, he seemed almost desperate to hold her. And every time they made love, she was left with the awful feeling that what they had could end at any moment. Jamie thought she'd known insecurity before. She realized now that she'd never truly known it until she'd fallen in love. She was convinced there was no state of existence harder on a person's nerves, more confusing and less likely to instill confidence.

She was dealing with that uncomfortable combination of feelings when she arrived home from work late one afternoon with the makings of a celebration Mitch didn't even know they were having.

Jamie had run into Dr. Thompson at the hospital shortly after Mitch's regular appointment with the doctor that morning. She hadn't seen Mitch, but the doctor had said something about champagne being in order tonight—then told her that Mitch had been released from his care.

"I told him I don't think he should tackle the Matterhorn yet," Dr. Thompson had said, because no one would have been surprised had Mitch planned on doing just that one day soon. "But Dr. Moody and I both feel he's recovered enough to do anything he pleases. He's made a remarkable recovery in the past six months. Frankly, I've never seen anyone heal so fast."

She could have told the doctor that she knew Mitch wouldn't be held down by norms. His determination had somehow reached her even in the stillness of his coma.

Mitch was on the phone when she entered the kitchen. His face was a little flushed, his eyes bright. She knew exactly what he was so happy about, too, and smiled back because she wanted to be happy for him—even though smiling wasn't something she felt like doing.

Setting down the groceries, she heard him say, "Don't worry. I'll be there," and felt the smile dissolve. "I'll still have to pass a flight physical to renew my pilot's certification but my medical certificate is valid for another six months. The doctors here said all my tests were excellent. They're not aviation examiners, though."

He paused, pacing. Listening.

"Hey, I won't let that happen," he said with a chuckle. "In another six months, no doctor will ever be able to tell I was hurt."

Except for the scars, Jamie thought.

She was sure he was speaking to someone at the company he was due to go to work for in less than three weeks.

It probably wasn't legal for him to use a medical certificate that had been obtained before he'd been so badly injured, but she knew that Mitch feared not being able to fly more than anything else. That he would do so any way he could didn't surprise her in the least.

It was with no small amount of relief that she heard him say goodbye—to Red. Red had hired another pilot for the tourist season, but Mitch had begun helping the older man look into ways to boost his floundering business. He spent a lot of time tinkering with the helicopters and planes Red owned, too, as much to help Red save on mechanic's fees as to ward off boredom. She should have known he'd have called him to share his news.

She didn't catch his slight hesitation before he hung up. All she noticed was that he looked like a little boy with a new bicycle when he turned around. "Guess what?"

"What?" She already knew what had him looking so much younger, but she wasn't about to deprive him of the pleasure of telling her. He'd waited too long for this news.

"No more therapy. No more tests. No more appointments. I can go back to work."

Her heart felt as if it were breaking in two. "I know," she said, resurrecting the smile as she placed her palm on his cheek. "Dr. Thompson told me." She kissed him, not letting herself linger, though she needed him to hold her more than she ever had. "Congratulations."

She moved away before Mitch could put his arms around her, and reached for one of the sacks. She wouldn't let herself think about what might happen tomorrow or the next day. She'd do what she'd done every hour for the past few weeks and concentrate only on the immediate. If Mitch had taught her anything, it was that the present was all a person could control. "Do you have any plans tonight?"

She knew he was frowning. She could hear it in his voice. "No. Why?"

A small circle of Brie and a bunch of grapes came out of the sack. "I want to take you somewhere."

"Oh, yeah?" he asked, watching her in a way that made her feel totally transparent.

"Yeah. You up for it?"

Deli ham and French rolls were set on the table. A moment later she folded the sack, shoved it under the sink and took two plastic bottles of mineral water from the refrigerator. Champagne would have been more appropriate, but the effects of alcohol could be a problem where they were going.

Mitch leaned against the counter, his arms folded over the white cotton T-shirt tucked into his scruffy cutoffs. He looked very male and a little confused. "Are you okay?"

"I'm fine. Why?"

"You just seem ... I don't know. Kind of ... rattled or something."

She used to be so good at keeping up a composed front. She still was. With everyone but him.

"I just want to hurry." Unwilling to meet his eyes, she headed into the laundry room, emerging a moment later with a bright pink backpack. "I don't want to miss the sunset."

She set the backpack on the table. Mitch took her arm.

He pulled her around to face him. But whatever it was he'd been thinking a moment ago had been set aside with her last comment. "We're going to the mesa?"

So much for surprises.

"I want you to see the view from there." Before you go, she added to herself.

"I'd like to see it." Because I know how special the place is to you, he thought.

She smiled and stepped back before she could do or say anything foolish. Ever since she'd spoken with Dr. Thompson, she'd had the feeling that the beginning of the end had started. No matter how hard she tried, she just couldn't shake it. "Then we'd better hurry."

Within minutes, Jamie had checked her backpack for the usual emergency stuff she carried in it: flashlight, first-aid kit, flares. Then, after she changed into a yellow tank, denim shorts and her hiking boots, they took off with the top down on her battered Mustang and headed out the dirt road leading up to the base of the Widowed Sisters.

All the way out, Jamie found herself hoping Mitch wouldn't be disappointed. She even told him that, warning him that where they were going was nothing like the spectacular climbs he'd been on; that the path leading up to the ledge where she liked to go was little more than a gentle incline with a few minor rocky spots. Nothing a little old lady in reasonably good shape couldn't manage.

He told her to stop worrying, that it felt good just to be out, and she knew he meant it. She knew he meant it, too, when they reached her ledge and he told her quietly, because the place demanded the low voices of a church, that he wasn't disappointed in the least.

The top of the mesa loomed above them, a hundred feet of sheer straight wall, when they reached their destination. Jamie never climbed any farther. She always stopped along the six-foot-wide natural ledge that ran for several yards above a huge tumble of boulders. This spot faced due west. From fifty feet off the floor of the plateau, the panorama stretched out for miles. Vast. Open. Completely untamed.

On the horizon, dense clouds had begun to build. The thunderheads were far enough away that they needn't worry about them, but every once in a while a jagged bolt of lightning could be seen against the heavy gray. Above them, the sky was the blue of early evening and streaked with clouds that the setting sun would color with the same salmons and pinks and reds of the rocks beneath Mitch's and Jamie's feet.

Sitting on the ledge, their backs to the rock wall and knees raised to support elbows, Mitch took Jamie's hand in his and looked out over the unspoiled vista. For a long time they sat in the silence.

"It makes everything else seem pretty insignificant, doesn't it?"

He didn't expect a response. She knew that. Just as she had known, somehow, that he would recognize what it was about this place that drew her. A person's perspective about a problem could be more easily gained when she realized that the millennia had left all this much as it had always been. Nothing really ever changed. *In the overall scheme of things,* as Martha would say....

"Listen." A delighted smile lit Jamie's eyes and she turned to see Mitch watching her. "Can you hear it?"

The sound was faint, low and mournful. For a moment Mitch wasn't even sure what she meant for him to hear. He hadn't been listening, anyway. He'd been wondering how he could tell her how free he now felt when he knew she didn't want to hear it.

It just wasn't fair. In Jamie he'd finally met a woman he wanted to share his feelings with—the one big complaint women had always had about him—and Jamie was the one person he felt compelled to protect from them.

The sound grew a little louder—a soft, eerie wailing on the evening breeze.

"What is that?"

She seemed amused by his puzzlement. "It's the wind blowing through the rock formations."

The expression on her face was hauntingly familiar. The soft light of her smile had once been a balm to him. It was his sustenance now.

"The Weeping Dove," he said, remembering the story she'd told him a lifetime ago. "Is that it?"

Pleased that he hadn't forgotten, her smile widened.

Oh, Jamie, he sighed to himself. I want to remember you this way always.

"You never said if anyone knows why she's crying."

She paused, thinking him utterly beautiful with the breeze blowing his dark hair back from his face. A century ago he could have been an Indian warrior standing in this very spot. He had that same nobility about him, that same affinity for such wide open spaces.

That same inherent need for freedom.

"The legend says she's mourning her husband. She'll weep forever because she cared about him so much."

"Some fate."

"It's hard to say goodbye to someone you care about."

His hesitation was not unexpected.

With a shaky smile she reached for the backpack, thinking to set out their small celebration picnic. This line of conversation was far too close to home for comfort and the way Mitch was watching her made it apparent he knew it, too.

He wasn't quite so willing to let it go. But he wasn't going to talk in euphemisms.

Stilling the fumbling of her hands on the pack, he made her look at him. He wouldn't address the dormant issue now, not here in this place that was so important to her, but there was something he needed her to know.

"No matter what happens, Jamie, I have never meant to hurt you. Please remember that."

She'd hoped for some assurance. His words left her with none.

"What's going to happen?" she asked, wondering if it wouldn't be easier to just get it all over with than to go on with the agony of wondering when the ax would fall. *If* the ax would fall.

She was terrible at being in love.

"Right now," he told her, because the hurt in her eyes was already there, "I'm going to thank you for bringing me here. No one has ever shared as much with me as you have," he told her, drawing her against him. "And no one has ever meant as much, either."

She clung to his words. As he held her and they watched the sun slip below the thunderheads, the words echoed in her mind, joining the mournful wail of the Weeping Dove. The sounds melded, his husky words and the keening sound, and in her mind he was now a part of this very special place. Realizing that, she knew she'd made a mistake bringing him here. This had been the one spot she could come to find peace. Now she'd never be able to come here without thinking of him.

She could only guess at what Mitch was thinking as he held her in those last minutes before the sun's rays disappeared and the spectacular sky faded to gray. She knew only that he was pulling deeper into his private self, the part she'd never been allowed to touch. As they left before the light was gone so they wouldn't be stumbling down the path in the dark, neither said very much. It was as if it had all been said anyway.

That sober silence accompanied them all the way home. It stayed with them even as they entered the house. That silence dictated darkness and by some unspoken agreement neither reached for a light switch as they moved into the shadows of the kitchen.

When Jamie heard Mitch stop behind her, she turned in the shaft of moonlight streaming through the window. "Make love with me," she whispered. "Please."

He drew her to him, his arms strong and warm around her. "Are you all right?"

"No."

He didn't ask what the problem was. He just gathered her closer and pressed his lips to the moonlight in her hair.

She was missing him already. "When?" she asked, her face buried in his chest.

"When what?"

"When are you leaving?"

He paused, drawing his hands down her back. "Tomorrow. How did you know?"

"I just did."

"It's only for a couple of weeks."

Relief swamped her. She lifted her head, swallowing hard, and tried to smile. "Oh."

Mitch tasted tears when he lifted her face to his kiss. He felt his gut clench. He'd never meant to make her cry.

Long after Jamie had fallen asleep, Mitch slipped from her bed and stood at the front window staring into the night. He'd known that their sleeping together would alter their relationship. Something had changed, all right. In him. It had started the moment he'd awakened to find her holding his hand and he wasn't at all sure how to deal with it.

He knew he could hurt Jamie. He already had. Knowing he had that power gave him no satisfaction whatsoever. What he felt was disgust with himself. He'd known from the beginning that he wasn't being fair to her. Even the fact that he'd warned her, that he'd told her he couldn't make her any promises, didn't alleviate the guilt he felt.

Guilt. As intimately familiar as he was with that one, he could almost hate her for making him feel more.

He turned from his shadowy reflection, standing naked in the darkness.

All along he'd been aware of the kind of woman Jamie was. The kind who needed a family. Permanence. Just thinking about those responsibilities made him panic. They always had, so he'd never even considered them. With them came obligations and the right for other people to make demands. To control. Jamie hadn't asked anything of him.

But tonight, tasting her tears, she had asked without the words. The very fact that she didn't want him to leave made it imperative that he do so. The demands would come.

This afternoon, when he'd told Red about being released by the doctor, the owner of Red Rock Air had come up with an offer Mitch couldn't refuse. It was the perfect cure for the vaguely claustrophobic feeling Mitch had been experiencing ever since people had begun asking him what his plans were for next month. Next year. The deal was only for two weeks, and that was all Mitch had planned on being gone. Now he wondered if it wouldn't be better for Jamie if he didn't come back at all.

He was still wrestling with that thought when he heard her putting on the coffee the next morning.

Jamie stood at the kitchen sink, her hair still damp from her shower and her robe loosely knotted. The relief she'd felt last night when Mitch had said he'd only be leaving for a little while had vanished when she'd awakened to find him gone from her bed. What replaced the relief was a definite sinking sensation. That sensation intensified as she turned, pot in hand, and saw him standing beside the kitchen table.

He hadn't bothered with shirt or shoes. Wearing only jeans, which he'd zipped but not snapped, and an expression completely devoid of any telling emotion, he took the glass pot from her. "We need to talk," he said, and dumped the water through the machine to start the brew.

It wasn't quite six o'clock in the morning. Not a good time even under normal circumstances for her to have a conversation. Especially not when she was due at work in an hour.

"Fine." She sank into the nearest chair at the table.

Mitch took the one next to her, looking very much as if he wished he were anyplace else at the moment. He leaned forward, pried one of her arms from around her middle and curled her hand into his on the table. "I told Red I'd be at his place at noon. So I won't be here when you get home."

She looked at their clasped hands. "What is it you're doing for him?"

"Research, basically. He knows some writer who's comparing raft trips down the Colorado for an outdoor magazine. Red wants me to go along and check out how the tours are run. See how the guides handle the different operations. That sort of thing. He's been talking about adding raft trips to his summer tours, but he wants to do something different than what's being done."

Jamie had almost forgotten that the main reason Mitch had come to Winston in the first place was to do some rafting himself. There were other things she'd forgotten, too. His need for freedom was never very far from her thoughts, but she'd somehow neglected to remember his love of risk, his passion for adventure. She'd been drawn by that recklessness, fascinated by it. Even envied it a little. Now she wasn't so sure why that had been.

"This sounds like the perfect opportunity for both of you."

His response to her conclusion was the faint tightening of his jaw.

"You said it was for a couple of weeks?"

His hand slid from hers. "Yeah."

He stood then and walked across the room. Stopping at the sink, he spread his hands wide on the edge of the counter and looked out at the early-morning light. A moment later she saw the muscles in his back expand with his deeply drawn breath. Letting it out, he lowered his head.

"I'm due in Houston the first of the month."

"I know."

"That gives me a week in between."

For several seconds the only sound to be heard was the gurgling of the coffeepot.

Jamie folded her hands in her lap. She, too, drew a deep breath. "Are you coming back?"

"I don't know."

"I see."

He turned then, his features dark and brooding. "Jamie," he began, then let whatever he'd been about to say trail off with a sigh. "I think it would be a mistake if I did."

"If you feel that way, then it probably would."

She wasn't going to argue with him. With her arms hugging her middle, she started across the room. There was nothing to argue about. He'd made his choice and it wasn't her. He'd chosen the life he'd known before. The one filled with the excitement and adventure and experiences he couldn't possibly hope to find in a town like Winston with a woman like her. She'd known all along that he wouldn't want to stay. He'd told her he wouldn't.

That didn't make it hurt any less.

"Can I ask you one thing?" She stopped at the coffeepot, feeling pretty good about the fact that she was actually able to pour herself a cup of the steaming brew without him seeing how her hands were shaking. "Would you mind telling me what it is that keeps you running?"

He didn't like the question.

She didn't like his tone. "What's that supposed to mean?"

"It doesn't 'mean' anything." All she wanted to do was understand him. That's all she'd ever wanted to do. "I'm just trying to figure out what you're trying to prove. And who you're trying to prove it to."

She wasn't doing such a hot job with the coffee, after all. Setting the cup down before she sloshed it all over herself, she folded her arms back over her stomach.

There hadn't been any demand in her expression or her voice. Jamie wasn't the kind of woman who could carry off a challenge, anyway. But that wasn't what Mitch saw and heard. Her words pricked at his conscience, reminding him of someone else who'd demanded answers to very similar questions. Questions he'd always avoided considering.

With the reminder came defensiveness.

"I don't have to prove anything to anyone." The tightness of his words betrayed a simmering anger. He knew the anger was with himself. Not with her. But he didn't differentiate. It was easier to do what he had to do with his temper guiding him instead of his heart. "That's not what this is about. You knew from the beginning what my plans were. I can't stay here, Jamie. This isn't what I want."

"This isn't what I want, either, Mitch. No." She held up her hand to ward off whatever he was about to say. He'd once told her to consider what she wanted for a change, and that was exactly what she'd do. "I'm not going to stand here and let you say a bunch of stuff I don't want to hear. If you say it's over, I believe you. I don't need convincing. And I won't argue with you. There isn't a thing I could say that would matter, anyway." She picked up her coffee. It spilled over the side. She didn't even stop to wipe it up. "I've got to go to work. Do me a favor and leave your key on the table."

Mitch watched her go, her head up, her shoulders trembling, and forced himself not to follow her. There was nothing he could say that would undo what he'd just done, so there was no point in trying. He was doing the right thing. The only thing he could do.

Swearing sharply, he went to his room and slammed the door. He'd been on the move for so long that he wasn't sure he even knew how to stop. All that had kept him going the past few months was the knowledge that he would get better, that he would move on.

That's what he was doing now. Moving on. But even as he threw his few belongings into his duffel bag and a cardboard box he'd dug out of the laundry room after he'd heard Jamie leave, he had to admit that the main reason he kept going was that he was afraid of what he might discover about himself if he did stop.

Part Three

Chapter Thirteen

Thursday, 7:00 p.m.

Jamie lay on her side, her back to the boulder, hugging her arms around herself. She'd have given anything to be able to sleep. Between the pain in her leg and being slightly petrified about being alone with a band of howling coyotes roaming not so very far away, that oblivion was impossible.

The moon was above the top of the tallest spire now. Ghostly shadows loomed around her. And everywhere she could hear the eerie silence that magnified every sound. An odd squeaking noise sounded not too far away. It was followed by more of the same, the small, high-pitched squeals seeming to ricochet off the canyon walls. A breath of breeze brushed her face. Dark wings passed in front of the moon.

Bats.

The squeaking was their radar.

She jerked upright and would have screamed if fright hadn't clotted the sound in her throat.

She did scream when the skittering of pebbles down the hill made her jerk to the side and she blinked at yellow eyes glowing in the dark.

Only when the unearthly beast, all eighteen slithery black inches of it, had turned tail and headed at a run through the moonlight did she manage to get the gun Mitch had left her. When she'd grabbed for it, her groping knocked it farther away. Now she held it so tightly a crowbar would have been necessary to pry it from her fingers.

She leaned against the rock behind her, her heart pounding so hard she could feel every beat in her head. Despite the fact that Mitch's jacket was buttoned to her neck, she was freezing, and her leg still felt as if someone had soaked it with gasoline and set a match to it.

Another noise. Another bit of motion.

If the venom from the snake didn't get her, her nerves would.

Oh, please, Mitch, she silently prayed. *Please hurry.*

She didn't know how many times she repeated those phrases. A hundred. A thousand. But she was repeating them again, rocking herself with the gun in her hand, when a new sound filtered through the night. A mechanical sound. Not the sonances of nocturnal creatures.

The droning grew louder, steadily escalating from a hum to a roar. Within moments, it seemed, the distinctive reverberations of a helicopter were rushing toward her and a bright light swept the floor of the little canyon a hundred feet from where she sat. The light swept a little farther away, turning black-and-gray boulders pink. Seconds later, the white and red lights of the chopper disappeared beyond the ridge and the roar faded to a hum. The sound seemed to hover at that faded pitch. Then, almost abruptly, she heard only silence.

Come back! her mind screamed, or maybe she did cry out in her desperation. "Mitch!" she called, and his name echoed back to her.

A tiny whimper met the echo. All that had made the past hour bearable was the knowledge that Mitch would be here. Soon he would be here. It hadn't entered her mind that he wouldn't be able to find her.

With her hand over her mouth, her other still clutching the gun, Jamie listened, straining to catch some hint of sound to indicate that the helicopter was returning.

All she could hear was the pounding of her heart in her ears.

It was only his first pass, she told herself, and even though he had missed her this time, just the knowledge that Mitch was looking for her helped hold down her panic. In her mind she could see the set of his jaw, the deceptively relaxed grip of his hands on the controls as he followed the beam of the searchlight over the jutting and jagged rocks. Then she remembered how difficult it had been to spot a victim even with daylight. Spotting one in inky blackness would be impossible unless his beam happened to land directly on her.

The only way that could happen would be for her to move away from the rocks and out into the middle of the ravine. She would have no protection there; she'd be even easier prey for the prowling coyotes and bobcats. But in the shadows he'd never see her. As soon as she heard the helicopter again, she would move out to where they'd found Tim. Just as soon as she heard it, she reminded herself.

But she didn't hear anything but the stirrings of tiny animals. And overhead all she could see were stars. Bright, beautiful, brilliant stars.

Ten minutes passed.

Ten more.

He wasn't coming back.

Between the debilitating pain in her leg, the awful shivering and the fear, Jamie hadn't thought there was room inside her to feel anything else. But what she felt when she repeated those words was the same aching emptiness she'd been fighting since the day Mitch had walked out of her life.

Mitch wasn't coming back.

The dull clunk of a small rock rolling into another sounded in the distance. The sound came again, followed this time by the whoosh of pebbles sliding down an incline. Jamie straightened, her body tense and trembling, and glanced in the direction of the noise.

The light of the full moon delineated every rock in surreal black and silver. Nothing moved among those sharp-edged shapes that she could see. Yet she knew what she'd heard. It was possible, of course, that the sliding had been the natural shift of rocks broken loose by their own weight. Or something else could have made that sound. Something big.

"Jamie?"

Like a phantom, Mitch emerged from the boulders across the flat floor of the ravine. She saw him stop as if he were searching the shadows, and called his name.

Relief swamping her, she scrambled to turn on the flashlight. The instant it went on, he headed across the moonscape of shale. Within moments he loomed over her. Then he was kneeling beside her.

"Thank God," she heard him breathe, and even as she reached for him he gathered her in his arms.

He pressed her head to his chest, holding her, rocking her. "I was so afraid," he said into her hair. He seemed to breathe in the flowery scent of it. "I didn't know what I'd find when I got here."

She wanted to tell him she'd been afraid, too. Terrified, actually. But it seemed more important that she just hold on. She desperately needed to absorb his strength. For now. For later.

He eased her away, loath to let her go when she was trembling so fiercely. "Jamie. Look at me." With one arm still around her, he pulled off the gloves he'd worn to keep his hands from splitting on the shale he'd scrambled down and took a flashlight from his pocket. "Dr. Moody told me what I need to do for you. I need to see your eyes. I'm going to turn on the flashlight. Okay?"

She nodded, not caring what he did so long as he didn't let go of her.

The light was blinding, his hands gentle, and after he'd made the cursory check for neurological involvement, he turned his attention to her leg. Started to, anyway. Remembering, he reached into his pocket, took out a small envelope, then opened the canteen lying on her backpack.

"You're supposed to take this."

"What is it?"

It was a tranquilizer, and Dr. Moody had told Mitch to be sure she took it. The sedative effect would help relieve her anxiety, calm her body's reactions to the toxin and antidote and help her rest. Mitch had taken the snake out with him— having stuffed it into the plastic pouch the mast trousers had come in. Dr. Moody had taken one look at the snake before sending it off to have its venom analyzed, asked what had been done for Jamie so far and promptly told Mitch what procedures to follow.

Mitch explained all that to Jamie, but he wasn't sure if his conversation with the doctor mattered to her. Even when she asked about the boy they had rescued and Mitch had told her that the kid had still been alive when they reached the hospital, she seemed a little numb—like someone suffering shell shock. But Mitch didn't know what to do about that, so he concentrated on what he could do and hoped it would be enough.

Fifteen minutes later, her swollen leg salved and wrapped, cold pack in place and medications presumably working, Mitch sat with her in the dark shelter of the curved rock. As dangerous as it had been for him to climb down to her with only the moon and a flashlight to guide his way, it would be suicide to attempt climbing out before daybreak. He hadn't been able to bear the thought of her being here alone. As he listened to the distant howling, he could only imagine how frightened she must have been.

He'd take care of her. As she'd taken care of him.

Tucking the blanket closer under her chin, he tightened his arm around her. Her head lay on his shoulder and he could feel her trembling clear through to his bones. It was killing him that she was so miserable.

He'd asked several times how she was doing. When he asked this time, she said the same thing she'd said before. "Okay."

He had to do something. The thought that came to mind was a long shot, but it couldn't hurt to try. She was restless with her pain. One minute her arms would be around her middle. The next she was tucking her hands under her chin. Then she'd try to put one under her cheek next to his chest. "Have you ever heard of *lunggom*, Jamie?"

Fretful, she stirred against him, her mumbled "No" not necessarily unexpected. "What does it mean?"

"It's a word I heard in Bhutan. Literally, it means 'walking on air.' The concept is a form of meditation that the monks at Taktshang use. It takes a long time to achieve, but those who master it can focus their energy and cover the ground with an almost superhuman stride."

Jamie lifted her hand, rubbing an aching spot on her forehead. He wasn't making any sense to her. He was sure of it.

He cupped her cheek with his palm to draw her eyes to his. In the moonlight she looked very pale, very soft—very uncomfortable. "If you focus your energy, you might be able to alleviate some of the pain. Do you know how to do that?"

She shook her head, frowning.

"Do you?" she asked, and even as she did she remembered watching him in the hospital as he lifted himself with the bar over his head.

"Not the way the monks do. Not by a long shot. But I know you have to make your focus be on something outside of yourself. Find a point and concentrate only on that. Make what you're looking at be your entire existence. You become part of what you see. That way, you forget about your body and anything about the way it feels. Do you want to try?"

She'd have tried hanging by her toes if he thought it would help. "What should I look at?"

The moon. A star. The peak of a spire rising above them. Any of those would have sufficed. And she fully expected Mitch to name one of them. Or rattle off the whole list. What she heard was completely unexpected.

A moment's hesitation preceded his quiet "Just keep looking at me, Jamie. Okay?"

"Okay," she heard herself return, and keeping her eyes on his, she felt his fingers brush along the side of her neck.

"Now. Talk to me."

Make what you're looking at be your entire existence. "I don't think this is a very good idea."

"Don't look away. Keep talking."

She couldn't look away. The beautiful lines of his face, his long sweeping hair, the stark concern in his expression were all too compelling. *You become part of what you see.* "I don't want to do this, Mitch."

"Why not?" He stroked the side of her neck, soothing her. "Don't you think it's working?"

As soon as he asked the question she remembered her leg, and that made her more aware of the dull burning. With her attention so focused on him for those few seconds, she *had* short-circuited some of the discomfort.

The trade-off was interesting. The pain in her leg for the pain in her heart. "I think we'd better keep talking."

With his hand on her shoulder now, he felt her trembling begin to ease. He wouldn't take credit for it. But he would let himself feel relief at knowing the medication was finally working.

"No problem." He tucked her head back to his shoulder, wondering if soon she might not be able to sleep. He hoped so. For her sake. "Tell me what you want to talk about."

Anything safe. "Tell me how you found me. I saw you go over, but I thought you'd gone right past."

The moon was directly overhead now and the temperature had dropped to the point where their breath was coming in vaporous puffs. Huddled as they were, though, the blanket draped over them, Jamie wasn't nearly as cold as she'd been before. So lying there, finally feeling some ease after the past harrowing hours, she listened as Mitch told her how he'd spread out the tools from the tool kit in the chopper around the top of the tiny tabletop mesa. And how, when he'd flown back over, the searchlight reflected off the handles and showed him where to land. He told her, too, how he planned on getting her out tomorrow, and though she wasn't keen on the idea of being carried out on his back, she didn't see that she had a lot of choice.

What Mitch didn't talk about was anything related to them. And though he held her, he made no attempt to kiss her. He was simply there for her. For the time being.

Which was how it had been before.

She fell asleep knowing that tomorrow she'd have to start getting over him all over again.

Chapter Fourteen

"Good God. It looks like a funeral parlor in here."

Barb Robinson walked through the doorway of Jamie's hospital room, hands on her hips and head turning from side to side as she checked out the flower arrangements on the windowsill, by the sink and on the table at the foot of Jamie's bed.

Setting aside the magazine she hadn't been reading anyway, Jamie smiled a little self-consciously. "Pretty obscene, isn't it? By the way, thanks for the roses."

Barb stopped by the bouquet of pink roses next to an arrangement of tulips and irises. She checked the card, commented that it was nice to see that the florist got her order right, then went on to see who had sent the rest. There were carnations from Stan, mums from Cub Scout Troop 644, the spring assortment from Mae Beth Potter from the retirement home, and a Hawaiian-looking vase with lots of foliage and a bird of paradise from Terese. Martha had sent a potted plant. Agatha was responsible for the bouquet of mylar "Get Well" balloons, which looked very much like those she sold in the gift shop.

"You hiding any other flora in here?" Barb asked, looking around before she sat down on the edge of Jamie's bed.

From the speculation in her friend's eyes, Jamie knew exactly what Barb was after. There was nothing from Mitch, though, and since Barb had already made her feelings known where Mitch was concerned, she didn't pursue the matter.

Instead, she grinned at the tiny blue flowers on Jamie's hospital gown. "Nice duds. Hardly a fashion statement, but functional. How does it feel to be on the receiving end of all this?"

"Weird," Jamie replied, then admitted, quietly so she wouldn't be overheard, that she could hardly wait to get out of there.

After spending two days in acute care, she had finally been transferred to a regular room. Thanks to the low toxicity of the snake that had bitten her, she probably wouldn't have to stay much longer. Except for the major swelling that had to be monitored to make sure the circulation in her lower leg wouldn't become restricted, she hadn't suffered any of the debilitating or disfiguring effects of a pit viper strike. The last snakebite victim to come through emergency hadn't been so fortunate. That particular gentleman had spent twelve days in Doris's relentless, regimented care.

Doris's militaristic approach to nursing had about driven Mitch up the wall, too.

The light in her smile faded. She did all right as long as she didn't think about the man who now seemed to be avoiding her.

"You made the local newspaper, you know," Barb said, attempting to bring Jamie's smile back. "The article was good, but the picture wasn't so hot. All you could see was the helicopter and someone's back. It was your shoulder and head, though. I recognized your braid." The body of the giraffe on her tan sweatshirt disappeared as she crossed her arms over it. "You should have been on the front page. Local hero stuff. You know."

"I don't think so," Jamie replied, relieved that the article hadn't been so prominent. When Martha had shown it to her, she'd also been relieved that the focus had been on Winston's unique system of cooperative effort between law enforcement, the medical community and private enterprise. The reporter had touched only briefly on the rescue and its complications. Mostly, Jamie was sure, because Mitch had run the young man off. "We were just doing a job."

"Yeah." Barb sobered. She remembered what else she'd read in the article. "I'm really sorry the kid you went after didn't make it."

Jamie was sorry, too, but despite Barb's astute change of subject—this time to recount what T.J. had done with his insect collection—Jamie's concentration on the conversation wasn't quite complete.

Mitch had given her the news about Tim Webster himself. When he had, he'd also told her he thought he now understood what it was she felt when she worked so hard on someone—only to lose him anyway. She knew she hadn't been fair just then, because Mitch had worked hard for Tim, too, but she'd wondered if Mitch ever would truly understand how it felt to lose someone. He walked away from everything so easily.

She'd said nothing about that to him. The sheriff and Dr. Moody had been in the room with them at the time. Stan had stayed only long enough afterward to let her know without quite saying it that he was sorry he'd had to ask her to go out to The Pinnacles. He'd had no choice, though. Jamie knew that. And she'd do it again if she had to. She was sure Stan knew that, too. After Stan had gone, Dr. Moody left—and Mitch went with him. She hadn't seen him alone since he'd brought her in.

Once she and Mitch had made the harrowing trip back out of the ravine, time had sped by in an almost undefinable blur. Martha and an orderly had been waiting with a gurney when Mitch set the helicopter down in the empty field outside emergency's automatic glass doors. Mitch had looked as exhausted as she felt, and she remembered Dr. Moody being concerned about Mitch's leg and telling him to go get some rest before he admitted him to the hospital, too. Then she was being pulled and poked and prodded and she remembered promising herself that the next time she worked on a patient she'd be gentler if she could.

She had slept for nearly twenty-four hours after that. During that time someone—Pam, perhaps—told her that Mitch had called. Then it seemed he was sitting by her bed, holding her hand, and bits and pieces of memory faded in and out about all the times she'd sat beside his bed and done the same thing.

Or maybe she'd only dreamed that part of it.

"Well, listen," Barb said, having concluded the recounting of her son's latest transgression. "I've got to get to the grocery store before the kids get out of school. Since you haven't been home the past couple of afternoons, they're expecting milk and cookies from me."

With a mock frown for the inconvenience, Barb pushed her auburn curls out of her eyes and stood up. She'd just opened her mouth to say something else when a deep voice came from behind her.

"Am I interrupting?"

The displeasure in Barb's expression was suddenly real. For the sake of politeness, though, she tempered it to simple tolerance. "Hello, Mitch. We haven't seen you for a while."

Had Jamie's attention not been focused on the tension she could see in Mitch's rugged features, she'd have blanched at her neighbor's coolness. The man filling the doorway was not Barb's favorite person at the moment. For a couple of reasons.

It was impossible to tell if Mitch realized that. "I guess that's because I haven't been around."

"It would have been nice of you to say goodbye. T.J. missed you. Well," she continued, turning her back on Mitch. "I'm out of here, Jamie. Let me know when you're ready to go home and I'll come get you. Tammy sends you this."

Barb gave Jamie a hug, was gracious enough not to glare at Mitch and took one last whiff of the roses she'd sent before heading out the door.

Mitch, his thumbs hooked on the pockets of his jeans and looking vaguely predatory in a black leather aviator jacket, stopped by the foot of the bed. "I don't think she's very happy with me."

"You hurt her son." It wasn't like Jamie to cause another person discomfort. And Mitch did look uncomfortable when she told him that. But he needed to know what he'd done to the kids by just up and disappearing. "T.J. thought you were his friend. So did the other boys on the team." Eddie Cuttler and shy little Troy Holt, especially. Troy had been near tears when he and Eddie had come over two days after Mitch had gone and Jamie had to tell them he wasn't coming back.

The muscle in his jaw jumped and Mitch turned his attention to the plants on the windowsill. They seemed easier for him to look at. Certainly, they were less accusing. "I was just on my way home and thought I'd stop to see how you were doing. Maybe my coming by wasn't such a good idea."

She didn't know what he expected from her. She did know she didn't expect to hear what he'd just said. "Home? What do you mean?"

"I rented a duplex over on Cottonwood Street. It's a little short on furniture, but I've bought what I need to get by for now."

She remembered him telling her he'd come back to help Red. But if he wasn't staying in a motel, if he was buying furniture, he must be planning on staying longer than she'd thought. "What about your job with the company out of Houston?"

"I quit it."

"You're staying for a while?"

It wasn't hope in her voice. It was defeat. When Mitch turned, it seemed from the rigidity in his features that he found it as disheartening as she to hear it there. "I'm buying into Red's business, Jamie. He can't do what he needs to do to make a go of it without more money. I've saved up a couple of dollars over the last few years and I think between him and me we can turn things around." He sounded a little defensive. He definitely looked it. "So, to answer your question, yes. I'm staying."

From across the room, Mitch waited for Jamie's reaction. He couldn't remember ever feeling as apprehensive as he had in the past two weeks—ever since he'd found himself fighting a storm between shore and an oil rig and wondering what in the hell he was doing there. It wasn't where he'd wanted to be. Ever since he'd left, he hadn't been where he wanted to be.

It was possible that he'd made that decision a little too late, though. Jamie simply looked at him with her huge hazel eyes, her features betraying nothing, then glanced toward the magazine on the sheet beside her hip and began fanning the corners of the pages.

He hated how she'd withdrawn from him, but he couldn't have expected her to act any other way.

"Do you remember the evening you found me out back? You were on your way home and I was sitting out by one of the service doors?"

The intricate weaving of her braid caught the light as, after considering for a moment, she nodded. She remembered, but it appeared that she wasn't going to enjoy any strolls down memory lane.

"What about it?" she asked, not looking up.

"I asked what had brought you to Winston from L.A. You told me you'd wanted to travel around for a while. That you'd thought you'd work here for a year or so, then try somewhere else. Alaska or Vermont, I think you mentioned. You didn't leave, though. You said there was no need to."

Her composure seemed in danger of crumbling. Doing what she always did when she felt threatened, Jamie sought to end the discussion. Distance always helped. Physical distance was best. Emotional would do in a pinch.

"It's not necessary for you to explain, Mitch. Not to me. There are a few others you need to talk to, though. Especially since you'll probably run into them sooner or later." Like you did with me, she thought, remembering how he'd said that very thing to her only a few short days ago. "I know why you needed to leave. I don't need to hear it again."

He stepped closer, his shadow falling over the sheets covering her legs. "What I was getting at," he went on, refusing to let her dismiss him, "is that you said you never left because there was no reason to keep going. You found what you were looking for in Winston. It might have taken me a while to realize it, but I did, too. We're both going to be living here, Jamie, and it'll be a whole lot easier if we can be friends instead of enemies."

"I won't be your enemy, Mitch." She could never hate him. Ever. "But don't ask me to be your friend."

"You're not being fair."

That was not the right thing to say. He knew it the instant her wounded glance jerked to him. He was beginning to feel a little desperate, though. He had to make her understand.

"How am I not being fair?" she wanted to know.

"By not listening to me."

"I've heard every word you said."

"Right. And you're so busy protecting yourself that you won't even give me a chance. Hell," he muttered, reaching. "You didn't even try to stop me when I did leave."

Not until the words slipped out did Mitch let himself admit how that had hurt. But even as he did, he realized that he'd stepped into an area he hadn't intended to address. Not yet, anyway.

"It wouldn't have mattered if I had tried to stop you," he heard her return with more heat than he expected. She turned away from him. "This discussion is ridiculous."

"It's also getting a little loud," Pam said, poking her neatly coiffed head around the edge of the door. "Why don't I close this?"

She reached for the door's handle. Mitch beat her to it. "No need. I'm going. Is she doing okay?" Since he hadn't had a chance to ask Jamie himself, he directed the question to Pam.

Pam, appearing totally nonplussed, responded as she would to anyone inquiring about a patient. "She's doing very well, actually."

"Good. Let me know if she needs anything. My number's in her chart. It's for Red Rock Air, but they'll get a message to me. I don't have a phone at my place yet."

"I'll do that," she said, and Mitch knew she'd turned to Jamie with her neatly penciled eyebrow arched as he strode away.

Ever since he'd come back, Mitch had tried to figure out how he could ease back into Jamie's life. Now he at least knew where to start. She didn't yet know all the reasons he'd come back. They might not even matter to her now. Even if they didn't, he needed to mend a few fences. And she needed time to get accustomed to the idea of him being around again. Time was the one thing he could give her—and the one thing he needed to repair the damage he'd done.

When Mitch's powerful strides carried him out the swinging doors at the end of the unit, Pam turned back to Jamie. "He's amazing, isn't he?"

"I don't think that's how I'd describe him."

"I meant physically. Watching him, you'd never know how badly he'd been hurt."

That was so true. Even as she'd leaned on him all the way out of the ravine, he'd shown no sign of weakening. "He's never been short on determination," Jamie had to admit.

As she said it, she thought she'd already seen him at his most determined. But a week later she began to discover there was even more to his resolve than she'd thought.

Barb brought Jamie home on Friday. Tammy, wanting to help though it wasn't at all necessary, came over early Saturday morning to fix Jamie breakfast. While she went back to her bedroom to finish dressing, Jamie left the child in the kitchen setting out cereal bowls. But when she came out two minutes later it wasn't Tammy's singing she heard. It wasn't cartoons, either. The television was still off. It was conversation.

Still braiding the ends of her hair, she heard Tammy's sweet little voice saying, "Sure. You can have some."

"Is there anything in there other than this colored stuff?"

At the sound of Mitch's voice, Jamie glanced up and went utterly still. Her hands fell, leaving the ends of her hair to lie loose over her shoulder. Standing in the doorway, she saw Mitch and Tammy smile at her.

She sounded more startled than displeased. "What are you doing here?"

"He's having breakfast with us," Tammy replied for Mitch. "He said his cupboards are naked."

"Bare," Mitch corrected.

"Bare," Tammy repeated, then shrugged because to her they were the same thing.

With pantherlike grace he stood, his glance roaming with intimate familiarity over the baggy purple sweatshirt she'd pulled over her jeans. His glance settled on her right leg. Seeming satisfied that she was able to put her weight on it, the quick concern left his expression.

"Actually, I came looking for T.J. His mom said he'd come over here for cookies to take to the park."

He looked entirely too appealing standing there with the sleeves of his blue chambray shirt rolled back and his eyes smiling at the way Tammy was counting out the ghastly pink, orange and yellow pieces of cereal so they'd all get an even amount.

Jamie headed for the coffeepot. "He left for Troy's house already. They were going to get some of their team together to play in the park."

"I know. I'm supposed to meet them there in an hour. I asked Troy if he'd call T.J. and Eddie and the rest of the kids. I'd sort of hoped to talk to T.J. alone first, though." Tammy stood up in her chair, the top of her head reaching Mitch's shirt pocket. She held out her hand, offering him a few of the extra pieces of cereal. Absently, he popped it into his mouth. He must not have thought it was too bad. He reached for another. "I wanted to apologize."

"Mommy makes me do that." Tammy selected an orange piece for herself and looked back at him with her nose wrinkled. "I hate to 'pologize."

"Me too, kid. But sometimes it's necessary. Even when the other person doesn't want to hear it."

"What's that mean?"

"It means that sometimes it's easier to keep being mad at someone than to believe they're sorry about what they did. Once you believe they're sorry, then you have to stop being mad at them. Some people don't want to do that. They'd rather stay angry."

"Why?"

"Well," Mitch continued, seeming as intent on the child as she suddenly was on him, "it can happen that part of what they're angry about is their own fault. If they stay angry, then they don't have to admit they were wrong, too."

Tammy's little brow furrowed. For several seconds she stood on the chair twisting one of her long cinnamon-colored pigtails and looking very much as if she were trying to comprehend. "Do you want some milk?" she finally asked.

"I'd rather have coffee."

"In your cereal?"

"No. Not in my cereal," he told the giggling girl and lifted her down to sit back in her chair.

Mitch hadn't so much as glanced at Jamie while he and Tammy had been engaged in their little conversation. Now he looked over only to ask if she wanted milk on her cereal, too, and if she wouldn't mind, if he could have a cup of coffee.

Not wanting to be rude in front of the little girl, not certain either what that little explanation of his was supposed to mean, she got the pot, let Mitch get the cups and sat down to her breakfast. She let Tammy and Mitch do most of the talking. Conversation seemed safest that way. At least it did until ten minutes later when Barb called wanting Tammy to come home because it was time for her to get ready for her piano lesson.

The door had no sooner closed behind the unhappy little girl when the illusion of safety vanished.

Mitch had seen Tammy out. Coming back to the table, he stopped beside Jamie's chair.

Jamie sat staring into her coffee cup. Finding nothing enlightening there, she leaned back, crossed her arms over her sweatshirt and waited for Mitch to say he was going now.

Apparently he hadn't planned on leaving just yet. Chair legs scraped on the floor as he pulled out the one nearest her. He was so close his knees almost touched hers and when he put his elbows on the table and reached across for his coffee cup, she could smell the clean scent of his soap.

"You don't approve, do you?"

If he wanted her off guard, he'd accomplished his goal. "Approve of what?"

"Of my meeting the kids this morning. I saw your face when I said what I was doing, Jamie. You don't like the idea."

"Whether I like it or not shouldn't matter. But no. I don't think it's a very good idea. The kids will just be disappointed when you leave again."

"I'm not going anywhere."

She didn't want to accuse. She didn't want to argue. But she did want him to know that she wasn't an idiot, either. "Mitch," she began as nicely as she could, "you told me yourself that in the last fifteen years you've never stayed anywhere longer than a year and a half. What happens if your arrangement doesn't work out with Red?"

"It'll work."

"You don't know that."

The muscle in his jaw jumped. That was never a very good sign, but his voice remained quiet. It was his eyes, though, that made her go still.

"What I know, Jamie, is that I want to stay here. I want it to work."

He picked up his cup, then put it down again. He seemed a little agitated. He also seemed to be looking for a way to say something that he'd rather have left alone.

Jamie felt she'd rather have him leave it alone, too. But the shadows in his expression prevented her from saying as much. She knew it wasn't easy for him to share the parts of himself he protected. That he was consciously trying to get past one of those walls now took too much of his effort for her to discourage. If she understood anything about him, it was how difficult it was for him to let himself be vulnerable.

"You've said before that you wanted to understand me," he finally began. "There's a lot that you already do. I'd already told you that when I left school I didn't give a damn about anyone or anything. I'd been pushed around for so long that all that mattered to me was doing what I wanted to do. So I got as far away from my parents as I possibly could and did the very things they'd forbidden me to do. And a lot they never even dreamed of. The more dangerous something was, the more it appealed to me. I didn't waste a whole lot of time trying to figure out what I was doing, but it didn't take a genius to know I was only trying to prove that I was my own man. But you already knew that." He paused. "What it's taken me this long to figure out was why I kept going once I'd proven it. I didn't see my parents for eight years after I left, Jamie. And when I went back, my mother was dead. My father said I'd killed her."

His words seemed oddly incongruous there in the peaceful surroundings of her kitchen. Sunlight streamed through the window, the barking of a dog could be heard from somewhere down a street, the coffeepot gave an occasional gurgle and the rich aroma of its brew scented the air. In that ordinary, Saturday-morning setting, she might have expected him to tell her that his parents had refused to speak with him. Perhaps they'd even threatened to cut him out of their will. But not this. She'd known about their control over him and that they were gone now. She'd known that thoughts of them turned him somber and brooding and sometimes made his temper short. But she'd had no idea this burden had been placed on him.

She leaned forward, reaching for something to say, but Mitch, by the way he shook his head, indicated he expected nothing from her. He only wanted to make her understand what it was that made him so certain of his decision to come back here. So he stilled her before she could speak.

"I'd never been close to them, Jamie. Never. All I could ever remember was feeling smothered by them, by their rules, by their expectations. I tried to tell my dad that I'd never meant to hurt either one of them. I really hadn't. But all he said was that after all I'd put them through, it would have been better if I'd never been born. He died the following year without ever letting me even get close to saying how sorry I was.

"All I seemed to feel after that was the guilt of not having gone home sooner. That and the fact that I didn't have a home anymore. Even though I hadn't gone back, I'd always known it was there. I'd thought it was there, anyway."

He pushed his fingers through his hair, shaking his head at his own inadequacies, his own selfishness. "The only reason I'm dumping all this on you is because I want you to understand why I came back. And why I'm not leaving. I found something here. I feel like I belong. As if this is my home. When I went to Houston, I was doing what I'd been doing for years. Escaping from having to think about what

I didn't have. I just didn't realize until I was gone that I had it all.''

The expression on his face was remarkably calm. He reached over and took her cup. ''I've got to meet my boys in a few minutes. I don't want to be late. You want more coffee before I go?''

She shook her head, wishing she knew what she was supposed to say. She felt confused, especially when Mitch stood, towering over her and meeting her eyes with the oddest combination of certainty and hesitation she'd ever seen.

''Think about what you do want, then,'' she heard him say. ''I've already made up my mind.''

A moment later, his footfall sure and heavy, he'd walked out the door.

The silence in the room seemed to echo with his words. For several seconds she sat stunned as those words repeated themselves. Then realizing what he'd done, she was on her feet, ignoring the twinges in her leg, and heading for the front window.

She pushed back the crisp white curtain in time to see Mitch reach into the cab of a new black pickup truck. He'd just turned away, baseball cap in hand, when she sank onto the sofa. She wasn't sure what she'd say to him. It seemed that, somehow, he'd just very neatly put the ball in her court. Only she wasn't sure why it was there or what she was supposed to do with it.

He truly believed he had found what had been missing in his life right here in Winston. And after what he'd said about what his father had done, and after thinking about the homeless feeling Mitch must have lived with for so long, Jamie didn't doubt him. He'd fit in too well from the beginning for her not to see how important this place had become to him. But he hadn't said a word about how he felt about her.

As she considered one of the studs on the painted trunk serving as her coffee table, she allowed that maybe that was her fault. It was entirely possible he didn't *know* how she felt. She'd certainly never come right out and told him she loved him. At the hospital the other day he'd even said she hadn't tried to keep him from going, as if her failure to do so meant she hadn't cared. That hadn't been the case at all. And though both of them knew she couldn't have stopped him, he couldn't take for granted how she did feel.

When Mitch had walked out, Jamie had acted the way she always did when she felt she didn't measure up, or couldn't compete, or wasn't good enough. She'd been protecting herself. She did that best by simply removing herself from the situation. She never stood up for herself. Never came right out and said what *she* wanted.

Mitch had recognized that in her.

Was he forcing her hand now? Could she put herself at risk by going after him? Was that what he'd meant when he said she was to think about what she wanted?

Those questions were still creating little knots in her stomach when, just before noon, she saw the game in the muddy baseball diamond across the street break up. A couple of the boys walked off to the east, another jumped on a bike and took off in the opposite direction and a few stayed behind to torment the girls on the swings. The only figure Jamie was interested in was that of the man with his arm draped over a little boy's shoulder.

From her living room window, which she'd checked with embarrassing regularity all morning, Jamie watched Mitch tousle T.J.'s hair before the grinning boy took off at an angle toward his own house. Mitch's stride slowed then and for a moment he seemed torn between heading straight across the street to Jamie's house or to the truck parked at the curb.

The screen door groaned when she pushed it open. "How was the game?" she called when he reached into his pocket for his keys.

If Mitch was surprised to see her standing on her porch, he didn't show it. His features betrayed nothing at all as he crossed her lawn, the winter sun reflecting silver lights in the dark hair lying over his collar. He came to a stop at the foot of the steps, near the clay pot that, in spring, held geraniums.

"We didn't play a game. We just tossed the ball around for a while."

"Oh."

He said nothing else. He simply waited while the breeze rattled the dead leaves on the paloverde near the driveway. Winter was a rather desolate time of year on the plateau and the cold air was making her shiver.

Or maybe it was just nerves.

"Do you want to come in?" she asked.

The blue of his eyes seemed deeper to her, more fathomless. "Is that what you want?"

"For now," she said, and thought herself very brave.

Mitch's eyebrow arched, but he said nothing as he came up the stairs and followed her inside. Something cinnamon scented the air, reminding him of the first time he'd come through that door. He'd learned so much since then, had grown to appreciate more than he'd ever thought possible. Part of what he'd learned had been painful, too. He hadn't realized the agony of losing someone until he'd thought about losing Jamie on that mountain. And he hadn't considered that he could feel that very same sensation standing with her perfectly safe in the home he'd come to feel was his own.

The door closed with a soft click. He stood by the sofa with its collection of mauve and blue pillows and she turned to him, looking decidedly hesitant.

"I need to know something," she began, clasping her hands in front of her. "Before you left for the park, you said you'd already made up your mind. You were just talking about staying in Winston. Right?"

"Partly."

Her heart bumped against her ribs. "What's the other part?"

He didn't look as if he wanted to answer.

He was only an arm's length away. Close enough for him to reach for her if he wanted.

Or for her to reach for him.

"Please, Mitch," she said, taking the chance and laying her hand lightly on his chest. "I'm not very good at this."

He glanced down at her hand. Something in his expression softened, almost as if a lock had fallen away. Taking her hand in his, he brought her palm to his lips. "The other part has to do entirely with you."

That was all he would give, but it was enough for her to know that she wasn't about to make a complete fool of herself. Encouraged by the feel of his arm settling over her shoulders, she curved her arms around his waist and let herself feel the first peace she'd felt in months.

"I love you," she whispered because even if he didn't love her back she needed him to know that.

"I love you, too, Jamie. I think I have since before I even saw you."

He spoke the words into her hair, saying them as if he'd never questioned what he felt, only what to call it.

He cupped her face when she raised her head, and he dared to let himself believe that all he'd been looking for had finally been found. "Now, there's something *I* need to know." He brushed his lips over hers, the caress achingly tender. He was trembling. He wondered if she felt it. "I need to know if you want the same things I do. I have a lot of lost time to make up for. And I think three would be nice."

"Three?"

"Children."

Mitch had once said that the reward and the risk were usually proportionate. Jamie believed him. Loving him was the biggest risk she'd ever taken and having him love her back was the best thing that had ever happened to her. He made her feel necessary in ways no one else ever could. And when he looked at her as if she were all that mattered to him, she felt like the most accomplished woman alive.

The smile on her lips was as warm as sunshine. "I had the feeling that's what you meant. Yes, Mitch," she said, melting into him as his head lowered to hers. "That's what I want, too."

Epilogue

Jamie stood with Mitch on the ledge, looking out over the vista from Weeping Dove. On the horizon, the sun sat like a great orange ball, setting the sky on fire and spreading an orange-pink glow out over the land. They weren't alone. Tammy, in new jeans and a white lace blouse, stood next to Jamie, who wore new jeans and a white lace blouse, too. Sam was there, next to Mitch and the rest of the small party gathered nearby. The gentle trail up the Weeping Dove had been lined with luminarias and Martha, bringing up the rear, had stopped to make sure none of the candles in the sand-filled brown bags had gone out, so the path would be lit on the way back down.

The minister, his robes flowing over his hiking boots, stood with his back to the view and smiled at Mitch.

Mitch was nervous. An interesting feeling, he thought, for something he wanted so badly.

"How are you doing?" he asked Jamie, and saw her look up from the bouquet of wildflowers and jasmine he'd asked her to carry. They reminded him of her. Everything soft and beautiful did.

"I'd be doing better if this was over." Anticipation lit her eyes. Along with a touch of anxiety. "I just keep thinking I'm going to wake up and none of this will be real."

"It's real." He touched her hair. She'd left it down for him, the pale colors of gold and wheat looking like a halo in the setting sun. "What I feel is real."

"I love you, Mitch."

"I love you, too, honey." His hand fell away. Tammy was tugging on his leg.

Bits of baby's breath had been tucked into the white ribbons on her pigtails. The tiny blossoms bounced as she looked up at him. "What's that?"

"What's what?"

"That sound?"

For a moment Mitch didn't hear it. Then the faint whistle of the wind grew out of the great vast silence.

He looked to Jamie. "That's the Weeping Dove," she said to the child. "What you hear is the sound of her crying."

"Oh." Tammy looked thoughtful. "My mom always cries at weddings, too. Are you going to kiss her, Mitch?"

"Your mom?"

She wrinkled her nose. "No. Jamie."

Mitch looked to the minister. "Go ahead," the gray-haired gentleman said with a grin. "The next time you kiss her you'll be married."

So Mitch did kiss her. And Jamie kissed him back. But as

she did, she thought that the sound of the Weeping Dove changed a little. It wasn't crying she heard. It was more like . . . a sigh.

*   *   *   *   *

COMING NEXT MONTH

AVAILABLE THIS MONTH:

Summer romance has never been so hot!

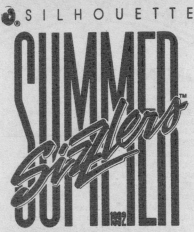

☀ SILHOUETTE

SUMMER Sizzlers 1992™

A collection of hot summer reading by three of
Silhouette's hottest authors:
Ann Major
Paula Detmer Riggs
Linda Lael Miller

Put some sizzle into your summer reading. You
won't want to miss your ticket to summer fun—with
the best summer reading under the sun!
